Kiss of the Texas Maverick

Brides of Bethany Springs
Book Two

Charlotte Dearing

The right of Charlotte Dearing to be identified as author of this Work has been asserted by her in accordance with sections 77 and 78 of the Copyright, Designs and Patents Act of 1988.

Copyright © 2023 by Charlotte Dearing.
All rights reserved.

No part of this book may be reproduced in any form or by any electronic or mechanical means, including information storage and retrieval systems, without written permission from the author, except for the use of brief quotations in a book review.

This is a clean, wholesome story of love and family set in late 19th century Texas.

It is the story of Amelia Honeycutt's second son, Simon, and the sparks that fly when the girl he teased as a child comes home.

Chapter One
Dumpling

Virginia Childress

By every measure, the evening had been a success. New faces with new money, old faces with old. All of them supportive and ready to help Governor Childress win reelection. The perfect gathering, Virginia thought.

Sadly, it didn't last.

Childress was a politician. A good one. He often talked with his hands, using them to punctuate and enhance his stories. Folks always had to give him a little space, room for the exclamation points, measurements and reenactments that animated his stories and brought them to life.

He wasn't a drinker. Wasn't used to imbibing. And yet, he was fond of fancy things and always looked for a chance to show how far he'd come. He'd eaten caviar, the horrid stuff, and he owned not one, but two, Henry Poole suits that hung in a cedar closet upstairs, ready for his next inauguration or meeting with the president. He wasn't just a cowpuncher from Bethany Springs. Not anymore.

He was the governor of Texas, and people of that caliber needed to show off from time to time. At least, that's what he told himself. So, when he was offered a glass of fine, French champagne, he took it, sipped it, agreed it was delicious, then promptly downed it, freeing up his hand for more storytelling.

Virginia hadn't seen her father with the glass of champagne. Had she noticed, she would have taken it from him, discreetly, of course, without him or anyone else realizing what she was doing. That's what Virginia did, she protected her father from anyone who might bring him down, especially from his worst opponent, himself.

Ten minutes later, after two more raucous stories, and a widening space for Childress to wave his arms, he proclaimed, "That's what I call a fine party!" His booming voice practically rattled the glittering chandeliers.

"Drat," Virginia muttered.

"Did I ever tell you boys about the time I outsmarted a pair of Oklahoma horse dealers?" her father asked.

"Blasted drat," she added, with more vehemence. She waited, hoping and praying he'd curtail his storytelling.

She'd planned this party for months, painstakingly combing through every detail, all the while keeping a wary eye on her father's upcoming election. For Virginia, it wasn't simply a matter of *wanting* to win reelection.

No. Her father *had* to win.

The sole purpose of his life, the reason he got out of bed each morning, was to be the governor of Texas. To be the center of attention. To opine, direct and entertain. To perform his one-man show, knowing full well that every person who could see him would watch his every word and gesture. If he didn't win, he'd be just another citizen, and Virginia could not imagine that calamity.

The evening had gone perfectly, but now her father might spoil things. While he never drank much, a glass or two would send Papa veering off to any topic. The worst topic, as far as Virginia was concerned, was anything related to her childhood. He might mean well, but his stories always humiliated her. She was nineteen. Not a child. She worked hard for her father and liked to think of herself as indispensable, not some sort of joking matter.

Her father fretted a great deal about the election. Lately he'd seemed consumed by thoughts of losing. His fine mind was distracted, drawn to frivolous matters rather than what was best for the good people of Texas.

As her father continued to perform, Virginia felt a growing panic. She couldn't whisk him away, not with the crowd gathered round, but she knew she needed to do something. Two nights ago, when she couldn't sleep, she'd written down talking points for her father. They were tucked in his coat pocket now, if only he'd use them.

"Your notes. Remember your notes," Virginia murmured involuntarily. "Talk about the orphanage in Fort Worth. Or railroad safety. Anything but me."

"I'm sorry, dear. What did you say?" Mrs. Westcliff looked affronted.

Virginia drew a sharp breath. She gathered her wits quickly and came back to Mrs. Westcliff and her new pet project, flower arrangements.

"I beg your pardon," Virginia said hastily. "You were saying something about the lilies. Or was it lilacs?"

Mrs. Westcliff returned to her favorite topic, the flowers she grew in her greenhouse.

Virginia tried to listen. She'd spent a great deal of time and effort on the flowers for the evening's event, making a point of including her favorite yellow roses, a private nod to her late mother. All thoughts of flowers flew from her mind as her attention fixed on her father.

"I never could say no to my little girl." Papa grew misty-eyed. "She always had me wrapped around her little finger."

He held up his hand, pinky raised to emphasize his point. "It isn't easy raisin' up a girl all alone. Especially a little mite that lost her mama so young and all."

Mrs. Westcliff droned on about spring blooms.

Virginia tried to coax air into her lungs.

Her father was just getting going. His voice rang across the crowded ballroom as he addressed the growing crowd. Beside him were two men she recognized, shipbuilders from Galveston.

"She loved her sweets, my little girl."

"Oh, no, not this," Virginia whispered.

Her father tugged at his tie. He didn't like fussy attire. Any minute, he'd yank the tie from his neck and shove it in his pocket. "I reckon she always will be my little Dumpling, even now that she's all grown up."

Mrs. Westcliff patted her arm. "Go on, dear. Everyone knows you're Orville Childress's right hand."

Virginia gave an apologetic smile. She made her way across the crowded salon, eager to stop her father's storytelling. Her path was slowed by various guests who wanted to say hello or compliment her on the lovely evening.

"I, personally, never thought she was stout." Her father's voice blasted across the din.

Virginia managed to keep a gracious smile as she threaded her way through the crowd.

"I just liked to see her happy. Course, now she's slender, hardly ever eats cake, but she'll always be my little dumpling. I'd never *seen* a child who could eat so many cream puffs," her father exclaimed.

Virginia came to his side and linked her arm through his. "Papa, don't bore these fine gentlemen with dull stories. I'm sure you all have better things to talk about."

"Here she is," her father crowed. "We Texans might not have a first lady, sadly. But we have a first daughter. She helps me with everything from speeches to minding my manners. Heck, I wouldn't be governor of Texas if it weren't for my daughter."

There was a murmur of polite appreciation. Virginia flushed with embarrassment. She didn't want to be the subject of her father's jokes, or praise. The entire reason for the party was so her father could rub elbows with notable Texas businessmen, and hopefully explain his plans for a second term. Now the group of men seemed to study her with curiosity.

"Such a lovely first daughter," the stockman from Abilene said, giving her a wink.

"Mighty pretty," said another gentleman.

"You can quit with your flattery." Papa laughed. "My little girl's never getting married. She's never had a sweetheart, never been courted. Shoot, she's never even been kissed."

"Never kissed?" the men exclaimed; a chorus of deep murmurings moved through the group. "Seems a shame. A real shame."

She rarely imagined her first kiss, but if she did, she wouldn't have imagined any of the men before her. The mere idea made her stomach clench. No, a first kiss ought to be given to one who was beloved, in a tender moment, after a great deal of yearning. Of that, she was certain.

A first kiss wasn't a prize. No. A first kiss was a sweet and precious promise.

After an awkward lull in the discussion, Virginia managed to collect her thoughts. "Now, Papa. Are you going to keep on embarrassing me or are you going to talk to these fine gentlemen about your plans to open an orphanage, and a veteran's home right here in Austin?"

The men regarded her with a note of surprise.

Papa valued her opinion much of the time, but not all men liked to hear females talk about political issues. From the looks on the men's faces, she suspected she'd overstepped. Still, she saw the moment as a chance to avoid any more awkward conversation. Schooling her features, she softened her voice. "I do hope you gentleman enjoy the evening."

The men nodded and muttered their agreement. She thanked them for attending the party and bid them good evening. Before leaving, she gave her father a pointed look, hoping he caught her meaning.

With that, Virginia swept away, returning to the festivities. There were guests to attend to, appearances to uphold and one more election to win.

Chapter Two
A Rude Awakening

Simon Honeycutt

Simon dozed, vaguely aware of a nearby movement. He mumbled a few words in hopes the disturbance was nothing more than a dream. He hadn't slept well. His throat felt like he'd swallowed a barrow full of sand. His head ached. Surely it wasn't time to wake up.

A nudge against his foot made him growl. "Quit that. Unless you want a fight."

He settled back into a peaceful slumber. Footsteps faded. Darned right. The rascal *better* leave him be. But no. A moment later the footfalls returned. Cold water splashed across his face. Drenched, half awake, he bolted upright with a snarl of rage.

"The heck you mean by waking a man like that?" he roared. He rubbed his eyes and squinted to find his mother standing a few feet away, holding a pail. "Mama?"

"Simon." She set the pail down and folded her arms across her chest. "Good morning."

"What did you do that for?" He wiped his face with a shirt sleeve. He looked around to find he was lying on the hay pile in the barn. The memory of the prior evening returned.

He'd gotten back after a week of hard riding across rugged range land. He was dog tired and should have gone straight home. Instead, he accepted an invitation from his family's ranch hands for a bite to eat. He stayed for a few rounds of cards that lasted till near midnight.

Instead of saddling up and heading to his cabin, he ended up bedded down in the barn along with the horses. He never expected anyone to find him there, certainly not his mother.

"You were a tad hard to wake," his mother said. Dressed in trim trousers and a starched cotton shirt, Mama wore her usual work attire. Her clothing was always practical, but she liked small feminine details like the pink scarf tucked under her collar.

She looked like she planned to saddle the big chestnut gelding, and check the yearlings, or perhaps ride the fence line. From her expression, he could tell she wasn't going anywhere till she'd given him a lecture or two, or five. She wore her favorite boots and tapped her foot slowly as she waited for him to pull himself together.

"Some reason you needed to wake me up so early, Mama?"

"It's almost six o'clock," she snapped. "I have an urgent matter on my hands, one that concerns you."

Simon grumbled as he got to his feet. Mama was in a grim mood. Again. Lately, it seemed he couldn't do anything right. No matter what, she was always sore.

Ever since Simon's older brother took a wife, Mama had gotten notions of more weddings. She wanted him and Zach to toe the line and get married too. Pronto. She'd threatened to cut them off by the end of the year if they hadn't settled down with a nice girl. Extra points if the new wife had a little one on the way by Christmas.

Simon couldn't think of anything he wanted *less*. A wife and kids? Shoot. Not him. He had big plans. Dreams that didn't include being a husband or father just yet. He intended to start his own brand of Brahma cattle which had only offended his mother further.

Mama didn't like the breed. Why? Because he did. And they were ugly. And ornery. No one within five hundred miles raised Brahmas, for good reason, she said. Why did he have to insist on doing things his way, she'd wanted to know.

Because that's the way it had always been. Simon liked to do things a tad differently. He was determined to start a herd of Brahmas, someday, but he'd have to buy his own land first. Mama wasn't having Brahmas on the Honeycutt Ranch.

He plucked the hay from his wet shirt. "How can I help?"

"Find Junior. He's missing."

Well, that was a surprise. Junior was the son of the ranch foreman. Mild-mannered and unassuming, rarely was he the subject of his mother's wrath so early in the morning. Usually, she reserved that for him or Zach. He frowned. "Junior?"

"That's right. He was expected home last night from his trip to the valley, and he never showed. Sheldon and Franny are sick with worry. They haven't seen him in nearly a week."

"I expected him at the card game last night. I figured he was too tired."

"He's not tired. He's missing."

"I understand." Simon stifled a yawn. "Junior's missing."

"Sheldon is beside himself. Franny's crying and carrying on. Which means, I'm short-handed. Sheldon's consoling his wife. Junior is who-knows-where. And Sheldon's not going to be worth a fig if Junior doesn't show up."

Simon scoffed as he raked his fingers through his wet hair.

Mama paced the span of the barn. "I have a bad feeling about this."

"I'm sure he's fine."

His mother pointed her finger at him. "You better pray he turns up. You are the godfather to his two boys."

Simon blinked.

Godfather? Him?

Water trickled down the back of his neck. His mother was correct. He was, in fact, the children's godfather. Junior's boys were said to be a handful and a half. Their mama, a scowling woman named Emmaline, had left Junior when the boys were little, taking them and an unexpected small inheritance from her grandfather.

For several years Junior hardly ever saw his boys, which was why Simon had mostly forgotten about them. Then one day Emmaline showed up, her money, and what little patience she had, run out. She didn't come to make amends. She came to leave the boys with Junior, saying she couldn't do it anymore.

It was time for Junior to act like their father, she said. He'd need to keep them. For a while, at least, till she and her new husband came back from their honeymoon. Simon had only caught a glimpse of the boys once or twice since they'd come to stay at the ranch. He couldn't imagine talking to them, much less caring for them.

"Who's minding the boys this morning?" Simon asked warily.

"Sheldon and Franny. But they're in no shape to put up with Ellwood and Tuck. Those two are worse than you and Zach."

Simon winced.

"Yesterday, one of those rascals swapped Franny's sugar and salt, ruining three pies and a dozen jars of pickles. Then they found a baby racoon and brought it inside. Sheldon spent the better part of an hour fending off an angry mama coon while Franny chased the baby round the den, trying to shoo it out the door."

Amelia went on. "By the time all was said and done, Sheldon had thrown his back out and Franny got a goose egg on her forehead."

Simon's brows lifted. Those boys did sound worse than him and Zach.

"The critters are gone, but this morning Sheldon's watch has gone missing. The boys claim the baby racoon took it. All this on top of fretting about Junior."

"Dang."

"You'd best keep in mind that if something's happened to Junior, they won't be able to manage those two little hellions."

Simon swallowed. He gave a small nod. "Yes, ma'am."

"Which would mean that raising those two youngsters would fall to *you*." She smiled in a way that always made him worry. He felt sure Junior would be just fine. It didn't seem possible otherwise, but Mama clearly relished the notion of him having to tend to the rascals.

"I expect you to get busy." Mama gave him a narrow look. "Quit sleeping all day and find out what Junior got himself into. I'll do my best to help Sheldon and Franny with the children until you get back."

She wrinkled her nose, clearly not relishing the prospect. "I'll send a letter to the governor while I'm at it. Just in case Junior got into trouble with the law. There's been a mess of robberies down by the border. The Texas Rangers have been arresting folks left and right. That's what concerns me the most. Junior's such a gullible fool."

"You're writing the governor?" Simon shook his head. He must be dreaming. Mama made no secret of her dislike of Governor Childress.

"I have to. Unfortunately. Call it women's intuition but I'm sure Junior's sitting in jail. Somewhere between here and Mexico. Ugh. I'll have to ask Orville Childress for his help. And I need to do it in a hurry. I'll send a letter with one of the men, so he gets it this morning."

Muttering under her breath, she turned on her heel and left the barn. Her footsteps faded till she reached the barn door. An instant later she slammed the door shut. The bang echoed through the empty barn.

Simon plucked a few more strands of hay from his wet shirt. He shook his head. Dread made his heart heavy. Junior in jail. It seemed impossible. Junior was the kindest man he'd ever known. Not the sharpest man around, but noble and gentle. He treated everyone with respect and care, even the ranch animals.

Simon took his Stetson from a hook, brushed off the dust and put it on. He sighed wearily. The day had gotten off to a poor start. He said a silent prayer that it wouldn't get any worse.

Pulling the door open, he squinted at the early morning sunshine.

"I'm sure Junior's fine," he said, speaking to no one in particular.

"I can't take in two boys. It's impossible." He shut the door, wincing at the sudden throb at the base of his head. "I don't even like children."

Chapter Three
A Grumpy Governor

Virginia

The morning after the party, Virginia heard a commotion from her father's room. He shouted and carried on, calling her name as he stalked the upstairs halls. Virginia, already dressed, hurriedly finished arranging her hair.

While her father was devoted to her, he had high expectations. If she appeared disheveled or unkempt, even in their private rooms, he complained vigorously.

A maid knocked and peered inside Virginia's room. It was a new girl, one who likely hadn't yet heard the governor in one of his moods.

Before she could say anything, Virginia spoke. "Yes, I know my father wants to speak to me. Please tell him I'm on my way. Then ask Edith to send breakfast upstairs."

"Yes, miss." The girl looked worried as if she dreaded speaking to the governor.

"Don't fret. My father's more bark than bite," Virginia said.

The girl looked unconvinced as she closed the door gently.

Alone in her room, Virginia finished tucking the last few hairpins. A moment later, she heard her father erupt, and Virginia couldn't help feeling sorry for the new girl. Heavens only knew why her father was so irritated that morning. Last night's party had gone very well, if not entirely for Virginia, for Papa and his fundraising.

Perhaps not enough of a success for his liking.

As a child, Virginia thought her father was the most amusing, most clever fellow in the world. By day, he worked in his law practice. She spent the day with her nanny. Papa arrived home at six o'clock on the dot. They'd eat dinner together every evening. After dinner, he'd read to her in the study. Often, he'd pretend to be one of the characters.

He invented his own characters too. Henry, the pirate monkey. Or Neville, the forgetful cobbler. He'd made her laugh until her sides ached. The servants and even her dour nanny would laugh when they heard his antics.

The years passed. Papa probably didn't even recall Henry or Neville.

Sometimes she thought he'd lost his sense of humor when he won the election.

She entered his room to find him still wearing his pajamas and dressing gown. He must have forgotten he had a luncheon later that day. She'd need to work quickly to help him get ready. The maid left the breakfast tray and made a hasty retreat as Virginia poured him a cup of coffee.

He glowered and waved a piece of paper in the air. "Have you seen the bill from the florist?"

"I have not."

"It's exorbitant. An outrage!"

"Most of the cost is from last night's party. You told me to spare no expense. I chose yellow roses, the kind that Mama liked."

If she thought mention of her mother's favorite flowers would soften his response, she was mistaken. His sour expression didn't waver.

He tossed the bill aside. "Cancel all the flowers. This morning."

"There's no need. I haven't ordered any. We won't be entertaining for the rest of the month."

He knit his brows and took a swallow of coffee. In his haste, he scalded his tongue, but at least that wasn't her fault. He said nothing as he sorted the morning's mail. Virginia began to set out the day's clothing. She left him to stew and mutter.

She held up a freshly starched shirt, frowning at the creased collar.

"What are you doing?" he demanded. "I'm not going out today, am I?"

"You have a luncheon at noon."

"I didn't recall I had an engagement," Papa grumbled as he rubbed his balding head. "I'd hoped to take a nap."

"It's on your agenda. Mr. Williams asked to discuss the proposed railroad line running through Tyler." Virginia tossed aside the first shirt and searched his armoire for a shirt with a properly ironed collar. When she found one, she set it beside a pair of gray trousers.

Her father grunted and began to read the morning paper.

Moving with brisk efficiency, Virginia selected a vest as well as a jacket, a four-button cutaway, and draped them across the bed. Adding a bowler hat to the ensemble, she stood back to look at her work. A governor's attire needed to be elegant but sensible.

The outfit would look good on her father, the dark colors concealing his portly frame.

Draped across the four-poster mahogany bed, the clothing looked especially handsome. Of course, the bed itself was a fine backdrop. When Sam Houston served as governor, his wife, Margaret, had given birth in the bed. Temple Lea Houston was Mrs. Houston's eighth child, but the first child to be born in the governor's mansion.

Eight children! Virginia always marveled at Mrs. Houston's fortitude, but she kept her opinion to herself. Papa didn't care for the notion of such things taking place in the governor's mansion. He pretended the childbirth story wasn't true. The details, he insisted, weren't fit for polite company.

"An outfit from New York is fixing to build a new shipyard," Papa read aloud from the front page. "They're not sure if they'll build in Houston or Galveston. Hmm. I'll have to ask Mr. Williams if he's caught wind of any news."

"That sounds like a fine idea. Just so long as you don't start talking about my love of sweets or if I've ever kissed an admirer."

He dropped the paper. "Why is that? Has Williams been untoward?"

"No. Not really. But I still don't want you to talk about whether or not I've courted. Like you did last night. Heavens, Papa, that was mortifying."

Her father chuckled as he returned his attention to the paper. "I'll just bet all those fellas wished they could call on you. Every one of them is a rogue. Each one likely thinks he'll be the first to steal a kiss from the governor's daughter."

Virginia cringed inwardly. "It's unseemly."

"It's a sight more interesting than beef prices."

"How flattering."

"I'm starting to believe that having a pretty and brilliant daughter makes a favorable impression on male voters. Every vote counts."

"In that case, perhaps I should set up a kissing booth on election day. I'll give voters a kiss in exchange for a Childress vote."

Her father looked aghast. "Don't be vulgar. Besides, the men relish the notion of a girl's first kiss. Not her hundred and first kiss."

"I can't imagine kissing one of your constituents. Especially in return for his support. That's hardly what I'd envision as my first kiss."

"Try not to fret. I hint at plenty of notions that I have no intention of carrying out. It's part of getting elected. Politicians make promises. Everyone knows that."

Virginia made a point of ignoring him as she straightened the books on his nightstand. Her father often claimed there wasn't a man good enough in the state of Texas for Virginia Childress. What had happened to that sentiment, she'd like to know. Nowadays, he prompted her to smile more, or to act a little friendlier at gatherings.

The other day, he'd asked her to hand-deliver a note to a judge. He encouraged her to stay and visit a spell. She had the distinct impression that Papa intended her to turn the trip into a social visit. She'd evaded his scheme by sending the note with a servant.

"It seems you ought to talk to voters about important matters," Virginia said, hardly able to hide her annoyance. "Not if I've ever kissed a beau."

Her voice wavered with emotion.

He looked alarmed and then conciliatory. "I'm sorry, sweetheart. I got carried away. Sit. Have some breakfast with your old father."

"All right." She gave him a pointed look. "But please don't shout at me about bills. I watch expenses closely."

"Of course. Of course." He rose and pulled out her chair and offered a gallant gesture. "Let's forget such matters, shall we?"

She took her chair without a reply. Pouring a cup of tea, she felt the tension ease from her shoulders. These days, her father was acting a little strangely, but it was to be expected. He was a busy man even without the worry of a campaign. The election was a few short months away. After the election, things would return to the way they were before. Thank goodness.

He set aside his paper and finished sorting the mail. "You won't believe who wrote, asking for my help. Our neighbor in Bethany Springs."

"Which neighbor?"

"Amelia Honeycutt!" He brandished the letter like a trophy. "Mrs. Honeycutt didn't mind cheating me out of a land deal. Oh, no. And then she refused to give one penny to my campaign. Stubborn woman. Doesn't care if I win in November but has no qualms about asking for help. No sirree. The old trout."

Virginia winced. Amelia Honeycutt had to be her mother's age, but she was hardly an old trout. Virginia had always admired the woman. Not that she and Mrs. Honeycutt were close in any way. No, Virginia had, for the most part, formed her opinion on what she'd heard of the formidable woman. Like anyone else, she knew of the woman's success as a rancher and business owner.

"I hope she's not asking on behalf of her children," Virginia murmured absently.

"I thought you detested those Honeycutt boys."

"The two younger ones were monsters." She grumbled under her breath. "*Especially* Simon."

"He made you cry. Is that right?"

She nodded. "He bumped into me at the county fair. It was an accident. Couldn't be helped. Still, I dropped my ice cream."

"Oh, darling."

"He knocked it out of my hand. And then he added insult to injury and laughed."

"Laughed? The cad."

"My thoughts precisely."

"No apology? Can't say I'm surprised. Amelia Honeycutt probably didn't raise her boys to be gentlemen."

"He laughed *and* called me a silly goose for crying. A *goose*. I don't even like people to call me Ginny or some other nickname. He called me a farmyard animal."

Virginia recalled Simon's glee. She could picture his grin. Simon had been eleven years old at the time, maybe twelve. She was seven. The memory made her cheeks burn with mortification as she pictured the incident.

Simon had offered to buy her an ice cream to replace the one melting on the ground. Perhaps it was his off-hand words or lack of remorse, but she'd refused to give him the satisfaction. She didn't want his ice cream. Not after he'd called her a goose. To her dismay, even the mere thought of the incident, made heat rise to her cheeks.

It hadn't stopped there. In the years that followed, she'd seen him at the county fair, and he always shouted the very same thing. "*Want an ice cream, Goose? Do ya?*"

Vile, odious boy. Of course, that *was* twelve years ago. Simon Honeycutt was long past boyhood. He probably didn't tease girls at the fair any longer.

It had been a long time since she'd visited Bethany Springs and she could hardly imagine Simon as a grown man. What she could imagine was a larger version of the loathsome, smirking boy. She was older too and ought to pardon his boyish teasing. She should forgive his trespasses. And yet, even after all these years, she couldn't let go of the niggling resentment.

"I'm sorry he was unkind to you." Her father tsked and shook his head. "The letter is not about any of her sons."

"Thank goodness." She shook off the memories. "I'm very glad to hear."

Her father raised a brow. "That so?"

"I didn't care for Simon Honeycutt, but his older brother was always kind to me. To everyone."

"Which brother?"

Virginia tried to look nonchalant. "Daniel. The eldest."

Father grunted. "I seem to recall he married. I read an announcement in the social pages."

"I'm so glad to hear. Tell me, why did Mrs. Honeycutt send a letter?"

Father scratched his jaw. "Amelia wrote about her foreman's son. Seems the young man has landed in considerable trouble. She's asked me to investigate matters even though she's not entirely sure where he's at. Maybe Victoria. Maybe Hebbronville. Maybe a dozen towns in between."

She buttered a piece of toast. "I wonder what happened?"

"Pah! Who cares? I'll take a look when I get the chance. If I get the chance, that is. The rascal is the son of a cowpoke. I'm not going to win an election helping some nobody."

Virginia winced. When her father first spoke of public service, he'd always talked of law and justice for the common man. For the past two months he'd thought only of appearances, and votes.

"You know who has a soft spot in his heart for Amelia Honeycutt?" he asked.

"Not you, clearly."

"My old friend, Wade McCord. He always says Amelia Honeycutt's the only woman he ever wanted to marry."

She smiled. "Mr. McCord? I figured he'd never consider settling down. To think. At his age."

Her father scowled. "What do you mean at his age?"

"Nothing. Sorry. I must have been thinking of someone other than Mr. McCord."

Her father didn't look entirely convinced but went on. "Wade gets stars in his eyes when he talks about her. Every time he goes to Bethany Springs, he tries to get his sister-in-law to arrange a chance meeting. He wants her to set him up with Amelia Honeycutt."

Virginia offered an extra-cheerful smile. "Speaking of Bethany Springs, I planned to speak to you about Mama's birthday next week."

Her father yelped. "Land sakes. Is it next week?"

"It is. We worked so hard on last night's party, I'd hoped we could make a trip and stay a few days. Perhaps even a week. I can arrange appointments on your calendar so that we have time to spend at the homestead and visit Mama's grave. Just like we used to."

"A week?" He clutched his chest. "I don't believe it would be prudent if I traveled to Bethany Springs just now." He frowned at Mrs. Honeycutt's letter where it sat beside his coffee cup. "I need to keep up the appearance of a busy governor. Not gallivanting across the countryside."

Virginia had guessed he wouldn't want to make the trip.

For some reason, his refusal made her want to go even more. They hadn't visited once since he'd become governor.

She longed to return to the place her mother and father had lived when they first married. Her father would call her sentimental, but she couldn't help the yearning she'd hidden in her heart. She couldn't explain her need to stand before her mother's grave. Or the desire to walk the land her mother had walked. Sit beneath the trees her mother loved.

He'd call her a sentimental fool.

She took a sip of tea. "Perhaps you could do without me for a week or so. I've promised to write an article for the *Texas Ladies Journal*. They requested a piece, one that might support your second election. The fresh country air would inspire my work."

Her father looked thoughtful. "You're not concerned about running into any of the Honeycutt family?"

An image of Simon Honeycutt's grin flashed through her mind. She flinched. Her father didn't notice, thankfully.

"Not in the least. I'm going in honor of my mother's birthday. And to take in the peace and quiet. I've had enough of dinners, parties, and crowds. I probably won't even venture off the homestead."

Her father looked petulant. She knew the expression well. He'd do what he could to keep her home and conjure up all manner of reasons why she should stay. Drumming his fingers on the table, he grew pensive.

"I have an idea for the article," she explained. "I'll write about the old Childress homestead. The family's deep Texas roots."

"That sounds fine."

"And how you raised me all on your own after Mama passed away."

"We didn't live there after your mother died. The house has been empty for some time now."

"That's true. But an article about the Childress homestead is sure to gain the attention of the good ladies of Texas. They can't cast a ballot but..." She let her words drift off.

Her father's eyes sparkled. "Those ladies can't cast a ballot, but their husbands will vote. Some will be influenced by their wives. It's true, my dear."

"I'll try to write my very best piece about Governor Childress."

While her father mulled over the idea, her heart fluttered with excitement. The prospect of time at the homestead, time away from the hustle and bustle of the governor's mansion, soothed a tender spot inside her heart. She imagined walks through the countryside. Peaceful evenings on the porch. Quiet days to do just as she pleased without answering to anyone.

Her father looked torn. He tapped his fingers on the linen tablecloth as he gazed out the window. He was used to having her near, used to asking for help with all sorts of matters, both big and small.

She waited.

"I promise to make you proud, Papa," she added, trying to prompt him to give his nod of approval.

"All right."

She smiled gratefully, but then reminded herself to school her features. It wouldn't do to appear so happy.

Her father gave a weary sigh. "You win. I suppose I can manage on my own. Go. Take a few days for yourself." He waved his hand in the air. "Go off to Bethany Springs. Stay in the old homestead and write your little article."

Chapter Four
Junior's Troubles

Simon

Shortly after Mama woke Simon with a bucket of water, he received word of Junior's whereabouts.

The news came from a young man by the name of Andrew, a fellow member of the Bethany Brotherhood.

The Brotherhood began in the desperate days following the War. It was a dark time. Texas had lost a fair number of her sons. Many of the returning men were wounded or crippled. It wasn't long before thieves and outlaws arrived, determined to prey upon the vulnerable widows and orphans.

The dire circumstances led to the creation of a small, dedicated band of men who took the law into their own hands. They were the first members of the Bethany Brotherhood.

Andrew's father had served, then passed the responsibility on to his son.

Lately, the men had enjoyed a span of peace and quiet. Thankfully.

Just the same, all of them remained alert to matters that pertained to Bethany Springs. Andrew came with that very news. One of the men learned that Junior had been hauled off to a remote jail a few hours' ride from Bethany Springs. A town called Sagebrush.

After learning the news, Simon saddled a horse and rode off to find Junior. He arrived in the town of Sagebrush in the late afternoon. There wasn't a lot to Sagebrush. A couple of saloons. A livery barn. A farrier.

And a jail.

Surprisingly, the jail was fairly considerable, much larger than the jail in Bethany Springs. For a town this size, Simon expected a one-room calaboose, but the Sagebrush jail looked like it could hold a fair number of prisoners.

Strange.

Junior had been arrested near the border. Why keep him here? Maybe the Rangers used the Sagebrush jail as an out-of-the way prison for certain outlaws.

Simon tied his horse and ascended the steps as he removed his cowboy hat. His boot heels thudded on the dusty planks of the porch. Stepping inside, he glanced around and spied the warden in a nearby office. The man dozed, hat pulled low, boots propped on the desk.

Someone shouted from the back. "Hey there, Simon!"

The cheerful greeting startled Simon. He peered down the hallway to the rows of cells. The lone inmate waved. "Over here. It's Junior."

Simon nodded Junior's direction and tried to wake the warden. With a light tap on the desk, he spoke quietly so as not to startle him. The man grunted, shifted in his chair, and went right back to his afternoon nap. His snores echoed across the quiet.

Simon cleared his throat. Twice. The only response came from Junior who chuckled.

"Warden's a heavy sleeper."

"Pardon me, sir," Simon said a little louder.

The man jumped. His hat toppled to the floor. His eyes, bloodshot and watery, widened to see Simon standing before him. "The heck?"

"Sorry to wake you."

"Least it wasn't me this time, Warden." Junior laughed. "Least it wasn't me."

"What do you want?" the warden asked Simon, his brow a deep furrow.

"I was hoping to have a word with your prisoner, sir. Sheldon Whitson."

"Junior?"

"Yes, sir."

The man's demeanor softened. He picked up his hat and brushed off the dirt, which was plentiful. Small puffs of dust wafted from the rim as the man eyed him speculatively. "He a friend of yours?"

"That's Simon Honeycutt," Junior called. "Remember? I told you about the time we got a herd of cattle back from Rio Grande rustlers. How we got home with a dozen extra yearlings and the cow with the cock-eyed horn? Remember?"

The warden grumbled an indistinct reply which was followed by a groan as he rose from the chair.

Simon spoke. "I've come to Sagebrush to bail Sheldon out."

"That so?" The warden squinted.

"Yes, sir. He's got two young boys waiting for their daddy to come home." Simon left it at that. He saw no reason to add that if he couldn't spring Junior from jail, he'd be minding the two boys on his own. Soon. As in that very afternoon. The boys had worn out their grandparents. Mama flat-out refused to keep them one minute longer than necessary.

Simon desperately needed to sweet talk, convince, bribe, or do whatever it took to get Junior out of jail. He was more than willing to pay bail. His mother owned the Bethany Springs Bank along with a couple others. Surely the warden would accept a promissory note. Then he and Junior could hire a second horse and leave Sagebrush.

One day he and his old friend would laugh about the entire misadventure.

"I'm happy to do whatever needed to help my friend, Junior," Simon offered, hoping to make his point perfectly clear. "I imagine this is just a small misunderstanding."

The warden looked unimpressed. "You can tell that to Judge Harper. He's going to hear Junior's case in Austin. Arlon Harper likely has plenty of questions for Junior, like why Junior had a saddle bag full of stolen money. After that, he'll arraign him. Mark my words."

Simon blinked. "Stolen money? Arraign him?"

"Five thousand dollars. A man doesn't normally carry that kind of money, does he?"

"They think Junior's the thief?" Simon asked incredulously.

"The money was in his saddle bag." The warden picked up a newspaper from his cluttered desk. He held it up to show Simon the headline. *Lone Thief Caught Red-Handed!*

The warden tossed the paper aside before Simon noted any details. It took him a moment to recover his shock. He decided the paper had to be mistaken. The article was likely about some other fellow, not Junior.

Simon regained his senses. "Sir, I can tell you for certain, Junior didn't steal five thousand dollars. He's an innocent man. Someone is trying to frame him."

"Sure." The warden's mouth curved into a slow grin. "First time I ever heard that one."

"Junior Whitson wouldn't pick up a lost penny from the sidewalk, much less steal thousands of dollars."

"That's all right, Simon. Don't you worry," Junior called. "I'm sure they'll figure out the truth by and by."

"Not worried about a thing," Simon replied, his heart sinking. "No worries here."

Junior added, "Just as soon as my friend John Smith gets back, we'll straighten everything out."

"Who's John Smith?" Simon asked.

The warden shook his head. "Search me."

"Would you mind if I had a word with Junior?" Simon asked.

"Not really supposed to allow visitors," the warden replied.

"Five minutes is all I need."

The man shrugged and returned to his chair. He waved Simon off, gesturing to the back of the jail.

Simon pointed to a ring of keys, hanging on the wall. "Mind opening the door so we can talk face to face?"

The warden shook his head. "Nothing doing. If you want to talk to your friend, you'll be on opposite sides of the bars."

Simon walked down the narrow hallway, noting the empty cells. His footfalls echoed. The jail didn't have the usual stench of sweat or other unpleasant smells. The Sagebrush jail must not get too many overnight guests. This wasn't the first jail Simon had visited. Usually they were rat-infested, filthy, and dark.

His suspicion about Junior's arrest grew. The Rangers were likely dealing with a series of robberies along the border. Maybe this was part of a larger problem.

"Mighty glad to see a familiar face," Junior said with his usual cheer.

"I want to ask you a few questions. Keep your voice down. Who is this John Smith fella?"

"He's a friend I made on the road out of Brownsville. He was on his way home. His wife was getting ready to have her first baby. His horse wasn't terribly fast, and he worried he'd miss the baby's birth. Shoot, I remember when Ellwood was born like it was yesterday."

Junior's stories usually provided more detail than was really needed, much more, in truth, and usually not the details that might prove helpful. Most times Simon didn't mind, but in this instance, Simon needed the *pertinent* facts so he could get him out of this mess. There was the issue of the two boys, sure, and that was motivation enough, but Junior was also one of the best cowboys in the state of Texas, strong as an ox, good in the saddle and an excellent roper.

Simon spoke quietly. "I don't have a lot of time, Junior. Can you explain why the Texas Rangers think you stole five thousand dollars?"

"No idea. I've never stolen so much as a piece of gum. My daddy didn't raise a thief," Junior said, with a touch of indignation.

"I believe you. I know you're as honest as the day is long."

Junior crossed his arms. "I don't believe John stole that money either. He's fixin' to be a new father, after all."

"Did he give you any money?"

"No."

"Okay, good."

"John asked me to keep an *eye* on the money."

"Five thousand dollars?"

"He was in a hurry, don't you know. His wife was about to have their first baby. A boy, if I recall."

Simon gritted his teeth. "John Smith knew it was going to be a boy, did he?"

Junior chuckled and shook his head. "Yep. Darnedest thing."

Simon rested his forehead against steel bars. He closed his eyes and said a short prayer. *Dear Lord, grant me patience.*

"It's real nice of you to come see me, Simon. Could you please tell my folks I'm fine and I'll be home soon as I can? There's a real nice widow who brings me vittles and does my laundry."

"That so? Well, you look all right, considering you've been in jail for a few days now."

"Can you believe?" Junior shook his head and grinned. "Funny how the good Lord brings folks into your life, isn't it?"

"Right. I wanted to ask another question."

"Just when you least expect it, too," he mused. "That's the curious thing about Velma coming around right when I needed her help. Seems sort of funny now that I think about it. Not ha-ha funny, more like scratch-yer-head funny."

"I hear you. Glad she's helping you out. About the money—"

"Velma's pretty too." He smiled, shrugged and his expression grew sober. "I'm sure things will work out fine. Still." He drew a shaky breath. "I'm worried about the boys."

"They're perfectly fine. No need to worry."

"I know you'll take good care of them. I worry about their mama finding out I'm behind bars. More than anything I've wanted to raise them up out on the ranch. Don't let their mama take them back. Promise me that, would you?"

"I promise. Don't fret." Simon rubbed his forehead, trying to recover his thoughts. "One more question about John Smith. Did he say anything else about the money?"

"Not that I recall. Let's see now. He asked to borrow my horse as we were leaving Brownsville because we ended up riding along the road at the same time. He seemed real nervous. I guess it's understandable considering his wife-"

"Right. She was about to have her first child. One that Mr. Smith happened to know was going to be a boy. So, you lent him your horse. Then come to find out five thousand dollars was right there in his saddle bags?"

Junior shrugged. "He said he'd left a little something he needed in his bags. That he'd get back soon as he was able. I didn't know how much money he had. I wouldn't ever feel right looking through another man's belongings."

"The Rangers didn't bother with those sorts of good manners."

Junior looked regretful. "They didn't even say please or thank you."

"I'll be darned," Simon said from between gritted teeth.

"I hate to tell John how they rummaged through his bags. Poor manners, if you ask me. John's going to be hot under the collar."

"When, exactly, were you going to chat with John?"

"When he comes looking for his horse. Soon. I reckon. If he can find me here in Sagebrush." Junior grew a little misty-eyed. "He'll show up. Just as soon as his wife has that little baby. Wonder if they'll call it John, then the boy will be Junior just like me. Wouldn't that be something."

"Yes," Simon said slowly, gripping the bars. "It'll be something all right."

The warden appeared in the doorway. "That's enough, Mr. Honeycutt. Them Rangers paid me extra to keep this one. I've heard the Rangers are mighty keen on stopping the outlaws that have been robbing the courier service. They're telling folks they've caught the ringleader."

Simon muttered under his breath.

"Don't worry, Simon," Junior said cheerfully. "I've got a perfectly reasonable explanation for the judge. Tell my boys their daddy will be home soon enough. Along with a few stories."

"Let's hope it's soon," Simon replied under his breath. "Real soon."

"I've got the whole thing figured out." Junior grinned as he tapped his temple. "Got it right in here."

"Sounds mighty fine," Simon said, hoping he sounded cheerful instead of panicked. He bid the warden a cordial farewell and left the Sagebrush jail.

Chapter Five
Back in a Week

Virginia

Virginia wished she could have left for Bethany Springs at once. It was not to be. She needed to make sure her father's week was planned out, every lunch, dinner, and nap. She'd already written instructions for his secretary and the cook, but needed to visit with them in person, to hand them their schedules and explain how to handle Papa in her absence.

She also needed to have dinner with Papa that evening, to go over the coming week and to reassure him that all was in order, and that everything would be fine for both of them.

She was eager to get away from the governor's mansion for a few days, truth be told. More than anything, she wanted some time away from Papa. He'd been worried about the election for months, his concern dominating half their conversations. It would be nice to escape his never-ending worry, to devote a little time to the memory of her mother.

Early the next morning, Virginia packed the last of her things in the trunks. Her maid had offered to help but Virginia dismissed her, explaining she'd rather pack her own trunks. In the quiet of her room, she heard the unmistakable sound of her father's footfalls on the marble floor. She waited and held her breath.

She said a silent prayer that he'd continue past her door. All morning, she fretted that he would change his mind. He'd proclaim her plan frivolous, insist she stay home and postpone the visit to the grave just one more year. Mother would understand, he'd insist, seeing as it was an election year.

The mere thought of the discussion tightened a coil of worry around her chest.

Father knocked gently and pushed the door open. He looked at her, a tragic expression etched upon his features. Shaking his head, he heaved a weary sigh. "How can you leave me, darling child?"

"It's only for a week. Mama's birthday is in six days. I'll come home right after. You only have a few dinners on the agenda. And they're all gentlemen-only affairs. You'll hardly miss me."

"Are you certain you'll be safe by yourself?"

"I won't be alone. Wilhelmina and her daughter left yesterday. They're picking up provisions, airing the rooms and tending to things."

"I barely slept last night." Her father spoke with a tragic tone. "This morning I could hardly touch a bite of breakfast."

He slumped against the doorway, eyeing her trunk mournfully. She doubted his sad tale. Likely, he slept like a baby. What was more, the servants reported that he'd eaten an excellent breakfast.

"You have crumbs on your vest, Papa." Virginia pointed out. She suppressed a smile.

He looked sheepish as he brushed the incriminating crumbs away. "Who is driving your carriage to Bethany Springs?"

"Harrigan agreed to take me."

Her father wandered around her room over the next half hour, doing his best to upset her travel plans. His methods were subtle and underhanded. First, he stood by the window and sighed heavily. Next, he eyed her trunks and commented on the contents. All the while, he spoke of the old home. It was drafty. Dusty. Likely it was home to all manner of vermin.

Virginia ignored his attempts to keep her in Austin. She explained how she didn't mind drafts or vermin. She was made of sterner stuff. He grumbled. She waved off his complaints.

When she finished packing, she sweet-talked him into fastening the trunks. He relented with a pained sigh and did as she asked. After, he directed the servants to load her trunks onto the waiting carriage.

The two of them, Virginia and her father, linked arms and went downstairs where he kissed her goodbye and helped her into the old Childress ranch carriage. She assured him he'd be fine, and that she would be fine too. He insisted, that in her absence, he'd suffer terribly and that she was heartless to leave him alone. She laughed off his complaints.

After all, she'd be home very soon.

The driver prodded the horses and the carriage rolled down the road, away from the governor's mansion. Virginia tried not to look too pleased about the trip as she waved from the back window. Papa, solemn and forlorn, lifted his hand to bid her farewell.

Chapter Six
Cowboy Lessons for Young Buckeroos

Simon

After talking to Junior in Sagebrush, Simon made the trip back to the ranch, first stopping to visit with Andrew again. He gave Andrew the meager information he had, that Junior was accused of a robbery of some five thousand dollars, and that he would likely spend the rest of his life in a prison cell unless the Brotherhood found this so-called *John Smith*.

The Bethany Brothers concerned themselves with the lands surrounding Bethany Springs. They didn't extend their jurisdiction or their concerns outside that region, generally speaking. This case was different, however, since Junior was a son of Bethany Springs. Andrew immediately understood what he had to do, and Simon agreed. Andrew planned to leave before sunset to start the long process of tracking down the real thief, this *John Smith*, or whatever his name might be. Simon told Andrew to send word every couple of weeks about his whereabouts and what he'd learned.

Simon bid Andrew good luck and continued his ride home. His mother met him at the corral. Mama listened to his report with a grim expression. She said little, aside from telling him that he'd need to mind the two boys for the next few days since Sheldon and Franny intended to travel to Sagebrush to stay with Junior. They expected he'd soon be transferred to Austin for his arraignment.

Simon, weary from his travels, wondered how he'd manage a pair of rascally boys. He felt bad, however. Maybe even a little guilty for not returning with Junior. If only he'd brought the boys' father home, all would have been settled. He could be arranging a pleasant evening of cards instead of child-minding.

He didn't grumble. Instead, he agreed with his mother's instructions, unsaddled his horse, and let it loose in the corral.

"I suppose you *could* stay at the ranch house," his mother said, likely surprised he wasn't complaining. "I *could* practice my cooking."

"That would be swell. I can hardly stand my own cooking. Usually try to show up at Molly and Daniel's around suppertime."

Mama sighed. "Go fetch the boys from Sheldon and Franny's. Bring them back. I'm sure Sheldon hopes to head to Sagebrush at first light."

Simon went immediately to Sheldon's house, some measure of relief in his heart. Sure, he'd need to sit and have dinner with the two boys, and maybe even fuss at them when they got out of line, but he'd be doing it at Mama's house, and that would make everything considerably easier. No concerns about making food or cleaning up.

When he got to Sheldon's house, the two boys were already saddled, sitting on a couple of small ponies. Sheldon handed the reins to Simon and wished him good luck, saying he wasn't sure how long he'd be gone. Simon wished him and Franny a good trip and headed home, ponies and boys trailing him slightly to his side.

It was already late, and the boys seemed like they were half asleep. *That works just fine for me*, Simon thought to himself. *Maybe this won't be so bad after all.*

Ellwood and Tuck, both with shirts misbuttoned and hair unkempt, minded Simon perfectly. They were just a year apart, one eight and one nine, and Simon could hardly tell which was which. He tried to address them by their names but they both answered each time. After arriving at the ranch, they took their bags to the spare room and bedded down.

Simon said goodnight to his mother and went to his room. While climbing into bed he had a thought that surprised him, that maybe his time filling in for Junior might not be so bad, and that maybe he should try to teach the two boys a little more about ranch life. Maybe he'd bring about a change in these two young'uns, a good change. He'd teach them what it meant to be a cowboy, and they'd remember Simon as the man who put them on the right course. The thought brought a smile to his lips as he lay down and put his hands behind his head.

While the two boys had spent time on the Honeycutt ranch over the years, they'd mostly lived with their mother and various family members. They weren't much for cowboying. He'd fix that.

The next morning after breakfast he announced his plans. "We're going to make cowboys out of you over the next few days. By the time your daddy gets back, you'll both be a couple of buckeroos."

"We heard horses bite," Tuck said as they trudged to the corrals.

"And kick," Ellwood added.

"It happens. You just need to treat 'em right. Show them kindness but let 'em know who's boss too."

The boys looked bewildered. And, truth be told, a tad fretful. Worse, they seemed afraid of horses. That didn't really surprise Simon. The night before they were perfectly happy to ride on the ponies, but the regular horses were at least fifteen hands tall, with withers a good foot above the boys' heads.

The boys hung back as Simon went into the corrals and came back with two older horses, a couple of buckskins that had lived on the ranch for as long as anyone could recall.

"Listen up. Horses can tell if you're fearful. No need to worry. This here is Dusty, and the other is Rooster. My brothers and I learned to ride on these horses. They wouldn't hurt a fly."

The boys weren't convinced. Simon told them that if they wanted to ride, they'd need to saddle their own horse. Reluctantly, they came to his side and helped ready their horses. Slowly, their worries eased. When it was time to mount up, both boys were smiling and seemed pleased with the prospect of riding.

Tuck was the first in the saddle. Simon instructed him to walk around the corral while Ellwood got on his horse. He turned to help the other boy. Before he could so much as tighten the cinch, Ellwood gave a high-pitched yelp.

Simon whirled around in time to see Rooster bucking. The bucks weren't more than a few half-hearted hops, but Ellwood seemed sure he was about to meet his end. White-faced, he clung to the pommel. Rooster probably couldn't remember having this much fun. The old buckskin hopped a few more times before tiring of the prank.

Simon watched intently, wondering what might happen next, hoping the boy wouldn't lose his nerve. Ellwood had slipped halfway from the saddle and scrambled to hold on.

Rooster could have shaken the boy off like a pesky fly. Instead, the old horse came to a halt.

Ellwood heaved himself back to the saddle. Sitting, wide-eyed, a slow smile curved his lips. "Shucks. That was something. I can't wait to tell my daddy I almost got bucked off."

"That's the spirit," Simon hastened to say. "You sure showed ol' Rooster a thing or two."

"He's pretty ornery," Ellwood exclaimed. "Think my daddy will like how I rode an ornery horse? Will you be sure to tell him how Rooster couldn't buck me off?"

"Why, sure I will," Simon said. "Everyone'll be plum amazed."

They'd be amazed all right. Rooster probably hadn't bucked in a decade but that was beside the point. Simon turned back to Tuck who waited to mount his horse. Tuck looked less sure than a moment before.

"Now don't you worry, son. I'm certain Dusty won't give you a bit of trouble."

Tuck looked a little pale but seemed willing to get in the saddle. Simon lifted him atop the horse and hoped that Dusty hadn't gotten any ideas. Dusty walked around the corral slowly. Meanwhile a broad smile lit Tuck's face.

The two boys rode side by side, arguing good-naturedly about who was the superior rider. Tuck claimed he was better since he'd kept his horse in a mannerly walk. He knew how to show a horse who was boss. Ellwood insisted he was the better rider. After all, he'd managed to stay on a wild bronc.

Simon assured them they were both mighty fine riders. "We'll have you out on the range in no time."

He watched the boys, a smile tugging on his lips. Even though serious matters weighed on his mind, it pleased him to see the boys enjoying themselves. He could recall learning to ride. Back then it was Sheldon Senior, the boys' grandfather, who showed him how to handle a horse. Seemed a tad peculiar how in a way, things had come full circle.

Daniel, his older brother, came to the fence a short time later. "I heard you're minding the boys."

"Teaching them to be ranch hands."

"How's it going?"

"They're doing all right. Thankfully. I wasn't so sure, starting out. Ellwood nearly got bucked off if you can believe. It's not easy minding a couple of boys. Sort of nerve-wracking. I don't know how Mama managed to raise three boys all by herself."

Daniel chuckled.

"They're doing fine here in the corral. Hopefully, they'll do all right riding the trails. I tell you what. Teaching a couple of boys how to ride is going to help my prayer life." Simon gave his brother a wry grin.

"I hear you. Speaking of prayers. Molly and I sorta hoped Junior would be home by now."

"You and me both."

Daniel rested his elbows on the rail and watched the boys. "Maybe the judge will look kindly on Junior when Franny and Sheldon go to court with him."

"Best bet would be if Junior's case got dismissed."

Daniel nodded. "Those boys need their daddy."

A pang struck Simon's heart. So many folks depended on Junior getting released. Not just Ellwood and Tuck but Sheldon and Franny too. If Junior's case went to trial, there was no telling what Junior would say. The man could talk a blue streak and might just incriminate himself along the way.

"Molly told me something interesting," Daniel said. "Something she heard at the mercantile yesterday afternoon."

Simon only half-listened. He was too preoccupied with Junior's plight.

Daniel went on. "It concerns Virginia Childress."

Virginia Childress. The name sent a jolt down Simon's spine. He jerked around to face his brother. "What now?"

His brother seemed to find his response amusing. "Thought that might interest you."

Simon narrowed his eyes. "I'm not interested. I'm just wondering why you might bring up her name?"

Daniel shrugged. "Nothing too special. Didn't mean to get you riled."

"I'm not riled. Who's riled? Not me."

"Of course, you're not. My mistake."

"I'm just mighty curious what the governor's daughter has to do with anything. Seems there's plenty other things to talk about."

"All right. Just forget it. Anyway, you've got your hands full with the two boys."

"Spit it out, would you? Don't make me ask Molly. She'd likely think I was asking because I was sweet on the girl."

"The girl?" Daniel shrugged. "You mean Virginia?"

Simon scowled, refusing to argue with his brother. He wasn't sure why he felt so perturbed, but he needed to keep a tight rein on his anger. Here he was trying to be a good example to Ellwood and Tuck. It wouldn't be fitting to lose his temper. The boys waved from the other side of the corral; their faces wreathed in smiles.

Simon waved back and called out a few words of encouragement. "Look at those youngsters. A fine pair of cowboys."

"She's come home to Bethany Springs," Daniel said, a smile playing on his lips.

"I don't believe you."

"It's the truth. Word is that she's staying a week."

"You're fibbing. No way old Orville Childress plans to stay a week at his homestead. That little cabin isn't grand enough for our governor."

"Orville didn't come. Just Virginia."

Simon didn't reply. Virginia Childress. Here in Bethany Springs. It was hard to believe. He could still picture her face back in the day. He recalled how badly she wanted to clobber him. All on account of a little misunderstanding. They'd met only a few times at the fair. Somehow, he'd made an impression. And, oh, how she disliked him.

He wondered if she'd remember him. Would she still want to smack him? His lips twitched. He could feel his brother's attention fixed on him.

"What? I just hope she has a nice visit."

"Right," Daniel said.

Simon schooled his features to remove any sign of amusement.

Daniel wasn't convinced. "Why don't you pay a neighborly visit? Tell her about Junior, how he's a good man, the last person who'd steal five thousand dollars."

This time, Simon couldn't hold back the smile. It seemed a terrible idea. Virginia Childress wouldn't take kindly to a visit, certainly not from him. Once more, he pictured her fury, the way she shook her fist at him when she couldn't catch him and thump the smile from his face.

"You think me and the two boys ought to talk to her?" Simon asked.

"The way I figure," Daniel explained. "If you take the boys along, they'll only strengthen your argument. She's a woman, after all."

Simon chuckled. "They say she's helped Orville win the election. I don't suppose she could have done that if she hadn't grown up somewhere along the way."

Daniel frowned. "I'm not sure if I follow, but what I'm trying to say is she'd have a woman's tender heart. The sight of those two boys. No mother around. A father wrongly accused and in jail, well, I reckon she might feel inclined to help."

"Possibly." Simon wasn't sure. Even as a child, Virginia had put on airs and talked like a grown-up. Especially after the ice cream incident. Her insults made her sound like someone's fussy maiden aunt. Whenever he saw her at the fall fair, they'd take up where they left off the year before. Her prissy words would ring in his ears all the way home, making him chuckle. First chance he got, he'd slip into Mama's study, slide the dictionary off the shelf and look up every bad thing she'd called him. *Vile. Odious. Reprobate.*

For some reason, her fine insults made him almost proud.

But then she stopped visiting Bethany Springs. Simon didn't know why. A few years later, her father announced his intention to run for governor. He'd won. Simon heard Virginia had written his speeches. He knew right away that little Miss Prissy had likely written the finest campaign speeches possible, ones that people talked about and felt good about. Ones that got Orville Childress elected as the Governor of Texas. The thought always warmed his heart even though she hadn't ever had anything good to say about him.

To Virginia he'd probably always be a rogue. Only she didn't call him a rogue, he recalled. No. She'd called him a *villainous* rogue.

He chuckled.

Daniel gestured to Ellwood and Tuck. "Go see her and take the boys along. She'll be more inclined to help Junior. She'll want to help them. It's natural for a woman."

Simon still couldn't picture Virginia all grown-up. The notion left him a little light-headed. He couldn't imagine what he'd say or even the very notion that she'd returned to the Childress cabin. The homestead had stood empty for years now.

"I'll go," Simon said simply.

Daniel grinned. He pushed off the railing, slapped Simon's shoulder and bid him goodbye. "Junior needs all the help he can get. I know you and Virginia weren't exactly on the best of terms, but I'm sure the two of you can let bygones be bygones."

"Of course," Simon said as Daniel walked away. "What did you expect?"

Daniel arched a brow.

"Well?" Simon asked.

Daniel turned away. Simon could have sworn he heard his brother chuckle. He called after him, asking again what he meant. Daniel kept walking, staying silent and without turning back, gave a dismissive wave over his shoulder.

Chapter Seven
First Morning at the Family Homestead

Virginia

The first night in the Childress homestead, Virginia spent alone. Utterly alone. No servants. No maids. For the first time in her life, Virginia Childress had spent the night by herself.

Several servants had come to Bethany Springs to tidy the house before her arrival, but Virginia had dismissed them an hour after arriving. The house still needed work, but the bedroom had been cleaned and aired out, and the bed had a new mattress, new pillows and fresh linens.

She felt a deep sense of happiness. Birds chirped. The breeze stirred the leaves of the nearby pecan tree, but the morning was quiet and peaceful. And thank goodness too. She was far from the hustle and bustle of the mansion. The cooks didn't need her help with the menu. Her father couldn't demand attention. There was no important event to plan or attend. The house was quiet.

Dawn filled the room with a soft, coral light. She lay in bed smiling as she gazed at the rough-hewn timbers spanning the ceiling. The old beams held a story, one she'd dearly love to know. Sadly, the stories were lost. Her father never spoke of early times. Virginia knew only that the beams had been cut by her grandfather when he'd claimed the land.

The story of her family's home made it as special to her as the distinguished history of the fine governor's mansion. More personal, of course. The homestead didn't fill her with the same awe as the mansion in Austin. And yet, the homestead offered something more, a link to her past. She'd never known her mother. At times she wasn't sure if she really knew her father. Yet, here in the old house, a warm contentment drifted across her heart, and she noted a bond to both parents as well as their distant kin.

Perhaps that was the reason she'd dismissed the servants. In truth, they were reluctant to stay. Not one of them saw what she saw. Instead of a rustic cabin, they'd seen signs of vermin. Instead of peaceful vistas, they fretted about outlaws. Instead of whimsical, unmatched furnishings, they complained about the crude accommodations.

And *that* was before they learned they'd be staying in the cook house, cabin that was even more uncivilized than the main Childress cabin. They'd voiced the same complaint. They'd been hired to tend to a governor's mansion, not a rustic hovel.

When Virginia listened to their harsh words about her family's home, she dismissed them and sent them back to Austin. She sent a letter for her father, telling him she'd do better without the fuss of servants and to send the carriage back in a week's time.

She'd never done anything like that before. It felt rebellious. He'd object, of course, but not so much that he'd make the trip to Bethany Springs to fuss. Virginia said her morning prayers, asking God to bless her short visit to the homestead and thanking Him for the chance to stay at the family home.

After she dressed, she prepared a simple breakfast from the provisions the servants brought.

Next, she reviewed her notes for her article. Sitting in the sun-filled parlor, she considered what to write. The editor of the *Texas Ladies Journal* was always willing and, in fact, eager to publish anything she wrote. Articles from the governor's daughter boosted subscriptions.

Still, Virginia fretted about the article. It would likely be the last she'd write before the election. For that reason, it seemed even more important than prior pieces. She didn't want to come across simply as a loving daughter. She wanted to show readers that her father was a man of honor.

Even more, she secretly wanted to prove she was a capable writer. There were times when she dreamed of working for the *Texas Ladies Journal*. She imagined writing or editing, perhaps when her father had finished his second term and no longer needed her constant help.

The morning passed as Virginia wrote, rewrote, and threw away a dozen drafts. The effort exhausted her. Why, she wasn't sure. In the past, she always had a hundred ideas. The editor would gently tease her for her lengthy pieces. Not today.

With a sigh, she set aside her writing and resolved to tidy the house.

The Childress homestead had been neglected for too long. The servants had cleaned everything but hadn't set things in an orderly manner. She decided upon the first project, the bookshelves that flanked the fireplace. Some of the old books needed mending. She set them on the highest shelf. The old farm and ranch manuals went on the second shelf, along with a pair of cookbooks.

Next came a handful of poetry and fiction volumes. She ran her fingers along the books, wondering if her mother had read them. Perhaps they belonged to Papa or his parents.

A small wooden frame lay on the bottom shelf. Virginia turned it over, careful of the brittle edges. The frame held an embroidered swathe of linen. Delicate, yellow blooms surrounded a single, embroidered word. *Hiraeth*.

She didn't know the meaning of the word. Why had the frame been hidden away? It seemed a shame. Such beautiful stitchwork ought to be shown off. She cleared the farm and ranch manuals from the second shelf and set them aside. The Childress land hadn't been farmed or ranched in ages, so the manuals weren't important for now.

In the middle of the empty shelf, she set the frame.

Taking a step back, she admired the handiwork. The mysterious artifact had come from one of her kin and she resolved to ask her father who had taken the time to stitch all the tiny blossoms. And just as importantly, what did *Hiraeth* mean?

Still feeling restless, she decided to set her writing aside until later. The sunny day beckoned. She'd go for a walk, take the trail to the hillside, and visit her mother's grave. As she stood on the porch, putting on her sunbonnet, she heard the sound of hoofbeats.

Startled, she drew a sharp breath and retreated to the cabin door. Three horsemen approached. Dust billowed behind them. As they drew closer, she noted two of the riders were boys. Only one was a man. Feeling foolish, she crossed the porch, stopping at the top of the steps to wait.

A prickle of distress wound around her heart. The boys didn't trouble her. That would be silly. Heavens, they looked as though they'd just learned to ride. But something about the cowboy riding between them made her yearn to retreat to the shadows once again.

She forced herself to stay put. Taking a stand was a matter of pride. After all, if she planned to stay an entire week, she could hardly scurry away like a frightened rabbit at the first sign of trouble. That wouldn't do at all. She came from stern stock. According to the stories Papa used to tell, her grandmother scared off a band of cattle rustlers at the age of eighteen. Grandmother had been a mere girl, a year younger than Virginia was now.

Virginia willed herself to remain rooted to the spot. She ignored the worrying thoughts.

The cowboy, along with the two young boys, rode into the yard and dismounted. The boys seemed unsure what to do with their mounts. They waited, looking around in confusion until the man took their horses and tied them to the weathered hitching post. A few words followed. Something about them staying put.

The man ambled across the stretch of overgrown grasses. Something about his confident gait vexed her. He swaggered, overly familiar, as if they were old friends instead of strangers meeting for the first time.

Her dread faded. A new emotion took off with her imagination. Childhood anger. Youthful indignation. There was only one person in the world who inspired such an array of heated, unladylike outbursts. Only one. Simon Honeycutt.

No.

She refused to believe. It wasn't possible. Surely, she was mistaken. Aside from the servants, few people knew she'd come to stay at her family's home. She'd been careful to keep her plans private and for that simple reason didn't expect anyone to pay her a visit. Least of all her childhood nemesis.

Setting her hand over her frantic heart, she watched as he strolled up to the house, a handsome smile curving his lips. He was tall, broad, and showed every sign of the same incorrigible boy of her memory. He stopped. With all the arrogance in the world, he took off his hat, rested his boot on her porch and nodded. "Afternoon, Miss Childress."

Her breath caught. She could hardly breathe, much less answer.

Simon Honeycutt was at least a foot taller than when she'd seen him last. His broad shoulders had widened considerably. His eyes sparkled as he offered a charming smile. He was handsome, terribly handsome, and for some reason this seemed particularly troubling.

Simon. Honeycutt. No. It wasn't possible.

This... this was like a terrible dream. Perhaps it was her punishment for trying to shirk her duties and hiding herself at the family homestead. She'd fled Austin. Deserted her father. And here was her penalty. Six foot and more of penance in the form of Simon Honeycutt.

She'd come home, finally, and the first person to call was the last person she wished to see. Ever.

He'd offered a greeting. Awaited a reply. She tried to offer something intelligible. What came out sounded like a garbled hiccup. Simon found this amusing. Of course, he did. He shrugged as if trying to suggest her clumsy reply was to be expected.

"It's been a minute, wouldn't you say?" Simon asked.

Virginia wanted to give a response that was both polite but firm. Words that came to mind included: Do I know you? Whatever do you mean? Do you realize I'm the governor's daughter?

To her dismay, she could not summon a single word.

Her attention drifted. Simon Honeycutt was no longer a vile, odious boy. Well, he might well be vile and odious, but in the last twelve years, he'd changed. Aside from his height, his light hair had turned sandy brown. A short beard darkened his jaw. His eyes sparked with warmth and humor. He was different. And yet the same.

At second glance, she noted how his eyes held the very same playful glint. His smile suggested equal parts mischief and charm.

"Simon?" she asked, primly. "Simon Honeycutt. Is it you?"

She wasn't sure why she even bothered with the question. Maybe because she hoped her mind played tricks. Maybe the handsome stranger hadn't ever teased or tormented her at the county fair. She held her breath and waited.

He nodded. "That's right. It's me, Simon Honeycutt. I'm mighty glad to see you, Goose."

Chapter Eight
Flowers for Mama Childress

Simon

Virginia Childress looked as though she might faint right there on her own front porch. Her deathly pale complexion put Simon into somewhat of a quandary. Should he offer to help her to a chair? Catch her before she tipped over or swooned or whatever governor's daughters did? Or should he keep his distance?

Mama had always taught him and his brothers to treat womenfolk with manners and courtesy. She'd drilled those lessons in when he was just a boy, and he could almost hear her stern instructions. Back then, he hadn't been what you might call a quick study, but he'd gotten the gist of things eventually.

A small murmur of distress fell from her lips.

He winced at her response. He'd been trying to be charming or at least pleasant. And yet, despite his best intentions, Virginia had scrambled back like he was some sort of dangerous criminal. It seemed she might have even called him just that a time or two a few years back. Or maybe it was dangerous reprobate.

Her distress troubled him for a moment before he let his gaze drift from her eyes to her lips and down the pale length of her graceful neck. A gentle thrill gathered around his heart.

The girl he'd chased so many years ago certainly looked different from the girl standing before him. Very different. He forced himself to attend to the matter at hand.

"It's all right, Virginia. I'm not going to harm you. I'm just here to pay a visit. Being neighborly. That's all."

"Neighborly?" she whispered.

"That's right."

Simon called to the boys, instructing them to bring the parcel from his saddle bag. Tuck hurried to do Simon's bidding and delivered the linen wrapped package. "Thank you, son. Go play with your brother while I visit with Miss Childress."

Tuck ran off and when he was gone, Simon held out the parcel. "My mother sends her regards along with a couple dozen sugar cookies."

"Thank you." She accepted the gift with a faint smile. "I've always thought highly of your mother."

She went inside to set the cookies on the table. Simon followed but stopped in the doorway and took in the details of the front room. It was tidy, rustic and dominated by a large dining table. Papers lay neatly in an even stack that looked like Virginia had used a plumb line to straighten them. Seemed about right. Virginia Childress liked things orderly. She'd struck him as that sort of girl when she was young and even more so now. That much was clear.

Just a few inches to the side of the papers, she'd lined up her inkwell and pens. They looked like tiny soldiers. Everything suggested precision and care. He could picture her sitting at the table, her back ramrod straight as she fretted over minute details.

His gaze drifted back to Virginia. She was a sight. Pretty but prim. All grown up, yet just the same. An urge to tease her about something, anything really, came from nowhere. In the middle of his careless reverie, he recalled Junior and especially the boys. Instantly he pushed aside his absurd notions of teasing and whatnot.

"I've only seen your family's home from a distance," he said, hoping a little friendly conversation would ease her mind. "It's mighty pretty."

"I do like it here. Very much." The tension around her eyes lessened. "I haven't come to visit for years."

"Are you here alone?" He frowned, looking around for a sign of others. "Surely not."

She didn't want to answer. He could tell as much. Likely she fretted about giving away any details. As if he'd try something untoward if he knew she was by herself.

He stepped out the door. She hadn't invited him after all and if he remained on the porch, she might feel more assured.

She followed him out and shut the door behind her. "Are those your children?"

"No, ma'am. I'm not married. Those are my godchildren."

"I see." She tugged at her sleeves with gloved hands. "How lovely."

He suspected she was relieved the boys weren't his. Probably thought he was still a troublesome rascal, not fit to raise children.

"The children's father is in jail," Simon said. "Might as well get straight to the point. I was hoping you could help. I've heard you play a part in your father's success. Perhaps you could put in a good word for Junior."

"Junior?"

"Sheldon Whitson. Everyone calls him Junior."

Understanding lit her eyes. "This must be the man your mother spoke of in her letter."

"That's right."

"My father mentioned the letter."

He nodded, grateful that she knew a little about the matter. If she was familiar with the situation, it might help things along. Maybe she'd forget about his pranks so long ago.

He spoke. "That's right. I don't like to trouble folks, but I wanted to explain about Junior's situation first chance I got. I wasn't sure how long you'd be staying in Bethany Springs."

"Six days." She cast a worried glance toward the boys. "I help my father with his work. As much as I can, but I doubt I could do anything for a man accused of a crime. My father prides himself on taking a hard stance when it comes to outlaws."

"Junior Whitson is no more of an outlaw than I am."

In an instant, he knew he'd taken a wrong turn. Virginia Childress had proclaimed him an outlaw some time back. From the looks of things, she hadn't changed her opinion.

She studied him with a skeptical look in her eyes. "I'm not sure if your comparison helps Mr. Whitson's case."

"Junior is one of the best men I've ever known," Simon said quietly. "He's good-hearted. Kind. Incapable of telling a lie. There's no way he robbed a bank. He traded horses with an outlaw. That was his only mistake. Now he's left holding the bag."

"I'm certain he'll get a fair trial and the truth will prevail."

Simon gritted his teeth. Virginia Childress was a little, snooty know-it-all. The same annoying girl he remembered from so many years ago. She was pretty. Yes. Very pretty. He'd give her that, but she hadn't gained much in kindness or sympathy or warmth. Junior sat in a jail cell, and she didn't give a darn if he got sent off for a crime he didn't commit.

He kept a tight rein on his irritation, however. Junior depended on him to fix things which meant Simon had to hold his tongue. For now, anyway.

"Ellwood and Tuck need a father." He hoped he sounded perfectly reasonable. "Their mama left the family. I'll end up raising them if Junior goes to jail."

"I wish there was something I could do."

"I'm counting on it," he replied, his tone firm.

Virginia pursed her lips. "It was lovely to see you, Simon," she said. She held out her gloved hand, clearly offering a gesture of farewell.

He had no intention of leaving till she agreed to help. Just the same, he couldn't resist the offer of her delicate hand. He took her hand in his. It was small. Fragile. He liked the way it felt resting in his palm. Pushing his thoughts aside, he forged ahead. "We're not done talking, *Miss Childress*."

She didn't reply. It seemed she found his touch unnerving, just as he did.

The feel of her gloved hand sent a tremor along his arm. For a moment, he could hardly think. He wasn't sure why and the entire notion aggravated him plenty. He dropped her hand and took two steps back.

She knit her brow. He watched as she carefully schooled her features to conceal her emotions. She knew how to guard her feelings. Not like when she was a girl. Nowadays she wouldn't let things fluster her. He had to admit that Virginia Childress had learned a thing or two since he'd chased her around the fairgrounds.

"You're concerned about the boys' father," she said thoughtfully.

Simon could tell she spoke in a measured, careful manner to keep her distance.

She continued. "You're a fine godfather. I can assure you that Governor Childress cares a great deal about justice being served."

Dang. She was good. He marveled at her ability to keep her wits about her while his thoughts scattered like frisky yearlings.

"That's mighty nice to hear," he snapped. "Just the same, I hope you might lend a hand. Maybe talk to your daddy and maybe even write a note to the judge. I reckon you know all those Austin bigwigs."

Her jaw dropped. His request shocked her to the point of stunned silence. Before she could gather her wits and argue, he went on. "I realize you don't know Junior, but you know me. You can take my word, can't you?"

Her only response was a look of deep dismay.

"Come on, Virginia. You and I go way back, don't we?"

Stone-cold silence was his answer. He gestured to Tuck and Ellwood. "I'm asking on their behalf. Surely you can help a couple of innocent kids from Bethany Springs."

The mention of children seemed to draw her back to the matter at hand. Her gaze drifted past his shoulder. The boys had wandered off and he could tell she was watching them. Their voices floated on the summer breeze. Innocent. Childlike.

At times, he wondered how much Ellwood and Tuck really knew about matters. Hopefully, they knew nothing about the trial. He prayed that Junior would be released before the trial. If that happened, Junior would return to Bethany Springs and the boys wouldn't ever be the wiser. Hopefully.

Simon pressed on. "Those two just got abandoned by their mama. Their grandparents can't manage them. Junior's all they have. Aside from me, which isn't saying much. I don't even like children. Not much, anyway. I'd be a terrible choice."

Virginia gave a soft murmur of dismay. It was clear she agreed.

The boys' voices grew louder. Their footsteps thudded on the path. Both boys were laughing and tugging on each other's shirts to reach the porch first.

"Miss Childress," Ellwood said breathlessly as he held out a straggly bunch of blooms. "We picked some flowers."

"They're lovely," she said softly.

She gazed at the children as if *they* were the ones awaiting some terrible sentence. Not Junior. She worried about them being in Simon's care and to some extent, she was right to worry. And yet, he couldn't help feeling a tad offended. He'd claimed to be a terrible choice, but part of him wished that she'd argued a little.

Both boys held out a bouquet of wildflowers. They looked up at Virginia with an expression of hope and happiness, as if they didn't have a care in the world.

"They're Indian Paintbrush," Tuck offered. "The field's full of 'em."

"Thank you, boys," she said gently. "Mama loved Indian Paintbrush flowers. That's what my father always said. She loved them almost as much as yellow roses. I'll leave them at her grave this afternoon."

"Her grave?" Ellwood asked.

"Yes." Virginia looked dismayed.

"Your mama died?" Tuck asked, white-faced. "She's passed away?"

"She did." Virginia did her best to compose herself. "I'm going to visit her grave this morning. I'll leave your flowers for her. Thank you."

"We'd better go with you, miss." Tuck attached himself to her side, firmly taking her hand in his.

"She can't go visiting her mama's grave all by herself, Uncle Simon," Ellwood proclaimed.

Virginia opened her mouth to reply as her eyes widened. Just as quickly, she closed her mouth, reluctant to dismiss the boy's offer. She gave Simon an imploring look, one he ignored.

"Folks always complain about us," Ellwood explained. "Like they don't want us around. Mama says we're a pair of nuisances. Grandpa says our mama's no good and we likely take after her, and our father says he doesn't know what to do with us, but he'll figure it out by and by. Just the same, we promise to be good if you let us come with you."

"Oh dear," Virginia murmured.

"We won't do a thing wrong, will we, Uncle Simon?" Tuck asked.

"Of course, you won't. You're a pair of fine boys. That's what you are." Simon suppressed a smile. "Don't you agree, Miss Childress."

Virginia swallowed hard. "I suppose that I agree."

"We'll just tag along as a sort of escort," Simon said, giving her a pointed look. "That would give us a chance to visit a little more."

Ellwood nodded. "We can pick more flowers for you on the way back, Miss Childress. After we say howdy to your mama's grave."

Virginia seemed flustered by the boys' show of kindness. After a moment, she composed herself and relented. "That would be lovely. Thank you."

She motioned to the path leading from the house. The boys began their trek along the trail, flowers in hand. They skipped along the path, laughing, and teasing one another. Simon and Virginia walked behind them side by side.

"They're very charming," Virginia said.

"They're all right, I suppose. Tolerable. Everyone thinks they're a pair of rascals. Especially my mother, but they're just normal boys. A little loud. A little rowdy. Regular boys."

They walked in silence for a long moment until she stumbled on a root and gave a cry of dismay. When she recovered, her face had turned a lovely shade of pink. Simon couldn't help noticing how pretty she looked when she blushed.

Of course, she was flat-out pretty the rest of the time too. Even when she wasn't blushing. He tried to push the thought aside. It was important that he pay attention to the matter at hand, not the soft blush of Virginia's cheeks.

"The path's uneven," he said. "Allow me." He held out his arm, daring her to refuse.

She studied him, some of that old wariness in her eyes. Tentatively, she set her hand in the crook of his arm. "I don't have much influence over my father, Simon."

"That's not what I've heard. Folks say you're smart as a whip. That your father depends on you."

"That's very kind. I help my father, but that doesn't mean he takes my suggestions. Not when they don't suit him." Her eyes sparked with wry amusement. "He wants my help. Not my opinions."

Simon pretended to look affronted. He shook his head. "Menfolk can be mighty stubborn."

He patted her hand, a gesture which was a little forward, considering. He could all but hear his mother lecturing him on manners, but he couldn't resist. Something about Virginia Childress brought out some of his less polite tendencies.

He pulled his hand away as he resolved to be friendly but polite to Virginia. He needed to avoid getting distracted. Junior's life depended on it. The well-being of Ellwood and Tuck depended on it as well, not to mention his own well-being if he suddenly became a father to two raucous boys. He'd have to do his very best to resist temptation.

After all, this was no county fair.

Not anymore.

Chapter Nine
The Walk to Mama's Grave

Virginia

The path to the family plot cut across a large meadow. An endless expanse of grass stretched to the horizon, the tall gold-green stems swaying in the late-summer breezes. The wind skimmed across the meadow like waves rushing to a distant shore.

The sight awed Virginia. The rush of the wind thrilled her senses even though it played havoc with her bonnet and tugged tresses loose. By the time they reached the top of the trail, she'd look a sight.

She didn't mind. Not a bit. How long had she yearned to come back to the homestead? It made her smile inwardly to think she walked her family's land on the arm of Simon Honeycutt. It was hard to believe. The entire scenario seemed like a dream of sorts.

She had to admit she was glad for his company and that of the children.

Visiting her mother's grave often filled Virginia's heart with mixed emotions. When she was a small child, the experience gave her bad dreams. Now, as an adult, visiting the grave made her both happy and melancholy. Perhaps it was best described as bittersweet.

She hadn't come to the homestead or to her mother's grave out of duty. Not anymore. It was more a sense of longing or missing her mother, though it was hard to miss a person she'd never met.

In addition to the mix of happiness and sorrow, a sense of guilt hung over her due to the grim fact that her mother had died in childbirth. It was a feeling she rarely talked about. Even with her father.

The truth of the matter was she couldn't recall more than a handful of times when her father had spoken to her directly about the painful subject. Instead, he referred to her mother's passing in vague terms. Euphemisms mostly.

The unspoken message was always the same. The matter was best left in the past. For the most part, she felt grateful he didn't mention the subject. Walking the trail with Simon, she prayed he would also treat the matter with some delicacy.

She smiled at him, sensing he'd carry on with his gallant manner. He smiled back, his eyes sparking with gentle humor. Warmth gathered around her heart, filling her with a rush of happiness. This short walk might be the only time she'd have with her old nemesis, but she was grateful for the new memories.

"It's sweet to see you with the two boys." The instant she said the words, she wished them back. He'd surely take the opportunity to return to the topic of Junior and the moment would be spoiled. Inwardly, she chided herself.

"I've enjoyed having them around. More than I'd expected," Simon said. "Don't know why everyone keeps saying they're so rotten. They seem just fine to me."

She very nearly laughed at his words. Simon had been a perfect little beast when he was younger, so it made sense that he'd view their behavior as acceptable.

"Then again," Simon added. "It's only been a day, so maybe it's too early to judge."

The two boys walked single file, each stretching out their hands to brush the tops of the tall grass. They laughed and joked and laughed some more. While she couldn't make out precisely what either boy said, their childlike exuberance brought a smile to her lips. She recalled Ellwood's words. The boy spoke of his grandfather's harsh criticism. To make matters worse, their mother had abandoned them. Virginia's heart felt heavy.

"I'm sure they're lovely boys," Virginia said. "Many people expect children to act like small adults."

"I reckon that happens."

"My father always wanted me to behave like I'd just completed finishing school. Especially when we were amongst his friends and colleagues. He'd fuss at me and insist I act ladylike, to use the proper fork, say please and thank you but not much else."

"Sounds pretty hard." He gave her a sympathetic look. "I still forget which fork to use. Though I do remember to say please and thank you. Most times."

"All I wanted was to come to the ranch and skip along the trails. I yearned to feel the grass on my fingers. To pick flowers. To play without care, but Papa always made his expectations clear."

"Did he?"

Virginia wasn't sure why she blathered on so. She ought to speak of pleasant things, not childhood disappointments, especially if they concerned her dear father, and even more so if she was talking to her old adversary. Simon seemed so attentive. And yet, she told herself to hold her tongue.

Distantly, she recalled a very different Simon Honeycutt, one that enjoyed tugging her pigtails.

"What did he expect?" Simon asked gently.

Virginia directed her gaze downward, noting the dirt clinging to her boots. "For one, he expected me to keep my shoes clean. If I scuffed my boots, he'd give me a long, long lecture."

"Keep your boots clean?"

She lowered her voice to mimic her father's tone. "Young lady, those boots came all the way from Paris. They cost a fortune. You mustn't be so careless."

Simon smiled. "That so? My boots came from here in Bethany Springs and first off belonged to Daniel which meant they were scuffed when I got them. Mama made me clean them every so often even though they got dirty again soon enough."

"Lucky you."

"Never thought about it."

"My father demanded perfection."

His brows knit. "And if that didn't happen?"

Virginia gave a light, dismissive laugh. It sounded hollow. Simon kept his attention on her. Why, she wondered, was she telling Simon all this nonsense? Thankfully they neared the top of the hillside. Maybe when they arrived, she'd manage to quit spilling her childhood complaints.

A moment later they reached the top of the hill. The boys stopped a short distance ahead to gaze across the landscape and take in the view. Virginia also found her gaze drawn across the land that stretched out to the horizon.

"Well?" Simon prompted. "What if you weren't perfect?"

"Oh, nothing too terrible. Heavens, he never scolded or struck me."

He smiled and patted her hand, a sweet gesture that made her breath catch.

"Mama didn't get too hot and bothered when we were in trouble. She just sent me and my brothers out to clear pastures. We had to pick up rocks and pile them along the fence line. That was all. Although once she locked my brother in a stall for a couple of hours."

"Surely not Daniel!" she said with mock indignation.

"No. Of course not Daniel. My big brother hardly ever stepped out of line. It was always me and Zach getting into trouble."

Virginia laughed softly. Warmth drifted across her skin. Her thoughts went to the subject of her father's disapproval. If he could see her now, walking arm in arm with Amelia Honeycutt's son, he'd be far more than disappointed. There would be no end to his sense of betrayal.

She wondered if Simon knew of the bad blood between her father and his mother. Curiosity tempted her to ask. She resisted the urge. Why mention any hint of strife between the two families? Especially when things were going so well between her and Simon. She had to admit she enjoyed his company and his attention. For once, she'd allow herself a small, harmless, stolen pleasure.

Chapter Ten
Two Acrobats near an Unmarked Grave

Simon

While Simon had every intention of talking more about Junior's trouble, the fragile look he saw in Virginia's eyes held him back. As they walked the path, he let himself enjoy her company. He was glad he'd kept his silence. After all, they were about to visit her mother's grave. Junior's troubles would have to wait. As they walked up the trail and approached the gravesite, she grew quiet.

He might not be the most gentlemanly of the Honeycutt brothers. Virginia wouldn't ever credit him with Daniel's effortless charm. Yet, he still liked to think he had some small bit of tenderness somewhere in his rugged heart.

When they arrived at the family plot, he took off his hat and gestured to the boys that they follow suit. They did as he asked and stood beside him, quiet and respectful. He gave them an approving nod.

The group bowed their heads in silent prayer. After a short while, Virginia moved to her mother's gravestone and ran her fingers along the top. "Mama was just twenty-two when she died."

"It's very sad." Simon grimaced at his clumsy words.

"It is sad," Virginia murmured.

Simon didn't reply.

"But it's happy. In a way. Daddy always said my mother loved the ranch and wanted to be buried here."

"That doesn't sound happy," Tuck said.

Virginia nodded. "Maybe not. I suppose my father wanted to make me feel better."

"Was she sick?" Ellwood asked.

"Ellwood." Simon cleared his throat. "Quit pestering Miss Childress. Understand?"

Ellwood nodded and offered Virginia a look of remorse.

"It's all right, boys. No need for the long faces. We're not attending a funeral. You can go play. I won't be more than a few moments."

Both boys looked relieved and scampered off to a nearby oak. While Virginia returned her attention to the headstone, the boys clambered up the lowest branch, laughing and clowning. Simon wished they'd find some other, less boisterous way to keep busy. It seemed untoward even though Virginia didn't seem troubled.

She folded her arms and gazed across the horizon. "Mama always liked this spot on the hillside. That's what my father told me."

"Isn't that something?" Simon wasn't sure what to say and hoped his words might comfort her or at least not make matters worse. He watched the boys, hoping they wouldn't tumble from the tree.

The boys looped their legs around the narrow branch and dropped back. Simon grimaced, half-expecting them to fall. Instead, they hung upside down, laughing like a pair of hooligans.

Virginia wiped a tear and laughed too, albeit far more softly than the boys. "I ought to bring them every time I visit my mother's grave. They lighten the mood considerably."

The boys swung back and forth.

"Let's show Uncle Simon a trick," Ellwood shouted.

Tuck laughed. "Ready?"

Simon's heart thudded with alarm. A trick?

The boys grabbed hold of the branch and shifted their legs. Then they hung upside down again and began swinging back and forth. They gathered momentum. The tree swayed. The branch bowed. Before Simon could tell them to stop, they swung wide and flipped, landing firmly on their feet. With a triumphant whoop, they held their hands up.

They jumped up and held their arms up in triumph. Virginia clapped; her tears almost forgotten.

Simon felt a twinge of nausea.

"That was marvelous," she exclaimed. "Well done, you two."

"Want us to do it again?" Ellwood offered.

"No!" Simon shouted. "Climbing is one thing but jumping from the tree is another."

The boys grumbled.

"Whose grave is this?" Ellwood asked as he crouched near a clump of grass. "It's sort of small. Puny."

Virginia went to his side and shook her head. "I don't know, in fact, I don't ever recall seeing it before."

Tuck gently tugged the grass aside. "Maybe it's a child's grave."

"I don't believe so," she said. "Although, I can't say for sure. The gravesite belongs to my family. Perhaps it's a cousin my father never mentioned."

"It doesn't have writing," Ellwood said matter-of-factly. "And your Mama's grave just has her name and the day she was born. Not the other day like they usually have. Seems peculiar, doesn't it, Miss Virginia?" He gestured to other headstones on the other side of the oak. "All the other ones have two dates along with the person's name."

"You're right about that. I keep telling Daddy to have the date added." She sighed and moved to the small marker. "I'm ashamed of our neglect. We ought to take better care of our family's final resting place. I'll be sure to have my father tell the engravers to add an inscription for this poor little soul."

The wind blew across the hillside. Virginia's bonnet ribbons fluttered as she knelt to study the small gravestone more closely.

"How peculiar," she murmured. "I wonder who this little one could be."

Chapter Eleven
Simon Teases Virginia

Virginia

Walking back to the homestead, her hand on Simon's arm, Virginia thought about her father. She missed him that afternoon there on the hillside and felt grateful for the company of Simon and the two boys.

How, she wondered, was her father faring without her?

Hopefully, he wouldn't miss her at all. He had something to do each day, things he liked doing. She'd taken great effort to make sure of that. With any luck, he'd hardly notice her absence.

She couldn't help but worry about him, though. A little. More present in her mind, she looked forward to a good day of writing, in the peace and quiet of the homestead.

The thought of the unmarked grave crossed her mind. She glanced back at the family plot on the hillside behind her. A sense of unease wrapped around her heart and a rush of worry fell from her lips. "Father won't want to talk about the unmarked grave."

Simon knit his brow with concern.

She chided herself. *Had she said that out loud?* It had been a private thought. One that Simon might use against her somehow. She fretted. Maybe it was the years of politics that left her wary and guarded. Then again, it might have been her earliest memories of Simon that honed her instincts.

To her relief, Simon didn't tease her. He regarded her with a warm look and gentle smile. "Some folks avoid graves. The memories are too painful. My mother, on the other hand, regularly visits my father's grave. She spends a fair bit of time tidying up and, you know... complaining."

"Complaining?"

He looked sheepish. "Mama talks to the headstone, giving it a report about her three sons. In her mind she's talking to my father, but if you just stand back and watch her, she's talking to the headstone. Usually, she's got a bee in her bonnet about something or other. Not that Mama is likely to wear a bonnet. More likely, she's wearing a Stetson."

Virginia tried not to smile. "Are you suggesting your poor mother has a long list of complaints?"

"Afraid so."

"Surely not about Daniel," she teased.

Simon shook his head. "Daniel's married if you didn't know. And he doesn't walk on water, just to be clear."

Virginia could hardly hold back a soft laugh. "Of course. And yet, I always thought him so kind, so honorable. I admit to a small fondness for Daniel. He probably doesn't even remember me."

Simon didn't reply.

"Just a silly, girlish admiration," Virginia added.

They walked in silence. Virginia stole glances at Simon, wondering why he'd grown quiet.

"I imagine all three of you Honeycutt boys are upstanding men," Virginia added in a conciliatory tone.

"Daniel's as fine a man as I've ever known. I appreciate your kind words about my brother, but I ought to give you a word of warning. Just in case you were to meet him while you were home."

"A word of warning? About what?"

"In a way, he's not the same person you might remember."

Virginia waited to hear what more Simon might say, trying to tamp down a rush of distress. She hated to think of anyone suffering. It pained her something awful.

"A while back he got in a scrape with a fellow."

Virginia waited and wondered where Simon's story might lead. A scrape could mean a fair number of things. There were plenty of rough characters around Bethany Springs. Still, she'd heard that Daniel was happily married. If he'd been injured, at least he had a wife to tend to him.

Simon set his hand over hers. A warm comfort washed over her. While she didn't like to speak of matters that might trouble him, she appreciated the shared moment. The wind swirled around them. The late summer sunshine gilded the trail.

For a moment, it was just the two of them, walking the trail she'd walked so many times before. The boys traipsed a short distance behind, far enough to be out of hearing distance. Her reverie stretched across the landscape like languid summer sunshine.

She grew aware of her scattered thoughts. She pushed them aside. Curiosity sparked. What *had* happened to Daniel? The longer Simon remained silent, the more she fretted. A quick glance at his grim expression didn't ease her fears.

"Are you going to tell me what happened, or do you want me to suffer and imagine all sorts of calamities?"

"He got hurt."

Simon's voice sounded taut. She heard the pain there and winced. She waited, hardly trusting herself to ask a proper question.

"For a while he didn't care to spend time with anyone. Nobody. Just his family. He's doing better now that he's married," Simon said quietly.

"I'm so very glad to hear."

"He and his wife are expecting a little one."

"Oh, that's wonderful."

Virginia felt a wave of relief. She still didn't know anything about Daniel's injury, but just the fact that he would become a father reassured her that he'd have joy in his life.

In truth, she hardly knew Daniel Honeycutt, aside from a few conversations at the fall fair where she'd found him to be kind and utterly charming. No. She didn't know him. And yet, she felt certain he'd make a fine father. "I can imagine he'll do well as a family man."

"Yes, no doubt."

Simon said the words with a hint of frustration, enough for Virginia to wonder.

"You sound like you don't approve."

Simon shrugged and grumbled softly. "My mother thinks Zach and I need to follow in his footsteps. She wants us married with families by next Christmas. I'm nowhere near ready for marriage. I figure if I can help Junior get out of jail, and help these two boys become respectable young men, she'll quit fussing at me about settling down."

"No interest in being a family man?" Virginia asked, playfully. After hearing his views about caring for the boys, she could have guessed his answer. Yet, she couldn't help teasing him a little. She deserved a little fun, didn't she? Surely turnaround was still fair play.

He arched a brow. "Maybe I do want to end up a family man."

She laughed aloud. "I'd like to see that."

"Maybe you will."

"Is that so?"

"If Junior winds up in jail, I'll need a wife to help raise the boys. Maybe I'll steal you away so you can help out, seeing as it would be your fault. Partly."

She shook her head. It had to be only a matter of time before Simon turned things around. Sure enough, she was right back in the middle of a fine mess with her old adversary.

"My fault?" she asked. "How so?"

"On account of your stubbornness," he growled, his eyes sparkling with amusement.

"Somehow, I felt sure you wouldn't manage this charade of charm and civility for too long," she said airily. "I just knew it was a matter of time before you gave in to some outrageous, devious line of teasing and torment. Steal me away? How would you do that, exactly?"

"Why would I give away my devious plot?"

Virginia laughed, hardly able to hold her amusement. "My, my, Simon Honeycutt. You're quite the charmer, aren't you?"

He didn't reply but the corners of his mouth twitched.

"Quite the romantic proposal," she added. "Threatening to steal me away."

"It'd be a fine arrangement. The boys would have a mama." He gestured to the pastures. "And I'd have a place to start my new cattle brand."

"And what would I have, pray tell?"

He held his palms up. "You'd have me, of course. Just what you've always wanted."

Virginia laughed again, wiping away tears. "Why, that sounds like the start of a very disagreeable dream."

"C'mon, Goose. You and me go way back."

"And that, you see, is the entire problem."

He set his hand on his chest. "Now you've gone and busted my heart."

They kept up a playful banter as they walked. Neither paid much attention to the boys who skipped ahead without a care in the world. By the time the group reached the house, Simon had explained his grand plan, one he'd clearly made up on a whim just to tease Virginia. He spoke of how he'd fence the Childress homestead. He detailed his favorite meals, ones he hoped she'd cook once they were married. He even talked about the day Virginia would be wagging her finger at Tuck and Ellwood, telling them it was time for them to get hitched.

Virginia explained how she'd toss out his entire cowboy wardrobe. Once his tattered clothes were dispensed with, she'd dress him head to toe in respectable attire, including proper suits, a few elegant vests to add detail, and some polished boots to round off things.

Simon declared her ideas an insult to cowboys across the fine state of Texas.

Back and forth they went. Mostly they argued playfully, sometimes doggedly, each certain they knew precisely how to fix the other.

When they arrived at the homestead, they looked around, searching for the boys. The children's voices came from the other side of the house. They whooped and cheered about heavens knew what.

Simon muttered something about finding them in case they were up to some sort of mischief.

Their voices floated on the late-summer breeze.

"That don't look too smart, Ellwood."

"It's fine. Quit bossing me."

"You're going to break it clean off," Tuck yelled.

"What do you know? Nothing!" came the gleeful reply. "That's what."

The pecan leaves rustled over the rooftop. Virginia gasped. One moment, the branches waved up and down, the next moment, the entire tree lurched to one side. Small branches snapped off and landed on the roof.

"What in the world?" Simon muttered.

One of the boys whooped.

The strange commotion continued, only now it wasn't just small branches breaking free. Bigger limbs snapped clean off and crashed on top of the house. Virginia watched in spellbound horror as the old pecan leaned one way and then the other. The old tree creaked ominously and shuddered as the largest limb of all fell with a resounding crash. Virginia held her breath, waiting as her heart hammered against her ribs.

Simon took off in a dead run. Virginia heard one of the boys speak, his voice small and forlorn. "That's bad."

"Yeah," came the other boy's reply. "Maybe no one will notice."

Chapter Twelve
Simon's Good Fortune

Simon

In the years to come, the incident would be referred to as the Pecan Tree Misfortune. This is what Virginia called it when she first gazed upon the broken limbs and wrecked timbers of the house.

A misfortune. Simon figured that was a bit of an understatement. It was more of a disaster. He didn't want to stir things up any more than needed, though. The boys were distraught, but he knew they hadn't been trying to destroy anything. It just happened. He appreciated Virginia's efforts to ease their distress.

Virginia hadn't cried or shrieked. Instead, she spoke gently to the boys to make sure they were unhurt. Then she directed them to sit on the back porch, far from the toppled tree. They sat quietly, or mostly quiet. They snuffled and wept softly while Simon studied the wreckage. He said little to the boys, resolving to discuss the matter later.

Virginia went inside and returned a short while later with a pitcher of lemonade and four glasses.

"Broken roofs can be mended more easily than injured children," she said cheerfully.

"It'll take a few days' work," Simon said gruffly.

She poured a glass of lemonade for each of them, serving the children first, offering them a comforting smile. Simon admired her composure. It wasn't until she handed him a glass that he noticed that her hand trembled slightly.

He took the glass and thanked her. He would have liked to take her hand in his and ease the worry she tried to hide. She seemed to read his mind. Her eyes widened. She turned away with a brisk step and withdrew to the porch.

"We're real sorry, Miss Virginia," Ellwood said tearfully.

Tuck nodded and tried to speak but his words dissolved into a new round of weeping.

"Now boys," Virginia said. "I know you didn't mean any harm. The important thing is that neither of you were injured."

She sipped her drink and sat down in a nearby chair. It creaked ominously and with a nervous laugh, she got to her feet. "You see, Tuck. Even the porch chairs are old and need mending."

Tuck stopped crying and eyed the bench he and his brother sat on.

Virginia smiled. "I think you're safe. Just don't climb on top of it and jump up and down."

Ellwood sniffed and managed a small smile. Tuck smiled sheepishly and took a swallow of lemonade.

Simon spoke. "Can we visit a spell, Virginia? Over by the pecan tree? I want to talk about repairs."

They set their drinking glasses aside and walked over to the downed branches.

"Are you doing all right?" he asked gently.

"I'm fine. Just a little shaken. That's all. It's peculiar. The moment I saw the boys were unharmed, I didn't care about what had happened to the house. It didn't seem important."

Simon offered his hand to help her over a large limb. She waved it off and managed on her own. They picked their way past the rest of the debris until they reached a spot where they could view the damage. The old Pecan tree still had some living branches, but more than half had rotted out and looked ready to fall any day.

The boys just hastened the process with their tree climbing and limb jumping. A once sturdy limb measuring a foot in diameter had broken free some twenty feet up and come down squarely on the house. The roof was broken, the back wall had collapsed. The resulting gap was wide enough for a man to stand erect and stretch his arms across.

"Oh, dear." Virginia drew a sharp breath. "That's my bedroom."

"I'm sorry about that. I truly am."

She pressed her lips together and nodded.

"Molly, my sister-in-law, has two brothers that can fix anything made of wood. I'll ask them to fix this for you as soon as possible. I'll pay for any damages, of course."

"Simon, I would appreciate any help with finding workmen, but I can't ask you to pay for the repairs."

He shook his head. "I'm not arguing. I'm paying. End of discussion."

She looked like she had an argument on the tip of her tongue. He went on before she had the chance to start. He knew she'd like the next part even less.

"You can't stay here."

"I could stay in the other bedroom."

"It wouldn't be safe."

"I'm not afraid. What's the worst that could happen? A few chipmunks come to visit?" She laughed at her own joke.

"You ought to come to our family's ranch and stay while the Collins boys repair the roof and wall. It wouldn't be more than a few days and I know my mother would be very pleased to have you in her home."

Simon expected Virginia to respond with shock. She'd probably be scandalized by his offer. He waited for a cry of indignation. After all, she was the governor's daughter. She couldn't accept just anyone's hospitality. So, it was with some surprise when her eyes lit with delight. Her lips curved into a sweet smile.

"Amelia Honeycutt," she said quietly as if speaking to herself.

Simon frowned and waited.

"Would your mother let me write an article about her?"

"Beg your pardon?"

"Occasionally, I write articles for a journal. I planned to write one about my father to help with his reelection. Once I'm done with that, I'd dearly love to write a piece about Mrs. Honeycutt. I've always admired her grit and fine mind. It would give me a chance to write something that didn't pertain to my father. You know? Something *interesting*."

Of all the replies, he hadn't imagined Virginia would ask this.

"Do you suppose she'd agree?" She set her hand on his forearm.

Her touch sent a thrill along the length of his arm. Sadly, his thoughts were in such turmoil, he didn't have the ability to enjoy her gentle touch. He rubbed the back of his neck, aware that she awaited his answer. He winced, not with pain but with a twinge of guilt. He swallowed hard and cleared his throat. "Could be."

Didn't sound terribly convincing. Despite that, Virginia's eyes sparkled. "Really?" she murmured as she laughed softly. "Could be?"

Could be. Well, it could be a lot of things. Could be his mama would have his miserable hide when she learned of this little chat with Virginia.

Still, he couldn't back down. Not now. If he didn't agree, Virginia would refuse his invitation. She'd stubbornly insist on staying in her broken, derelict home.

He nodded. "I'm sure she'd love to talk to you, Virginia. After all, she admires you too."

She gasped and lifted her hand to her mouth. "Oh my!"

"Let me talk to her first, all right?"

"Of course." She clasped her hands in front of her. "That would be the prudent course of action. Thank you, Simon."

He told Virginia to pack for a stay of several nights. He'd be back shortly to get her. He rode home, taking the boys along.

Back at the ranch, Ellwood and Tuck eagerly helped with what they could. Simon showed them how to unsaddle the horses and where to store their saddles and bridles.

They loaded oil tarps onto the buckboard and a bucket of nails, a hammer, saw and some other tools. He intended to close up the house well in case there was rain, but first he'd have to cut away the branch that was partway in her bedroom.

He instructed one of the ranch hands to send word to the Collins boys. He wanted to speak to them about the repairs that would be needed, what materials and tools they should bring. They offered to head out immediately, but Simon asked them to be at the Childress homestead early the next morning. With surprise he realized he did not want the Collins boys or anyone else talking to or distracting Virginia. He'd enjoyed the walk with her and didn't feel like sharing her with anyone else.

Shortly after lunch, when he and the boys had the buckboard hitched, they set out for the Childress homestead to collect Virginia.

Virginia waited on the porch, a smile lighting her pretty face.

Simon's heart skipped a beat as they approached the cabin. The boys sat on the bench beside him, chattering about something or other. He didn't hear much of their conversation. His attention was fixed firmly on Virginia. She was coming to stay in his family's home. He prayed this would bode well for Junior. And he couldn't help feeling pleased for his own selfish reasons. He admitted to himself that he looked forward to time with Virginia.

Perhaps the Pecan Tree Misfortune would prove to be his good fortune after all.

Chapter Thirteen
An Unexpected Guest, and a Shattered Window

Amelia

Amelia arrived home from the back pastures just as Simon left with the buckboard. She wondered what he might be up to, but just assumed he was teaching the boys how to drive a wagon. There was hope for that boy yet.

When he returned later that afternoon, with a guest, she wondered if she might be seeing things, but no. The surprise guest was none other than Virginia Childress. Orville's pretty daughter was all grown up of course, and she'd be staying at the Honeycutt home for a spell.

Amelia sprang into action, quickly airing the spare room. If only she'd known she was to have company, she would have made special arrangements. She could have bought some pretty soaps, the jasmine-scented ones that Sophie was so fond of. And she could have made a special dinner, too. Something fancy. Something better than a simple roast.

Simon, along with one of the ranch hands, hauled Virginia's trunks upstairs. Amelia caught bits and pieces of the Pecan Tree Misfortune amidst the hustle and bustle. She was more than a little taken aback.

"I'm sure they didn't mean any harm," Virginia insisted as she unpacked a small valise, setting the items on the bedside table.

Amelia snorted. She was about to explain that Tuck and Elwood were quite the naughty pair and, if they weren't careful, they'd scamper back to the homestead and clamber back up the pecan tree to finish the job. Simon could tell she was about to expound on her theory and stopped her with a shake of his head.

"It's mighty nice to have you here," Amelia said. She meant it too. Virginia Childress was a rare type of woman who understood how to hold her own among the bigwigs of Texas. "I'm happy for the company."

Virginia blushed. "You have a lovely home."

"It's nicer when I'm not the only one in it."

Amelia crossed the room and peered out the window. Simon and his helper unpacked the last of the trunks. A north wind gusted. To her surprise a dark wall of storm clouds had rolled across the horizon.

"Looks like we're going to have some weather," she said. "Glad you got here before the rain."

Virginia glanced out the window. "Thank heavens."

A burst of wind rattled the windowpanes. The back of Amelia's neck prickled. She scanned the barnyard, searching for Tuck and Ellwood. She excused herself and went downstairs. Simon stepped inside with the final load of Virginia's possessions. Land sakes, the girl didn't exactly travel light. This parade of luggage was almost as bad as traveling with Sophie McCord.

"Seen the boys?" Amelia asked.

Simon shook his head. He looked perplexed.

"Don't worry. I'll find them."

She turned on her heel and went directly to the kitchen. Cookie pans sat on the counter. She'd left them to cool just when Simon arrived with Virginia. It came as no surprise that a fair number of cookies were missing. Close to a dozen had been filched.

Muttering under her breath, she collected the remaining cookies and put them in a tin. She set the tin inside another, larger tin and tucked it in the broom closet. They wouldn't find the cookies there. Unless of course they recruited Simon's help. He'd know right where she'd hidden the cookies, having filched scores of them as a boy.

Leaving the kitchen, she searched the house for the culprits.

As she checked the rooms, she had to wonder why the good Lord kept giving her so many pesky boys? After raising three of her own, all she wanted was a grandchild, preferably a granddaughter.

She hated to complain.

She loved her three sons something fierce. She loved Sophie's children too. Sophie had been lucky. She was blessed with four children, one sweet, angelic girl and three rip-roaring boys. All four were Amelia's godchildren, Lord help her.

In addition to all *those* troublesome boys, she had watched over the multitude of cowboys who worked the ranch over the past twenty-some-odd years. Some of them had begun work so young, they'd hardly needed to shave. She'd taken them in and done her best to guide them along the straight and narrow. She'd done her part, or so she liked to think.

Yet here she was… saddled with more pesky boys. Junior's two boys. Two small children who'd managed to topple the back wall of a fifty-year-old homestead. Part of her found the notion amusing. Probably the vindictive part of her. She liked to imagine Orville's face when he heard the news of his family's home.

Served him right. Orville Childress, the cantankerous old toot, hadn't lifted a chubby finger to fix a thing for Junior. Of that she was certain. No. He was too high and mighty to take care of his constituents in Bethany Springs.

After searching the downstairs, she found the cookie thieves hiding in their room. They tried to look innocent but failed miserably.

"Hello, Miss Amelia," Tuck said brightly. "You look mighty pretty."

"Yes, ma'am," Ellwood agreed.

"Oh hush. Don't try your tricks on me. I didn't fall off the turnip wagon yesterday."

They eyed her warily. They'd better be worried. She and the boys had a little history. She'd met with some of the boys' mischief even before today's so-called mishap. In the few short weeks since coming to the ranch, they'd accumulated a list of offenses. There was the biscuit incident. And the garden calamity. Along with the barnyard duck disaster. Junior might be as dumb as a box of rocks, but his conniving boys seemed plenty smart.

"Why don't you explain what happened today."

The boys paled. The room grew darker with the approaching storm. Thunder rumbled nearby.

"I'm trying to understand the sequence of events," she said, pacing the room. "You were playing in the back of the homestead. That right?"

"Yes, ma'am," they said in unison.

Ellwood nodded. "We intended to pick pecans. Didn't we Tuck."

Tuck agreed.

Amelia gave a cool smile. "In June?"

"Yes, ma'am."

"Mighty nice of you," she said sweetly. Two could play this game. Or was it three?

"We were only trying to help Miss Childress." Tuck said, eyes wide, the very picture of innocence. "We didn't realize the branch would break when Ellwood jumped up and down."

"I thought it was sort of funny, the way the great, big tree sort of waved side to side." Ellwood swayed to emphasize his point.

Tuck looked somber. "Real glad my brother didn't get hurt."

"Well, that's true," Amelia had to admit.

Neither boy had so much as a scratch. They looked pensive, as if an injury would have been a nuisance. Boys never liked to consider the outcome of their shenanigans. No, at this age, they figured they were immortal. Ellwood and Tuck likely didn't worry much about their father either, simply assuming things would turn out fine. Just fine.

Lightning flashed. The bright, white light lit the room for an instant. In that brief moment, Amelia noted the boys' fear. It came and went as quickly as the lightning, but she saw it, and felt some satisfaction to know that the boys *could* be scared, of something, if not her. It was good to know.

"I'm glad too," Amelia said.

"Ma'am?" Tuck asked.

"That you boys didn't get hurt." She glanced out the window. "My word, that's quite a storm brewing out there."

Neither boy spoke.

"We get different types of storms in Texas. Ever noticed?"

"No, ma'am," one boy replied.

"Never noticed," said the other.

"One of my first ranch hands came from a German family. He used to talk about *Landregen*. Land rain. He said it was the sort of rain that was slow and steady. A rain that filled ponds and helped the crops. Usually, the storms drifted up from the south."

She heard the wind gust and turned to see dust devils twirling in the barnyard. The storm was practically on top of them. Out of habit, she checked the haybarn to make sure the doors and windows were secure. Sheldon usually tended to such matters, but he was visiting Junior in jail. Fortunately, the other hands had closed everything up tight.

Amelia moved away from the window but kept a wary eye fixed on the heavy, swirling clouds.

"Simon's father, Mr. Honeycutt, had his own phrase for this sort of storm." She smiled, recalling the deep timbre of George's voice. "He called them the wrath of God."

The boys both drew sharp breaths. Just then the sky opened up, unleashing a torrent of rain. Hail followed. The first hailstones were no more than the size of a marble. They bounced off the roof. It wasn't long before they grew in size. Soon, much larger hail drummed the house making it impossible to hear each other speak.

Amelia edged further from the window. The rain, wind and hail filled the room with a deafening roar. Just a few miles away the Childress homestead was most likely getting pummeled and soaked by the storm too. She pictured the lovely Childress home, one that had withstood the ravages of time but hadn't survived the Whitson boys. Now the storm might ruin the interior of the home along with the family's possessions.

As the moments passed, the hail diminished. Just when Amelia thought it was done, a hailstone smashed the window. A parting wrathful shot. The glass shattered. Wind blew past the shards, carrying drops of rain. Most of the rain, thankfully, blew past the broken window. The storm rolled on. A short time later, the hail was done. The wind died down. The rain slowed.

The hailstone, big as her fist, rested amidst the glass shards. She picked it up and marveled at the size. George would have grumbled about the broken window, but he would have also marveled at God's mighty power.

"Ever seen one this big, George?" she asked under her breath. "I haven't."

George had been gone many years, but part of her still awaited his answer. He didn't reply, though. Of course, he didn't.

She turned to show the boys. To her surprise, they no longer sat, grinning like little imps, on the side of the bed. In fact, they were nowhere to be seen. A movement caught her eye. She pulled up the lower edge of the blankets and peered beneath the bed. In the dim light, she spied Ellwood and Tuck, their faces pale and their eyes filled with genuine terror.

Amelia chuckled to herself. She never could stay mad long, not when it came to children. Ellwood and Tuck had been yanked this way and that, first by their mama hightailing it out of town and then their daddy getting arrested. She could clearly see they were terrified and felt her heart soften almost instantly.

She held the hailstone out for their inspection. "No need to fret. It's just a chunk of ice. No need to worry. God brings the storm, but in His mercy, he blesses us with rain and sometimes flowers. Which one of you is ready to toss this back out the window?"

The boys seemed to want to think things over for a few seconds, but by and by, they wriggled out from under the bed. To her surprise, it was the younger boy, not the older, who took the hailstone and tossed it out the window.

Rascally boys. Maybe it was her lot in life to tend to all these pesky boys. One of these days, she'd get a girl to spoil rotten. In the meantime, she'd do what she could for her allotted boys. All in God's time.

She smiled as she tousled the boy's unkempt hair. "All right. Come along. You've got extra chores to make amends for those stolen cookies."

Chapter Fourteen
Papa's Grudge Against Amelia

Virginia

Virginia changed her dress for supper. It was her custom. Amelia might not dress for dinner, but Virginia resolved she'd do as she always did. After she'd fixed her hair, she left her room and made her way downstairs. As she walked the length of the hall, she paused to look at the various pictures on the wall.

The frame at the end of the hallway held a sketch of George Honeycutt as a young man. Virginia was struck by the similarity between Simon and his father. Both men had the same smile and the same expressive eyes. She stood rooted to the spot for a long while, studying the man's image.

Finally, she let her attention drift to the next frame, a map of the Honeycutt ranch, dated 1860. Likely the land holdings were several times that much now, several decades later. Amelia had worked hard, not just to provide for her family, but to prosper and give her boys a good start in life.

Virginia had heard a number of stories about Amelia. Most of them had to be nothing more than tall tales. Amelia was a strong woman, yes, but surely, she didn't lasso Longhorns while blindfolded.

She smiled. If she could write an article about Amelia, she'd be sure to address that tall tale as well as a few others.

Downstairs, Tuck and Ellwood set the dining table, working quietly with solemn expressions.

Amelia worked in the kitchen, finishing the last of the meal preparation.

"I should have come to help," Virginia said, embarrassed by her poor manners.

Amelia smiled as she stirred the contents of a pan. "Never mind. You're our guest."

"That's very kind." Virginia felt relieved. She had few cooking skills and didn't want Amelia to know how little she knew.

"It's very nice to have a little female company," Amelia said. "I'm sure you hoped to stay in your own home for a few days. It seems like it's been a long time since you visited Bethany Springs. Last time I saw you, you were just a girl."

"It has been too long."

"I'm sorry about the boys and their pranks. Hurts my heart to think of a tree falling on the old Childress place."

Amelia poured tea into a pitcher and added sugar. Virginia came to her side and wordlessly took on the task of mixing the tea with a long wooden spoon.

"I'm grateful the boys weren't injured," Virginia said.

"Simon's going to talk to the Collins boys this evening. He intends to ask them to check the rest of the house. He'll make sure the structure is sturdy."

Virginia felt a pang of guilt for everything Simon was doing on her behalf. She wondered what he expected in return. If anything.

"That's very kind of Simon," she said quietly. "I know he hopes I can help the boys' father, but I don't have that sort of influence over my father."

"I understand," Amelia said. "All you can do is put in a good word. If you're willing."

Virginia nodded. "I can try. I'll return to Austin next week and will do what I can."

Amelia continued with the cooking. She opened the oven and slid out a cast iron pan, setting the heavy pan on top of the stove with startling ease.

For a slight woman, Amelia Honeycutt was surprisingly strong, Virginia decided.

Lifting the lid, Amelia waved off the cloud of steam billowing upward. A savory aroma filled the kitchen as Virginia's stomach rumbled, much to her dismay.

Amelia gave her a wry grin.

Virginia smiled despite her embarrassment.

Amelia took the roast from the cast iron pan and set it on a wooden cutting board. She let it sit while she heated the remaining contents of the pan. When it came to a brisk boil, she lowered the damper. Next, she poured milk into a bowl, added flour, and whisked the mixture before adding it to the pan.

Virginia drew closer to Amelia. From a few paces away, she peered past Amelia's shoulder to take in the details. Her mouth watered and she wondered if she ought to learn how to cook. One day. Perhaps when she was finished helping Papa fulfil all his political ambitions.

"What will your father say?" Amelia asked.

Virginia startled and gave a nervous laugh. "Pardon me?"

Amelia set the pot aside and turned to face her. "What will he say about you staying here? Surely, you intend to send word."

"Well, yes," Virginia stammered. "I ought to send word. Certainly, that would be the right thing to do."

"Won't he worry if you're not at the homestead?"

"Hardly. He likely won't check on me. He's a very busy man."

Amelia arched a brow. "Too busy for his daughter?"

Virginia knew she ought to take offense at the blunt observation. Amelia's words were brusque. For some reason Virginia couldn't find it in herself to argue. Papa was too busy for her. It hadn't always been that way, but with a second election looming on the horizon, her father gave little thought to anything aside from winning.

Amelia shook her head. "He might not give his blessing. The notion of you staying in my home might gall him."

Virginia didn't reply with the words that were right on the very tip of her tongue. Did Amelia wonder if Papa might withhold his blessing? That was putting things mildly. Papa would be *furious*.

Usually, Virginia fretted over such things, but something about coming to Bethany Springs eased her worries about Papa's displeasure. He'd simply have to step back and allow her a few moments of happiness and quiet.

Amelia went on. "He won't want you to stay with me because he still holds a grudge."

Still? Grudge? Virginia held her breath, wondering what Amelia could mean. She knew there was bad blood between them but assumed it was simply a matter of personality, not a grudge.

Amelia chuckled. "He likely resents the time I bought some land out from under him."

"I see. Possibly." Virginia said the words without thinking. She didn't know the first thing about the matter. She let the silence linger in hopes that Amelia would fill the quiet space.

Amelia took some butter from a nearby shelf and added a portion to a pan of potatoes. She chopped some chives and tossed them into the pan and stirred the mixture.

Virginia wondered if she would say more.

After a long moment, Amelia went on. "It was just a little squabble. Hardly worth mentioning. There was a pretty little stretch of land between our properties that ran along the Bethany River. Your father wanted to buy it, for some reason. As did I. Unfortunately, there was a dispute over the title. Two men claimed title to the land. Both had documents to prove ownership. Your father hired a couple bigwig lawyers to fight them, to prove one held legal title."

"That sounds like my father," Virginia said. "He would have had faith in the letter of the law."

Amelia scoffed. "Of course. But I knew what that land was worth. And I knew what it would cost to hire lawyers and to fight in the courts. So, I just paid both families their asking price."

Virginia drew a deep breath. Suddenly she understood a little of the animosity between her father and Amelia Honeycutt. He didn't want the land. He wanted to keep her from getting it and she'd outfoxed him with a shrewd tactic. No wonder his pride was wounded.

Virginia noted a sense of sympathy for her father. At the same time, she admired Amelia.

Amelia went on. "Paying extra for the property stung a fair bit. But not for long. Since I didn't have to pay all those legal expenses, I came out ahead."

Virginia nodded slowly, trying to imagine the chain of events. Daddy was a proud man. Everything was a contest, one that he had to win, and it must have especially pained him to lose to a woman.

"Papa hates to lose." Virginia sighed. "More than anything, Papa hates to lose."

Amelia chuckled. "I suppose I'm just as bad. I get the bit in my mouth, and nothing stops me."

"How long ago did this happen?" Virginia asked.

"About ten years ago."

"He never mentioned anything to me."

Amelia's eyes sparkled. "I'll bet. Men don't like to talk about these sorts of things. Especially when it comes to land deals. Trust me. Men think land is their domain. They don't want some troublesome female outbidding them or outwitting them. It's the worst sort of insult for the menfolk of Texas."

Virginia tried to keep from smiling at Amelia's irrepressible sass. She'd never imagined such determination. Or such steel.

"It's the truth." Amelia's tone held a note of teasing. "Texas men pride themselves on being gentlemen. They do a fine job when it comes to manners but tend to get a tad ornery any time a woman buys a piece of land right out from under their nose."

"I can just imagine," Virginia said. Silently, she resolved to wait a good long time before telling her father about staying with the Honeycutt family.

Chapter Fifteen
Repairs to the Childress Homestead

Simon

Simon spent the night tossing and turning. He tried not to think about Virginia sleeping in the guest room at the end of the hall. It seemed like a cruel joke. The one girl he'd loved to torment so many years ago, now tormented him, albeit unknowingly.

Unable to sleep, he tossed aside the covers and went to the window. He threw open the sash and inhaled the cool night air in hopes the fresh air might clear his mind. He let his gaze wander the night skies, taking in the twinkling stars. To his dismay, the thoughts of Virginia remained.

Virginia slept just a few steps away.

In his family's home.

She'd grown into a beautiful, graceful woman who made him yearn for things he ought to ignore. How would it feel to trail his fingers across her skin? How would her unbound hair feel against the palm of his hand?

He spent a sleepless night trying to banish thoughts of Virginia. At dawn, he gave up on sleep. He dressed, left his room and checked in on Ellwood and Tuck, who both slept peacefully. He'd forgotten his morning devotions. He said a quick prayer of thanksgiving as he stood in the doorway.

Lord, I thank you for the boys' tranquil sleep. I pray I can help Junior and his young boys.

He closed the door quietly and went downstairs. Mama was in the kitchen, judging from the aroma of coffee and clatter of pans. He wandered outside, not quite ready for conversation. The first rays of dawn burnished the horizon. Soft light lit the barns, sheds, and ranch house.

From the yard, he spotted Virginia. She sat by the window; her head bent over some early morning work. His breath caught in his throat. His pace faltered. He stared like a fool, unable to look away.

She glanced up, smiled, and waved before returning to her task.

Last night, she'd seemed solemn and pensive. It stood to reason, after all. The day had been one calamity after another. First, the shock of him arriving on her doorstep. Next, the visit to her mother's grave and the discovery of a mystery headstone. After which, Junior's boys had demolished the back corner of her beloved family home. The string of calamities was topped off with an unplanned stay at the Honeycutt ranch house.

Many females would melt into a puddle of tears. Not Virginia. He felt a twinge of pride and admiration. Forcing his gaze from her window, he turned away and chided himself. He needed to keep his thoughts fixed on helping Junior.

If Junior's case went to trial, he'd find a way to get himself convicted. Simon was sure. What then? Simon would have to raise the two boys. Land sakes, he'd only watched them a short spell and they'd caused more trouble than he could shake a stick at.

By the time he returned to the house, Virginia had come downstairs and was visiting with Mama. She sipped a cup of hot tea and wished him good morning.

"You were up early," she murmured.

"You too," he replied. "Writing speeches for the governor?"

He hadn't intended to start the day with teasing banter but couldn't help himself.

"Not this morning. I'm working on my article."

Mama set a platter of bacon on the kitchen table. "Did you get a chance to write your father? You might want to let him know what happened."

Virginia took a swallow of tea as she mulled over the question. "I meant to write him."

"You afraid he'll storm back to Bethany Springs?" Mama chuckled. "That would be a sight."

"I'm not afraid of my father." Virginia poured herself more tea. "Why would I be afraid of him?"

"That's the way," Mama asserted. "You can't back down. Not an inch. Men like Orville Childress are either at your feet or at your throat."

Virginia didn't seem to know how to reply. She remained quiet. Mama turned back to the stove and the task of scrambling eggs. She hummed as she stirred the contents of the iron pan.

Simon grumbled under his breath. He'd hoped Virginia might write her father and mention a few words about Junior's case. She hadn't even told her father about her own circumstances. He had to wonder if she might, in fact, be a little intimidated by her father.

Regardless, he needed her to help Junior. He planned to ride out to the Childress homestead and see how the repairs were coming, and to make sure the Collins boys checked the structure of the entire house. He resolved to take her along, the trip would give him the chance to explain the urgency of Junior's plight.

After breakfast, he hitched the buckboard. He drove the wagon up to the front of the house and hitched the team to the post. Virginia appeared from the front door with Ellwood and Tuck close behind. The boys stammered, begging to come along, and promised to be good as gold.

His mother followed, eyeing the boys with mild annoyance. The youngsters, in turn, eyed his mother with deep concern. Simon was starting to think the boys were afraid of Mama.

"Please let us come along," Tuck pleaded.

"We could do chores," Ellwood added. "Help clean up and whatnot."

Simon stood by the buckboard, weighing his options. He would rather leave the boys behind with Mama so he could have Virginia to himself.

Virginia came down the steps, a smile playing on her lips. "Let them come. Why not?" She fastened the ties to her bonnet. "What's the harm in bringing them along?"

Mama snorted. She leaned against the railing and gave the boys a pointed look. "What's the harm? I wouldn't ask if I were you. Don't want to tempt the two little mischief-makers."

Simon shrugged. "Reckon I can put them to work while I talk to the Collins twins."

With that, the boys scrambled aboard the wagon.

His mother chuckled at their hurried retreat.

Simon helped Virginia to the buckboard, bid his mother goodbye and set off for the homestead. While he'd carefully planned on what to say to Virginia, his plans scattered like leaves on the autumn breeze. Sitting beside Virginia confounded his thoughts. Her scent, floral and feminine, made him yearn to draw closer.

"Goose, you smell nice," he blurted. Almost at once he regretted his words. To his surprise, she wasn't a bit offended. Instead, she appeared bemused by his comment.

Sparks of laughter danced in her pretty eyes. "Why, Simon Honeycutt, aren't you the charmer?"

He grumbled under his breath. Her lighthearted comment bothered him even more than the notion of her rebuke. They rode in silence for a spell. When he glanced her way, he found she still looked plenty amused, ready to tease him mercilessly. It seemed odd, her ready to give him grief. How the tables had turned.

She lifted a gloved hand to her lips. "I'm so terribly sorry."

"For what?" he growled.

"I ought to return your delightful compliment. Where *are* my manners?"

Unsure how to respond, Simon tried to summon an intelligible answer. He wracked his mind to no avail. Before he could say anything near reasonable, Virginia spoke.

She patted his arm. "Simon, you smell nice too."

From the back of the wagon came the sound of the boys' laughter. Simon glared at them. They sobered at once and offered expressions of apology. He turned back to Virginia.

"You're all grown up now," he muttered. "You don't lose your temper like you did when you were a girl in pigtails."

She looked prim. "Don't sound so surprised."

"You're not even mad about the boys knocking down half your family home."

Her smile faded. "I'm thankful no one was hurt. The house can always be repaired. Besides that…"

Her words trailed off. He waited for her to continue as her gaze drifted across the countryside.

"You were saying," he prompted. Part of him hoped she'd say something about spending time with him.

"As much as I enjoy helping my father, I'm grateful to have a little time to myself." Color rose to her face. "Perhaps it's selfish, but I relish spending time away from town."

"Even if it's to repair an old house?" He smiled and was pleased when she returned the smile.

"I love that house. I always hoped my father would want to return, but he had his heart set on politics."

"What about you? What's your heart set on? It sounds like you're not entirely fond of life in Austin."

"I don't mean to complain."

"You're not. It's just a simple question."

"I like politics too. I want to help my father in any way I can. He's a fine man. Honest. Upstanding. A loyal Texan."

Simon nodded. "Listen to you. Seems to me you've learned a thing or two about politics. Maybe *you* should run for governor."

Pressing her lips together, she shook her head. He suppressed his laughter at the memory of Virginia's outbursts so many years ago.

He ought to leave it alone but couldn't resist. "Goose for governor."

"Oh, hush," she retorted, trying not to smile. "You're impossible. Really."

They rode the rest of the way, talking amiably. Simon wisely stuck to light conversation and refrained from mentioning his old pranks. Virginia talked about her grandparent's farm, their milk cows and fruit orchards. She sounded nostalgic even though she hardly knew her father's parents.

When Simon and Virginia arrived at the homestead, they found the repairs already underway.

The Collins boys along with a crew of a half-dozen men had started work at daybreak.

Jack and Will greeted them with broad, eager smiles. Simon introduced them to Virginia. They replied with polite words before they began to talk of their plans to reconstruct the back wall as well as the roof.

They excused themselves and returned to their tasks. Will tended to the old tree, working with several men to clear branches. Simon instructed Tuck and Ellwood to lend a hand, hauling brush away from the house. Jack sketched plans and drew up an order for materials.

"You two boys seem very young to take on such work," Virginia told Jack and Will as she eyed the project. "But I feel confident you'll do an excellent job."

Will and Jack both blushed at her praise. Virginia picked her way through the wreckage, remarking that things weren't as bad as she'd feared. Several of the workers seemed awed by Virginia and spoke of their admiration of her father.

"Thank you kindly," she replied. "I certainly hope we can count on your vote in November."

"The governor ought to whip Congress into shape," one fellow said, grumbling good-naturedly.

"I agree whole-heartedly," she replied cheerfully.

"Be nice if he'd see to fixing the roads around Bethany Springs," another man suggested. "The ruts get so deep that you could lose a horse in 'em."

Virginia nodded. "I shall pass on your concerns. I happen to think the roads are atrocious as well."

Simon watched as Virginia listened attentively to the men as she wandered around the worksite. She took in the men's concerns. With each exchange, she promised to speak to her father about the issues. Simon marveled at her poise. She produced a small notepad; one she'd tucked in her pocket and jotted down their comments and concerns.

After a short while, he found Virginia in the kitchen. She seemed lost in thought, gazing out the window.

"Reckon we can head back when you're ready," he said quietly.

"Thank you, Simon."

"Are you really going to tell your father about what the men talked about?"

She looked surprised. "Of course."

"What about Junior? Are you going to ask him to look into that matter?"

"I can try, Simon. That's the best I can do."

He crossed the kitchen, came to her side, and noted her gaze fixed on the boys playing in front of the house. "Ellwood and Tuck need their daddy."

Virginia swallowed hard and pressed her lips together into a grim line. Keeping her attention fixed on the boys, she grew pale.

"You lost your mother," Simon said quietly. "You must understand the importance of Junior's case."

It wasn't fair to bring up the death of Virginia's mother, but Simon was perfectly willing to use any desperate, underhanded means to get Junior free.

"I trust my father," Virginia said, her voice tremulous. "He's a man of honor. I can write him every day but, in the end, I have to believe he'll always do the right thing."

Simon wasn't so sure but couldn't find the words to explain. In the end, he believed Orville Childress wanted to be governor. Period. He'd step over anyone to achieve his goal. Maybe even Virginia.

Chapter Sixteen
An Offer to Governor Childress

Amelia

Amelia hadn't planned on writing Governor Childress again, but she sensed Virginia might dilly-dally. If there was one thing Amelia disliked, it was waiting for others to do what needed doing. She spent the morning writing various letters, trying her best not to sound impolite.

Dear Orville, you worthless piece of donkey dung.

Donkey dung. She liked the phrase and thought it apt but felt it lacked the right tone. She crumpled the paper and tossed it aside.

Dear Orville, your daughter is twice as smart as you.

Dear Governor, when are you going to start acting like a governor?

The pile of crumbled paper grew. She considered taunting him by praising his opponent but couldn't recall the man's name. He was a cattleman from the panhandle, older than dirt, suffering from consumption who might not even live till November. It didn't seem a worthwhile insult even if she could recall the fella's name.

She wasn't entirely sure why she disliked Orville Childress so. Maybe it was because he reminded her of all the men who'd tried to take advantage of her when she was a young widow. Not right away, but as soon as they noted her small successes.

After she sold her first herd of cattle to a military camp down by the Rio Grande, men came out of the woodwork. They wanted to cheat her or woo her or both. They wanted what she had. Every time they tried a new trick, her heart hardened a little more.

Her love and loyalty belonged to her three boys.

Besides, she'd lost the only man she'd ever love. George was gone. She'd never love another. Not when she'd already had the love of her life.

She'd resolved to devote her life to her family. And making money. Sometimes she felt a little ashamed of how much she loved making money. It was a game she was determined to win. And for that reason, it pained her to realize she'd have to offer Orville an expensive concession.

Right now, nothing meant more than getting Junior's life back. Even if it meant handing over the land along the Bethany River that she valued so much, the same land she bought all those years ago by paying two different men for one piece of land, transactions that irked her at the time for paying twice what she should, but also gratified her because it was the only way to beat Orville Childress to the punch.

She wrote the new letter carefully, offering to give Orville the land, free and clear. Then she tore it up. She couldn't stomach giving the land to him. She started a new letter, and this time she finally felt like she got it right. She offered the land to *Virginia* in exchange for Junior's release, though she didn't mention Junior once in the letter.

She mentioned notions such as, *pending the favorable outcome of a certain matter*. She included, *given the long and mutually beneficial relationship between the families*. She made a point of avoiding terms that hinted of an outright bribe, while at the same time giving Orville the easiest decision he ever needed to make.

Make one call, you old largemouth, and in exchange, you will reclaim the one piece of land that ever eluded you.

Amelia smiled as she tucked the letter in the envelope. Giving Virginia the land would kill two birds with one stone. She'd get Junior out of a scrap, and she'd give Virginia land that Simon would gladly take for his cattle venture. If he really wanted to start his own brand, he could just marry Virginia Childress. Amelia sighed. She hardly dared hope.

The Childress girl didn't seem to have a great deal of horse sense, not when it came to ranching, certainly, but she was whip smart when it came to other matters. Amelia could just imagine a little granddaughter with Virginia's beauty and brains.

"I'd name her Pauline. After my grandmother," Amelia said the words aloud, startling herself. She chuckled. Thankfully, she was alone, and her words wouldn't invite a hundred questions from Simon, or worse, Virginia.

She rode to town, left her horse at the livery, and set out for the post office. When she got a block or so from the red brick building, she paused to offer a quick prayer. Usually, she prayed in private and felt a twinge of awkwardness.

Just as quickly, she dismissed the discomfort.

What difference did it make if she prayed outside the post office right there in broad daylight? She didn't care who saw. All she wanted was that the good Lord watch over Sheldon's son, keep him safe and protect him from harm. Deep in her heart, she was sure of one single thing. Junior was innocent.

Heavenly Father, I pray that you keep that fool boy safe. And if it's not too much trouble, I'd like Simon to marry Virginia.

She couldn't let herself dwell on Simon marrying Virginia. That might be asking too much of the Good Lord.

Instead, she pictured Junior's cheerful smile and recalled his gentle nature. He was as kind as the day was long. If Sheldon's son was a thief, than she was a jack rabbit. That fella couldn't harm a fly, much less steal a small fortune from a courier service. He simply didn't know the first thing about defending himself or keeping his mouth shut. No, Junior liked to blather on and on about everything under the sun which would only make him appear guilty as sin.

Dear Lord, remind Junior to mind his tongue, to keep from getting himself deeper into trouble.

"What's wrong?"

The question startled Amelia. Drawing a sharp breath, she opened her eyes. Standing a pace or two away was her dear friend Sophie, watching her with a mixture of alarm and curiosity. Sophie's husband, Robert, stood beside her, a smile lighting his features. He doffed his Stetson and murmured a polite greeting.

"You look *awful*," Sophie said, eyeing her from head to foot. "More so than usual."

"Sophie, darlin'," Robert objected. "That's a mite harsh. Amelia doesn't like to get gussied up."

Amelia was used to Sophie's criticism when it came to her choice of attire. Sophie probably took an hour or better to dress each morning on any given day, and that was if she planned to remain at home. If Sophie were setting out for town, she'd take far longer, trying on various dresses to find the perfect one for her outing.

Not Amelia.

Much to Sophie's dismay, Amelia wore the same types of clothes most days. Practical clothes. She chose trousers and shirts over dresses and petticoats. How else could she run a ranch or earn and keep the respect of menfolk?

"I'm working today," Amelia sniffed. "Not heading to a tea party."

"I'm not referring to your clothes. You're pale and haggard."

Robert clucked his tongue and offered an apologetic shrug.

Sophie was undaunted. "You look like you haven't been sleeping well. What's wrong?"

Robert remained silent.

Amelia brushed off Sophie's words. She had good reason for looking tired. She lay awake many nights, worrying about Junior. During the day, she worked double-duty, taking care of Sheldon's tasks. She was tired. Still, she had no desire to explain.

This was hardly the place or time to confess her hope that Simon and Virginia might one day wed. Nor did she wish to explain the details about Junior. Just thinking about the two matters plum wore her out. Besides, the matter was in the Lord's hands now. What else could she do?

"I suppose I haven't been sleeping quite as well," Amelia said lightly. "I thank you for pointing it out to me. I'd been wondering what your opinion might be about the matter."

Sophie looked contrite as she set her hand over Amelia's hand. "You must come for a visit, *mon amie*."

Before Amelia could respond, another voice came from behind Sophie.

"I think she looks as lovely as a summer morning." Wade McCord sauntered down the walkway, a lazy smile curving his lips.

Amelia gritted her teeth. Things were going from bad to worse. The last person she felt like chitchatting with was

Sophie's brother-in-law. Wade McCord seemed to think he was the world's gift to ladies. An aggravating mix of arrogance and fast charm. She'd rejected his charisma time and again. Over the years, he'd come to view her as a challenge. She'd like to smack the smirk clean off his face. One of these days, she might give into that temptation.

Adding to his list of faults was his friendship with Orville Childress. They'd gone to law school together and the governor often invited Wade to his la-di-da functions. Wade had supported Orville's run for governor the first time around and would likely do so again, which only proved that Wade wasn't near as smart as he thought.

She could ask him to help Junior but couldn't bring herself to stoop that low. It would be a cold day in Hades before she asked Wade for help. He'd be delighted to lend a hand but would likely presume all sorts of nonsense, like she owed him something.

She narrowed her eyes as she considered a blunt reply. As usual, he kept blathering on.

"I can't imagine Amelia Honeycutt looking haggard," Wade said to Robert. "Can you?"

Robert looked around nervously. If he agreed with his brother, he'd risk his wife's wrath. On the other hand, he didn't want to say anything that might be construed as ungentlemanly. Robert McCord prided himself on his fine, Southern manners.

He pretended not to have heard Wade's question.

Instead of getting mixed up in a thorny subject, he remained silent and began examining the brim of his cowboy hat as if he just noticed some irregularity.

"Of *course*, he can't imagine Amelia Honeycutt looking haggard." Wade spoke on Robert's behalf, his smile widening. "In my opinion, Miss Amelia, you look as fresh as a daisy."

Sophie frowned with clear disagreement.

"Oh, hush, Wade." Amelia grumbled. "I haven't looked daisy fresh since Sam Houston was governor."

The mention of Sam Houston drew her thoughts to Orville Childress. She tried to keep from scowling at the letter. The scalawag had better lend a hand to one of Bethany Springs' native sons. If he kept on ignoring pleas for help, she might just pay the good governor a visit in the house that she and the rest of the Texas citizenry paid for with tax dollars.

"I know something is bothering you." Sophie narrowed her eyes. "You can't hide your troubles from me."

Amelia waved her envelope. "The only thing troubling me is this letter I need to post. If I don't hurry inside, I'll be too late to send it today."

Sophie pursed her lips and lifted her chin, clearly disbelieving Amelia's words.

"We'd best not make Amelia late," Wade said.

Finally, the man had something sensible to say. Sophie and Robert both looked perplexed.

"Why don't you two go on," Wade said to Sophie and Robert.

Sophie's lips tugged into a smile. She bid Amelia goodbye and tugged Robert down the walkway. He said a hasty farewell and squired his wife away from the post office.

"Where are they going?" Amelia asked.

"To the greengrocer and the butcher," Wade replied. "Sophie and Robert might raise fine cattle, but my sister-in-law insists on buying her beef from the butcher. She's tender-hearted, don't you know."

"Oh, I know," Amelia said.

"I am as well, Sophie," Wade said.

Amelia managed, barely, to resist rolling her eyes. Wade McCord was nothing more than a slick, smooth-talking fella who enjoyed cards and brandy and lively parties in Houston, San Antonio, and other towns.

He straightened his tie and cleared his throat. "May I escort you into the post office?"

"What for?" Amelia demanded.

"I'd like to make certain you get prompt attention." He winked.

Amelia's jaw dropped. She couldn't recall anyone ever having the nerve to wink at her. Even George, her husband for all of five years, never winked. Not once.

Wade took advantage of her surprise and offered his arm. "Would you do me the honor?"

"Oh, for heaven's sakes, Wade."

He knit his brow with exaggerated dismay. For a long moment, they stood in silence, each waiting for the other to back down. Amelia refused to budge. To make herself clear, she folded her arms.

Wade raised his hand and set it over his heart. "You wound me."

Passersby grinned at Wade's antics. Amelia felt her cheeks warm with embarrassment. It wasn't like her to blush, and her response only irritated her more.

"Oh, fine! I'll take your arm. I can't stand to see a man make a spectacle of himself."

He took her hand and set it in the crook of his arm. Her cheeks flamed as her blush deepened. Suddenly, she wondered if she might be the one making a spectacle of herself. She'd only allowed one man to take her arm, and that man had gone off and gotten himself killed in the war.

Walking in silence, she tried to ignore the shocked expressions of bystanders. Amelia cringed inwardly. This was how rumors started. It wasn't much later than ten in the morning, but she knew tongues would start wagging. By lunchtime, friends and neighbors and shopkeepers would have come up with an entire story just from a glimpse of her and Wade. They'd likely have her engaged, married, and living happily ever after with Wade McCord.

She might hold his arm as she walked, but she told herself it was to avoid making more of a spectacle. There was nothing to the gesture. Certainly not anything like what people would conjure up.

And yet, she had to admit that clasping his arm wasn't *terrible*.

Her thoughts scurried about like chickens in a coop, trying to avoid a wily fox. Refusing to let Wade, the notorious charmer, disrupt her calm, she made a point to ignore the feel of his forearm beneath her palm. She disregarded entirely the way he put himself between her and the busy road. And she paid no attention, whatsoever, to his manner of squiring her past several rough cowboys.

Thankfully, they soon arrived at the post office. To her surprise, Wade set his hand on her back to usher her through the doorway. The chickens began their fretful scurry once more.

Wade McCord was incorrigible.

She ought to object, to put him in his place, but for the first time, Amelia couldn't summon an argument to object to the gallantry of Wade McCord.

Chapter Seventeen
Virginia Starts to Bend

Virginia

After they left the homestead, Simon, Virginia, and the boys drove back to the Honeycutt ranch. Virginia chatted with Ellwood and Tuck as they traveled along the tree-lined road. They asked a hundred questions about the governor's mansion.

As the miles passed, Tuck became so pleased by the topic that he announced his plan to run for governor when he was older. "Maybe when I'm fifteen," he said, his eyes lit with possibility.

"You'll have to be a little older than that, Tuck," she said.

His smile vanished. "Older than fifteen?"

"You have to be thirty."

"Thirty?" he exclaimed. "That's so old!"

Virginia laughed. "Perhaps I could show you around the mansion one day." The words tumbled from her lips before she could stop them. She knew her father wouldn't look favorably on a visit from the sons of a man charged with robbery. How would that look if word got out?

"Can I come?" Simon asked, his tone playful and even a little flirtatious. "I'd like a tour as well, Miss Childress."

"We'll see," she replied primly. While Simon liked to tease, he never used a flirtatious tone. He only toyed with her in this way because he wanted to get Junior out of jail. It bothered her. What bothered her even more was how her heartbeat quickened and part of her yearned to hear more of Simon's flirting.

That afternoon, Amelia returned from town with a letter from Junior's parents. They were in Austin, staying at a hotel a short distance from the courthouse. They sent news that Junior's trial would be in two weeks' time.

Amelia, Virginia, and Simon sat on the porch while the boys played in the yard. Simon paced. Virginia tried to keep her composure as she sat on the porch swing.

"The worst part," Amelia said, "is that the judge is known for his quick and harsh opinion. He prides himself on his rate of convictions."

Amelia set the letter aside and wandered off the porch, joining the boys by the corral where they watched a cowboy work a young horse. The silence stretched between Virginia and Simon.

"I admit to fretting about Junior," she said quietly.

Simon nodded with a wry grin. "Me too. If your father can't help him, I reckon I'll have to bust Junior out of jail myself."

"Simon Honeycutt!" She wasn't sure if she should laugh or argue.

"What?"

"You can't bust Junior out of jail." She nodded toward the boys. "You have *obligations*."

Simon heaved a sigh as the edges of his lips lifted. "I'm sure I could manage a jailbreak. If I can't, who's going to tend to these pesky boys?"

Virginia rubbed her forehead. For some reason, it had begun to throb. "Simon," she whispered. "This is hardly a joke.

Not like when we were children. The entire matter strikes me as so very, very serious."

Simon's smile faded. "That's right. That's exactly right. Matters are very serious on account of young lives in the balance."

A shudder drifted down her spine. The boys looked so small. So innocent and vulnerable. They depended on her help to sway her father's opinion. If she failed, Junior might be found guilty of a crime she was sure he hadn't committed. "Lord protect these poor innocent children."

"Maybe we ought to pay your father a visit," Simon offered. "You could give us a tour of the mansion and the governor can meet Tuck and Ellwood."

Virginia didn't answer right away. She recalled the list of engagements her father had that week, hardly believing that she would entertain the notion of traveling to Austin with Simon and the boys. It dawned on her that her father had most of the day free at the end of the week, the day before he expected her home. She kept quiet, however, hardly daring to suggest such a venture.

Chapter Eighteen
Daniel Pays a Visit

Simon

Simon's joke about busting Junior out of jail had been an attempt to make light of grim circumstances. The next morning, he woke early spent the first few hours of the day tending to Sheldon's chores. He returned to the house to find Andrew, the young cowboy who went in search of the real thief, the one Junior called *John Smith*.

The men shook hands and Simon led Andrew to the orchard, far enough from the house to have a private conversation.

"What's the good word?" Simon asked.

"I don't have one really, I'm sorry to say. I've been to Austin, Victoria and Galveston and ten cities in between. I haven't learned anything I didn't know when I started."

"I see."

"The only good news I have, if that's what it is, is that there have been three robberies over the past two weeks, all of them similar to Junior's. If the thief keeps stealing, he'll eventually get caught."

"Right. Well, if that's the best news we have I'd say things don't look too hopeful."

"Simon, I'm not giving up. I need to be home for a few days to tend to some things, but then I'm heading out again to see if I can track down this man down."

Simon and Andrew shared a parting handshake, then Andrew rode off. Simon knew it was a long shot for Andrew to traipse around the state of Texas, hoping to be at the right place at the right time, but that's the only option he had. He was grateful to have one of the Brotherhood's most dedicated and energetic men on the job, and he said a short prayer ask for Andrew's good health and good fortune.

Simon walked back to the house and found Virginia standing on the front porch, a cup of coffee in her hands. She offered it to him as he walked up the steps.

The sight of Virginia in the morning sunshine was powerfully distracting. She wore a dress the color of the summer sky. Her hair hung in a loose braid down her back, much like the way she wore it as a girl. Her braid was the only thing that reminded him of Virginia as a young girl. Other aspects of her dress and demeanor made clear that Virginia was a lovely young lady now.

The dress showed off her narrow waist. The soft blue fabric contrasted with her fair skin. She looked as if she was made of porcelain, even though Simon knew she was anything but delicate.

He felt like a fool, his mouth suddenly dry and sweat on the back of his neck. He probably looked like a fool too.

"Mornin'," he said, a little more gruffly than he'd intended.

Ellwood and Tuck came out and eyed Virginia and Simon with curiosity.

Virginia offered a shy smile. "I saw you over by the orchard and thought I'd bring you a coffee. But you came back before I could bring it to you."

"That's mighty kind of you," he said, his teeth gritted for some reason he didn't understand.

The boys regarded them with bewilderment. Simon could hardly blame them. He felt a tad bewildered too. Virginia picked up a small black music case off the porch.

"I found my mother's violin at the house. I thought I might try a tune."

"All right." Simon wasn't sure what he was supposed to say. So far, everything coming out of his mouth wasn't more than a heap of nonsense.

The boys elbowed each other, their confusion giving way to amusement.

"I'd like to play here on the porch if that's agreeable," Virginia murmured.

"Fine by me. I don't really have an opinion, one way or another." Simon narrowed his eyes at the boys, who seemed to think the entire situation was a fine joke.

"I didn't want to disturb anyone. Your mother is in her office. I'd assumed you were out and about." Virginia waved her hand the direction of the corrals. "Doing… cowboy things."

This made the boys chuckle.

"I'm not doing cowboy things," Simon replied. "Not anymore. I got my cowboy things tended to first thing."

"We'd like to hear Miss Virginia play music," Ellwood said as he sat on the porch swing.

Tuck sat beside him. "We've never heard anyone play a fiddle."

Virginia shook her head. "It's not a *fiddle*."

The boys giggled and wrestled on the swing, each trying to shove the other off. The swing creaked, the wooden slats complaining about the rough treatment. It swung wildly.

Simon was about to tell them to settle down, but Virginia spoke first.

"Gentlemen," she said. "I only play for respectful audiences. And that means a quiet audience."

She lifted the violin, tucked it beneath her chin and drew the bow across the strings. The boys settled down and sat silently, watching her with interest. Virginia played a few notes as she tuned the instrument. Simon leaned against the railing and watched as intently as the two boys.

"Actually," Virginia murmured, "I've never played for an audience. Papa forbade it. He said a governor's daughter ought never to give a public performance."

"Why not?" Simon asked.

"Papa fretted that if I didn't play well, I'd reflect poorly on him. I completely understand his concerns. Still, I'd like to think that my music isn't all that dreadful."

Ellwood rested his chin on his hand. "I bet you play real pretty, Miss Virginia."

"That's right," Tuck offered. "We'll be sure to let you know if it's dreadful. Won't we, Ellwood?"

"We sure will, Tuck. We sure will."

Simon grumbled. "Seems a father would be proud of his daughter's music."

Virginia didn't reply. She tuned her violin with a studious expression. Simon's irritation about her father faded from his thoughts. He watched Virginia's entire demeanor change as she prepared to play. She was a pretty girl, to be sure, but in that moment, he thought her even more lovely.

When she was finished adjusting the instrument, she began to play. The delicate notes of her song filled the air and drifted across the porch. Simon stood transfixed. The boys grew still. They listened attentively, hardly blinking as they watched.

Simon felt the music wash over him like a delicate swath of silk. Virginia's gaze softened. She swayed gently as if the melody worked its magic over her as well. When she finished and the final notes faded into silence, the boys applauded. Simon joined them and smiled as Virginia's cheeks pinked.

"That was something," he marveled.

She shook her head. "Please, Simon."

"I mean what I'm saying. I've never heard anything so pretty. Hope you intend to play more than one song."

She gave him a chiding look.

"I'm telling the truth." He brushed his palm over his forearm. "I got chills listening and I never get chilled unless it's cold."

Goodness, just being around Virginia turned him into a jabbering fool.

She didn't look convinced.

He grinned. "Come on. Would I tease about something as important as fiddle playing?"

"Simon." She shook her head. "You're impossible."

The boys begged her to play more.

Before she could reply, a sound distracted them all. Simon's brother walked up the path and offered his applause. Daniel had come to the house to talk to Mama. A smile lit his features as he climbed up the steps.

Daniel didn't often greet folks with a cheerful smile. For a long time, he'd been a reclusive fellow, preferring his own company, living in a cabin on the other side of the ranch. His reticence came about after he'd been wounded in a brawl with a rustler. Badly hurt, he ended up with a grisly scar and an eye patch to cover the eye he lost.

After he got married, he'd come out of his self-imposed exile. He and his wife set up house in the old Honeycutt homestead. Everything had changed after Daniel met Molly Collins. Daniel no longer seemed to care about his scars. Probably because his sweet, kind-hearted wife seemed to think he was the finest, handsomest fella in the state of Texas.

Simon recalled how Virginia had gone on about Daniel and how kind he'd been to her years ago. He couldn't help an unpleasant pang of jealousy. Simon didn't care to hear Virginia wax poetic about his brother. Simon wanted Virginia to admire him. Not Daniel.

"Why, Virginia Childress," Daniel exclaimed. "I thought stories of you staying with Mama were just a passel of rumors."

"Daniel. How nice to see you!" Virginia set her instrument in the case and offered Daniel her hand. "It's lovely to see you. Heavens, you Honeycutt boys grew tall."

"We get our height from our daddy," Daniel said.

"Tall *and* strong," Virginia blurted. She blushed at her words.

It wasn't often Virginia looked embarrassed. Simon might have been amused if he hadn't felt annoyed. Daniel was tall *and* strong bit not as tall as him. Why didn't Virginia ever say such words to him? He gritted his teeth.

Daniel chuckled. "Mama taught us the value of hard work."

"I'm sure she did," Virginia added hastily. "Your mother works harder than any woman I know. It explains how she's done so well for herself."

Virginia and Daniel chatted amiably about marriage and the baby Molly expected. Simon felt his shoulders relax a little. Virginia seemed to have recovered her senses and talked to Daniel in the same friendly but polite way she spoke to the men at the Childress homestead. If Daniel's scars and eye patch troubled Virginia, she gave no notice.

Daniel deftly turned the conversation to the matter of Junior's trial. Virginia, with equal skill, sidestepped any promises.

"My father prides himself on his sense of justice," Virginia said evenly. "I'm certain Mr. Whitson will receive fair treatment."

"We're counting on it, aren't we, boys?" Daniel asked Tuck and Ellwood.

The boys nodded.

Mention of the boys made a little of the color drain from Virginia's cheeks. Her smile faltered. She recovered quickly. The smile returned. Simon marveled at her composure. She'd learned a thing or two, helping her father climb the political ladder.

"I don't mean to suggest your daddy isn't the smartest fella in Austin," Daniel said. "But I've heard that *you're* the secret to his success."

Simon smiled inwardly. He had to hand it to his brother. Maybe Daniel was equally skilled in the art of flattery.

Virginia shook her head. "Oh, now, Daniel Honeycutt. That's hardly true."

Daniel shook his head. "I've heard you even write his speeches."

Virginia's eyes sparkled. "Perhaps one or two."

Daniel nodded. "I certainly hope he'll remember the folks here in Bethany Springs. One in particular."

"I know," Virginia said, lowering her voice. "I'll try to do what I can when I return to Austin."

Daniel gave a tight smile. "Thank you."

Virginia went on. "I hope to convince my father to give the matter his personal attention. I never ask him for anything. He's so busy, you see."

She paused, looked over her shoulder at the boys on the swing before going on. "Surely, he won't begrudge me one small favor."

Her gaze drifted to Simon. Silently, wordlessly, a sense of understanding and yearning stretched between them.

Simon nodded. "Hopefully."

Chapter Nineteen
News of Stranded Cows and Calves

Amelia

The second morning after Virginia Childress came to the ranch, Amelia woke at dawn. She rose, said her prayers, and dressed. She went downstairs to start breakfast. It surprised her how much she'd grown to enjoy preparing meals. Perhaps it was because she had folks to feed. It was never as gratifying to cook only for herself. Why bother?

When she had family and friends around, the entire venture took on new importance.

To her delight, her son Zach arrived just as she finished making coffee. He brought some bad news. Several cows had been stranded on the far side of the Bethany River. Zach guessed there were three of them, each with a new calf, so six animals altogether.

They talked in the kitchen in the predawn darkness. Zach filled his coffee mug and sank into a nearby chair with a weary sigh. "Sorry to add to your troubles, Mama."

Amelia pressed a pie dough into a pan. "I don't mind one bit."

"I figured with Sheldon gone and the youngsters here, you were short-handed."

"True. I've been doing my chores and his too, but Simon's been a good help."

Zach took a swallow of coffee. In the flickering lamplight, she noted his furrowed brow. He was likely too tired to ask many questions, especially after a night of riding the north pasture.

"I can round up a few men and ride back out this morning. Maybe after catching a few winks. The O'Brian brothers are mending the hay crib. I'll take them along. See if we can get those mamas and babies across the river. They're raising a ruckus, fretting they'll be left behind."

"They're worried about coyotes or mountain lions helping themselves to a calf."

"I'm worried too. That's why I want to get them across today or tomorrow at the latest."

"Mm," Amelia said absently. She filled the pie pan with sliced apples, sprinkled cinnamon and crimped the edge of the pie. When she was done, she held it up for Zach's approval.

"That looks right pretty. When did you take up baking? Are you wearing an *apron*?"

Amelia chuckled and brushed her palm over the pretty apron. "You like it? Molly made it for me. She's such a wonder with needle and thread. That Daniel certainly married a smart young lady. Lovely too. Mind you pick out a girl as pretty and sharp as Molly, you hear?"

Zach shook his head but didn't argue about the wife comment. Instead, he complimented her attire. "It looks very nice on you, Mama. It'll take a little getting used to, but it's right pretty."

"I'm getting domestic in my old age. All I need is a couple of grandbabies."

She sighed, glanced over her shoulder, and found Zach offering a wry grin.

"Don't bother setting out for the strays just yet. I'll pack up the wagon, Junior's two boys as well as Simon and Virginia. We'll make a day of it. Maybe even spend the night, camping. Land sakes, I can't recall the last time I spent the night on the range. I reckon that's one good thing about Sheldon having to stay in Austin."

"How so?"

"That Sheldon." She slid the pie into the oven and brushed off her hands. "Such a mother hen. He never liked for me to camp out. He said it wasn't fitting. He always insisted I send hired men to ride out to the far reaches of the ranch."

"He's got a point." Zach got up and served himself another cup of coffee. "I believe you're the only female I know who enjoys sleeping in a buckboard."

Amelia chuckled. "I used to go out with your father, a couple days at a time. He said I was the best camp cook around. Wasn't true, of course. I burned near everything, but my cooking saved your daddy from worse food. Or having to cook for himself."

Sadness tugged at her heart. It seemed a different lifetime. And yet, the memory of those nights sleeping under the stars was fresh in her mind. She could almost feel George's arms around her as they fell asleep on the bed of the wagon, after a long day's work, then waking at first light to the sound of mourning doves.

Oh, George. I miss you so. Still...

Pushing aside the memories, she returned her attention to breakfast and began slicing bacon.

"You sure you want to take this on?" Zach asked gently as if sensing her mood.

"It would be a fine idea. Junior's boys could do with a venture. They're both so worried about their daddy. Moping all day long, not even enough gumption for pranks, poor little tykes. And Virginia's every bit as fretful. Simon's not much better. I'll just round up the whole lot. We'll leave after lunch."

Zach leaned against the counter. "I'll come along. Lend a hand."

Amelia smiled. Standing in the soft lamplight, Zach reminded her of George. Her boys all looked like their daddy. They had his mannerisms too. The three of them had been her reason for going on and fighting so hard to put a meal on the table. There were times that she'd look at them and get misty-eyed. Her heart would fill with tenderness. Her throat would get a lump.

"If you're feeling up to it, Zach. It would be nice to have you along. Nothing better than spending time with my boys."

"Yes, ma'am," Zach said. "I'll be happy to help. Mind you pack your frilly apron."

Amelia waved off his words. "Oh, hush. Go. Rest a spell. I'll set your breakfast in the oven."

He grinned, set aside his mug, and strolled out of the kitchen.

"Rascal," Amelia grumbled. "Never sure which one is worse, Simon or Zachary."

Chapter Twenty
Work Boots for Virginia

Virginia

Virginia had to wonder what she'd gotten herself into, staying at the Honeycutt ranch. She'd wanted to stay with the family and get to know Amelia Honeycutt but fretted about the woman's outlandish plans that included wagon rides to distant parts of the ranch, meals cooked over campfires and sleeping in the wilderness.

First off, they were heading to the north pasture, the furthest extreme of the Honeycutt ranch. They'd spend at least a day, probably the night too. There, Amelia would make them a fine dinner over a campfire. The boys could fall asleep under the stars and when all was said and done, three stray cows and their calves would be rescued and reunited with the herd.

Virginia listened to the plan over lunch, sitting in the family dining room. As much as she yearned to write an article about Amelia, she wondered if such a venture was worth it.

Her gaze drifted from Amelia's excited expression to Simon's thoughtful demeanor. Somewhere along the way, she'd expected one of them to inquire if *she* cared to go. No one asked. There was no chance to object. None. Before she knew it, the meal was over, the dishes cleared. Simon whisked her and the two boys to a back room to try on boots in preparation of the trip.

"I'm sure we have boots to fit all three of you." He knelt beside a trunk and rummaged. Boots clunked against the sides of the trunk. Every so often, he tossed one or two aside as he chuckled. "I recall wearing this pair... why, look at these dandy boots... can't believe Mama kept my very first pair..."

Before long, he had both boys in a pair of boots. They seemed pleased at first, then began to worry, or so it seemed to Virginia. They fretted about thunderstorms and hail and sundry threats. Simon laughed and dismissed their worries. They might get rained on but so what? As for hail, it only smarted for a short while. Neither boy looked a bit reassured by his words.

"Virginia, I need one of your shoes," Simon said.

She laughed nervously, backing away a few steps. "I don't understand."

He gestured. "Come on now. Don't be shy. Give me one so I can compare it to the boots. That will help me find a good fit. Otherwise, I'm just guessing your size."

While she had no desire to clamber onto a buckboard, she felt a certain degree of responsibility to the boys. In her worst moments, she agonized, wondering if Junior's fate rested in her hands. Was it her fault he still sat in a jail cell? Could she have written her father and begged him to intervene? Probably not. Especially since she hadn't even written her father to say she was staying with the Honeycutts.

Meanwhile, Simon Honeycutt wanted to fit her to a pair of boots. Virginia winced as she took in Simon's expectant look. He held out a hand. Clearly, he awaited one of her shoes. In exchange, he'd give her a pair of boots that fit her foot.

Even the boys watched and waited. Ellwood and Tuck seemed almost pleased to set out on the camping trip across the Honeycutt lands. For the first time in several days, the boys wore slight, tentative smiles. They waited. Everyone waited. Virginia felt the weight of their expectation.

"Fine," she muttered. She tugged off a shoe, a delicate kidskin half-boot she'd bought in New Orleans last year. Simon frowned as he turned it this way and that. A flush of mortification rose to her cheeks.

"Your feet are pretty small." He said matter-of-factly. "Let's see what I can do."

After a few moments of searching, he presented her with a scuffed pair of cowboy boots. He helped her tug them on. The gesture startled her, but he seemed to think nothing of it as he sat back on his heels, awaiting her reply. Standing, she wriggled her toes and found them comfortable enough.

"Go ahead and walk around." Simon gestured to an open area of the room.

"If I must," Virginia said as she took a few steps. The heavy boots thumped the floorboards. "Heavens, I sound like a Clydesdale."

"What's a Clydesdale?" Tuck asked.

"A very large horse," Virginia replied.

Ellwood shook his head. "You sound like a medium-sized horse."

"What a relief." Virginia gave Simon a pained look. "I'm perfectly happy to remain here at the house."

"You gotta come," Ellwood said.

"Please, Miss Virginia." Tuck looked at her with wide, pleading eyes.

Guilt stabbed her heart. A small rush of resentment followed. If only her father was the type of man to help an innocent man. If only he could set aside his own interests, she could look at the boys with a clear conscience.

Simon nodded. "Go on. Walk a little more. Try 'em out. Trust me. You don't want to be miles from home in a pair of boots rubbing your feet raw."

"Indeed." Virginia walked the length of the room. The boots felt fine, just heavy. Each step sent a thud across the floor.

Inwardly, she cringed. While she'd never been one for the fanciest of attire, she'd somehow wound up with a wardrobe of fussy, overpriced, impractical clothes. She'd never worn a pair of cowboy boots. Not once in her life. No, her father always insisted on a feminine, elegant appearance.

With a glance at Ellwood and Tuck, she reminded herself why she was doing this. While she relished the chance to know more about Amelia, she yearned for something else, a more important goal. To offer some small solace to Junior's boys.

She'd go on the trip and work up her nerve to return to Austin and demand justice for Junior. She might even wind up taking the boys to see the mansion. Maybe even Simon. The notion swirled in her mind, still too outlandish to envision.

The boots felt too heavy and too clumsy. It couldn't be helped. She resolved not to complain. Instead, she turned and thudded her way back to the middle of the room.

"Well?" Simon asked. "How do they feel?"

"They feel adequate."

"Let's see." Simon studied the tips of the boots, protruding from her hem. "Can you raise your skirt a couple inches?"

She gave him a pointed look. He responded with an exasperated huff. The boys simply watched the goings-on with interest.

"That's an indelicate question," Virginia told the boys. "For your information."

Simon frowned. "I'm trying to save you from a few blisters. Tell me how the boots feel, already."

"Fine." Virginia gave a huff of indignation as she lifted her skirt a few inches. "Perfectly fine."

To her astonishment, Simon pressed his thumb to the tip of her boot. Too surprised to reply, she watched as he moved his hand to her instep and ankle. Both times, he squeezed the boot.

"I reckon those will do." He sat back and looked up at her. "If you're comfortable."

Virginia weighed her answer, wondering if she fully understood the question. She didn't care for the notion of traipsing across a cattle pasture. Not even if it meant helping the boys or lending a hand to some stranded cows. She ought to feel sympathy for ailing animals, but she couldn't find it in her heart. Why not let them just stay put? Everyone knew that Longhorns were practically feral.

"Virginia," Simon prompted. "What about these boots? Think you can manage a short ride across the ranch?"

"Yes." Virginia glanced down at the scuffed, well-worn leather and gave a smile she usually reserved for political gatherings, one that masked her feelings. "They're perfect. I'm ready."

Chapter Twenty-One
Bethany River Campsite

Simon

Simon rode beside the buckboard. Zach rode on the other side as they traveled along the well-worn path to the north pasture. Mama drove the team. She looked pleased as punch, dressed in a new jacket she'd bought with Sophie the last time they'd gone on a shopping trip to Houston. She'd even worn a fancy belt with a silver buckle, maybe to impress Virginia.

Virginia wore a simple, cotton dress Mama had lent her for the trip. Even though it was nowhere near as fancy as her own dresses, Simon thought she looked mighty pretty. He tried, best as he could, to keep his gaze from wandering to where she sat on the buckboard.

Ellwood and Tuck perched on the second bench behind the women. Both looked around, taking in the sights with wide grins. Their happy expressions warmed his heart. He liked to think the trip supplied a small ray of sunshine in the midst of their turmoil.

The covered wagon creaked as they made their way on the rough road. The contents of the buckboard clattered each time the wagon bumped or swayed. Mama had packed enough provisions for a trip to Laramie, not a short jaunt to the north pasture. She, too, looked pleased as all get-out.

"It's been a long time since I've taken Barbara on a trip." His mama spoke. "The old girl likely felt a tad neglected."

"Did you polish off her dust?" Simon asked.

Zach chuckled.

Mama looked affronted. "Of course. I can't take Barbara out for a ride without sprucing her up beforehand. I cleaned and oiled her too. Polished her pretty walnut stock."

The boys didn't pay much attention to the conversation. Instead, they scanned the horizon, searching for storm clouds or who knows what sort of threat. Simon had already explained there likely wasn't a storm cloud in all of Texas.

Virginia scanned the landscape with as much interest as the boys. She didn't seek rampaging buffalo or dastardly outlaws but admired the beauty of the land. She turned to Mama to ask, "Who is Barbara?"

Mama winked at Simon. "One of my most trusted friends."

Virginia caught the note of amusement. Her lips twitched and Simon watched as she gave in to the fun. "It's so nice to travel with friends."

"Certainly is," Mama replied.

Virginia went on. "I didn't happen to see anyone else in the wagon. I suppose Barbara must be a petite sort of friend."

Mama shook her head. "Not really. She's sturdy. Stout."

Virginia clicked her tongue. "Poor Barbara. Stout. Seems quite an insult."

She looked to Simon for a hint of who Barbara was, but Simon remained tight-lipped. Mama would explain by and by. It wasn't much of a mystery, after all. After they rode a quarter mile, Mama gave in and spilled the beans.

"Barbara is the gun I carry whenever I head to the north pasture. I never know if I might encounter a pesky varmint."

"Are you going to shoot a gun, Mrs. Honeycutt?" Ellwood asked.

Mama pondered the question. "Probably not. But it's better to be armed, ready for trouble and not need a gun, than the other way around."

The boys squinted as if trying to work out what mama had said.

"Goodness." Virginia fanned herself. "I've never gone on such an outing. Never mind. It's never too late to learn new ways. I'm sure my father's father and grandfather were no stranger to weapons."

Mama scoffed. "Not out on that family homestead. The men knew their way around guns, but I can assure your father's mama and grandmother knew how to shoot a weapon too. Not just the menfolk."

Virginia lifted her brows.

Mama patted her knee. "One day I'll show you how to shoot your own Barbara. You'll need to know."

"Why would I need to know how to shoot?" Virginia looked aghast.

Mama didn't reply right off but seemed to consider her words carefully.

Simon wanted to know as well. He didn't like to think about Virginia needing to shoot a gun. Ever. A sudden realization came over him. If Virginia ever needed a gun, he wanted to be there to protect her. She seemed far too refined to manage a gun. She didn't belong in the country, certainly not alone.

"Why do you say my grandmother and great grandmother would know how to shoot?" Virginia asked.

"Because they were among the first folks to claim land here in Bethany Springs. Just like my husband's family. A couple of generations back, folk had to contend with wolves and bears, not to mention outlaws."

Virginia, as well as the boys, took in this bit of history with solemn silence. They looked around the land as if expecting a bear to charge the buckboard. The boys were delighted with the prospect. Virginia not so much.

"I suppose I always imagined Bethany Springs as a sort of paradise," she mused. "I never thought of all the dangers folks had to contend with."

They continued on their way, riding to the north pasture and stopping by the river to make camp. The river was twice as wide as he'd expected. Strange, especially since he hadn't heard reports of rain upriver. The water streamed past, a murky, swirling torrent, carrying branches and other debris.

Simon and Zach shared a glance, silently communicating their concerns about the swollen river.

"River looks fine," Mama proclaimed. "Glad I don't need to fret about it running low this summer."

"It looks yucky," Ellwood said as he stood a safe distance away.

"It looks like mud," Tuck chimed in. "I bet the fish are sad."

"How can they see anything?" Ellwood asked.

"They can't. That's why they're sad," Tuck explained.

Mama lowered the back of the wagon and pulled out her cast-iron cookware. "They see just fine. Especially after they put on their spectacles."

Virginia smiled, as she pushed up her sleeves and began to unload the wagon.

The boys looked unconvinced as they stared at the raging river. Simon and Zach tended to the animals. They left the wagon for the women to manage.

"All right, gentlemen," Mama said to Ellwood and Tuck. "Make yourselves useful."

The boys scurried to lend a hand. They unpacked the wagon, minded directions, and set up the campsite. Simon watched as he unsaddled his horse. He noted a small glimmer of pride. The two boys worked hard and didn't stop till Mama told them they'd done a fine job.

When he finished tending to the horses, Simon went to the riverbank to search for the cattle. This was the usual crossing point. Cattle were creatures of habit. He'd expected to find them wandering the area, bellowing for the rest of the herd but there was no sight of them. None.

Cupping his hand to his mouth, he shouted, using the customary cattle call, the same his mother taught him years ago. "Sook, sook, sook."

Normally he'd hear a response. At times it might be a quiet, tentative moo. Other time it would be a loud, indignant bawl. He heard nothing.

"River's rushing," Zach muttered. "It's too loud. Drowning you out."

Simon called again. Waited. And tried once more. Behind him, he heard the women and children setting up the campsite.

"That's how you start a campfire," Mama announced. The children whooped and cheered. Virginia's polite clapping followed.

Simon tried calling the cattle again. Not that he'd collect them that afternoon or evening, but he'd hoped they might be nearby. Longhorns were ornery, not usually skittish, but the cows had youngsters. They were apt to be uneasy, watchful for coyotes or other predators. New mamas were always nervous. Even Longhorns.

Zach shook his head. "I don't recall seeing the river this high. You sure about this? You think we ought to worry about a few cows and calves?"

Simon had to admit Zach had a good point. In a way, the trip had been a means to distract the boys from the grim facts. Even now as Simon stared at the raging river, he could hear them chattering about the campfire.

With a pang of sorrow, he noted their excitement. Their heart-wrenching innocence. Their daddy might not hang, or Simon certainly prayed he wouldn't, but Junior could well end up in prison for the rest of his life.

When Simon first considered the possibility, he'd worried about his own circumstances. Simon winced at his own selfishness. In the beginning, he'd fretted that if Junior went to jail, he'd have to raise the boys. That hardly mattered anymore.

Oh, how things had changed in a remarkably short time. Now, Simon worried more about justice for Junior. The longer Junior stayed in jail, the more Simon worried he might not be released. An innocent man could spend years behind bars. The idea weighed heavily on Simon's heart, the dread as profound and powerful as a raging river.

"We're crossing in the morning," Simon said matter-of-factly. "Those strays belong with the Honeycutt herd and we're going to bring them back home."

Chapter Twenty-Two
Childress Homestead for Sale?

Virginia

Ellwood and Tuck finished their supper, taking seconds of the peach cobbler Amelia made in an iron skillet. The boys ate with gusto while they argued, between bites, why they ought to sleep in the wagon. Amelia listened with a bemused smile. Virginia couldn't help feeling a tad sorry for the boys as they listed the perils of sleeping outside.

"Scorpions, centipedes, toads," Ellwood said, counting off the various dangers on his fingers.

"Spiders, mosquitos, earwigs," Tuck added.

Virginia wondered if those things existed. Earwigs? She'd never heard of such a thing and tried to picture a creature with enormous ears that wore wigs. She wanted to laugh aloud but assumed she'd misunderstood. Surely.

Meanwhile, Zach and Simon reclined on their bedrolls on the other side of the fire. Both men laughed about the boys' worries. Propped up on their elbows, Zach and Simon basked in the soft glow of the campfire. Virginia could well imagine them offering even more fearsome threats, scaring the boys and her too well beyond reason. Thankfully, they held their tongue.

Not so with Amelia. She was more than ready to add troublesome, nocturnal threats. "Don't forget about snakes, coyotes and mountain lions."

The boys looked stricken. "Mrs. Honeycutt, please let us sleep in the wagon."

Amelia scoffed. "Sorry, gentlemen. The wagon is for ladies only. You get to sleep by the fire. You'll be fine. It'll do you good."

The boys grumbled and begged to no avail. Virginia was about to take up their cause when she heard Zach start a campfire story. The boys grew still, nestled in their bedrolls as Zach began a tale about a wild bandit and a brave Texas Ranger.

As Zach told his story, Amelia ushered Virginia into the covered wagon, holding the flap aside to let her pass. A moment later, both women sat ensconced inside the wagon. A lamp cast a soft glow across the interior. Amelia had heated water so they could wash before bed. The detail struck Virginia as touching and kind. She thanked Amelia, who at once brushed off her gratitude.

"I might be a rancher, but I like going to bed clean and with a little perfumed lotion. Don't tell anyone I like such feminine comforts."

Virginia smiled. "Why not?"

"It would ruin my reputation. I don't want folks to know I have a soft side."

"Your secret is safe with me."

As Virginia prepared for bed, she noticed Amelia's gown. She wasn't sure what she'd expected, but it certainly wasn't a delicate lace gown. The gauzy trim looked impossibly fragile. The collar spanned Amelia's narrow shoulders, accentuating her slim form.

"Don't look so surprised." Amelia combed her hair. "I might be a widow, but I still like to sleep in something pretty."

"You really *do* have a soft side," Virginia murmured.

Amelia held her finger to her lips. She gestured to a rumpled garment, lying at the foot of her bedroll. "I'm also fond of other fabrics. Take my robe, for example. It's just old, tattered flannel. And yet that robe once belonged to my dear husband, George. Of course, I had it altered. Otherwise, I'd be swimming in the old robe. I like my pretty, French lace, but I love the warmth of George's flannel too."

Virginia smiled.

Amelia sighed. "I probably sound like a crazy fussbudget. Talking about nightgowns and robes. It's because I'm so pleased to have a woman's company. That's why I'm such a chatterbox. I can't imagine sharing this with my boys. Molly, yes, but she's a new bride. I'd never expect her to spend a night in the wild with her old mother-in-law."

Virginia wanted to hasten to give a reply. She hardly thought of Amelia as old. As she considered the notion, she realized that she couldn't quite figure how old Amelia was.

Simon's mother had some grey hair, and a few lines on her face, but in a way, she seemed ageless. One moment, she'd talk of the time she dressed down a railroad tycoon in his own boardroom, chastising him for cheating stockholders. The next moment, she got tears in her eyes as she talked of a motherless kitten she'd nursed back to health. Or an orphaned foal she'd saved from coyotes.

Amelia Honeycutt seemed indomitable. She was fragile, yet strong. She spoke her mind and refused to suffer fools or blowhards. Virginia could well imagine how much Papa disliked the woman. Amelia was a force of nature. And yet, she insisted on wearing soft, feminine nightgowns even while camping on her north pasture.

Distantly, Virginia recalled the notion of writing an article about Amelia. Somehow the idea had lost some of its appeal.

"You're very pretty," Virginia whispered. "Not old at all."

Amelia tied a ribbon around her braid. "Not near as pretty as you."

Virginia flushed.

"And so, I do hope you'll forgive me when I tell you what I intend to do."

Virginia frowned. "What do you mean?"

"I received a letter from my land agent this morning. He had some interesting news. There's a rumor your father wants to sell the homestead."

Virginia's breath caught. It wasn't possible. Surely her father would talk to her if he wanted to sell the family land.

Amelia pulled back her blanket, settled on her side of the wagon and drew the covers up. "I realize this must come as a shock. It did to me."

Virginia sat on her blanket, unmoving, wishing more than anything Amelia would claim the entire thing was a joke. She clung to the hope that Mrs. Honeycutt liked to play tricks on people. After all, she *was* Simon's mother.

"I don't believe you." Virginia breathed the words as her heart thumped against her ribs. "It's not possible. Daddy wouldn't do that. He wouldn't betray me. My mother is buried on the land."

"I understand. But you must know as well as anyone that your daddy isn't sentimental. In fact, he's eager for a quick sale. I told my agent not to barter, to make sure the governor got my offer before he had time to change his mind."

Virginia gave a breathless laugh. "No. This isn't happening. I'm dreaming. Or perhaps you're having a joke at my expense."

"I'm not joking. I'm a businesswoman. I never joke about business."

Virginia pressed her lips together, determined not to show her distress. Her father was always fretting about money. He often grumbled about expenses. Still, it was impossible that he'd sell the homestead.

Amelia lifted to one elbow. "Just marry Simon. He'll have land to raise those appalling, hunchbacked Brahmas and you'll get to keep your birthright. I'll buy the land and give it to you as a wedding present."

The discussion was growing more outlandish by the moment.

"I will never marry," Virginia replied. "I can't. It's not possible."

Virginia considered explaining how her mother had passed in childbirth. She'd assumed Amelia knew the story. Didn't everyone know that Mama had died giving birth to her?

"Never marry?" Amelia's eyes widened. "Never, *never*?"

"Never, never."

"You're going to be a spinster?" Amelia's lips quirked. "Seems a shame."

"I planned to live a quiet life on my family's property. Alone. But content."

"Hmm. Well, I'd like to point out that women need a husband. It's not natural for them to live alone."

Virginia lifted her chin. "Fine words indeed. If you believe that, why don't you get married? You've been widowed how many years?"

Amelia narrowed her eyes. "That, my dear girl, is none of your concern. I married once. He was the love of my life. No one gets a second chance when it comes to one-time love. We're discussing *your* circumstances, Missy."

Virginia shook her head. "I'm not getting married either."

Amelia grumbled and fell back in her bed. "Sassy girl. I suppose this is what it's like having a daughter. I'd always imagined they were pliable and somehow easier than sons. So much for that notion. You don't want to marry because you've spent too much time around Simon."

"Pardon me?"

"Simon doesn't intend to get married either. I threatened to cut him off if he didn't, but then Junior got himself arrested so I had to take back my threat. I told Simon if he can get Junior free, I wouldn't force him to get married."

Virginia blinked. What on earth was she talking about? "You threatened him? About marriage?"

Amelia pressed her lips together into a grim line. "I did. If there's one thing that I dislike, it's having to take back a threat. Which was precisely what I had to do when Junior got himself thrown in jail. Taking back a threat is a poor idea. Very poor. You do that a time or two and people start assuming you'll back down from other matters, if you know what I mean."

"Not really," Virginia said slowly.

Amelia waved a dismissive hand. "Trust me on this. It's terrible to walk back a threat. Especially when dealing with obstinate grown sons. Give them an inch. They'll take a mile."

Virginia still wasn't entirely sure she followed the thread of the conversation. Her mind returned to her main concern. "I can't believe this is happening." She murmured the words, speaking more to herself than to Amelia. "How could Daddy part with the land?"

"I intend to acquire the land. And when I do, I'll give it to you and Simon. Once you're married, that is." Amelia settled under her blanket and sighed as she closed her eyes. "We'll talk after I've secured the deal. Good night, dear."

Virginia waited a long moment. When Amelia didn't say more, she dimmed the lantern, crawled across the buckboard, and slipped beneath the blankets. Instead of drifting off to sleep, she fumed. Papa would never sell the ranch. She'd heard him grumble about money, and knew he worried, but he wouldn't ever part with the Childress lands.

Surely not.

And yet there was a niggling shard of doubt. An election cost money. A great deal of money. Lately, he'd refused to show her the expense ledger. He declined to discuss finances. What if he'd decided to sell the ranch to pay for the expenses of a second election?

"No. Papa. No." She whispered the words into the darkness.

The worry faded. Her devoted father might have his weaknesses, but he'd never betray her trust by selling the land. He knew the homestead was precious to her. She'd return to Austin in several days and speak to him first thing. That would still give her time to stop him from completing a sale. In the meantime, she'd set her worries aside.

She let out a deep sigh. Her fears drifted off. She refused to let Amelia's words spoil the camping trip. Instead, she mulled over a very different detail. Simon refused to follow his mother's mandate. He might marry one day but in his own sweet time.

Typical.

A smile tugged at her lips as she tried to imagine Simon Honeycutt's beleaguered wife. Immediately a flicker of jealousy flared. For the life of her, she couldn't imagine where her feelings of envy had come from. She pushed aside the jealous thoughts and went back to imagining Simon's wife. The woman would likely suffer endless teasing, tricks, and pranks.

Perhaps not all the time. There might be small moments of happiness. Few and far between, Virginia assured herself. Simon could be kind one moment yet infuriating the next. Her thoughts drifted to the way he comforted Ellwood and Tuck when they fretted about their father.

Simon *could* be sweet. She had to admit he did have a little tenderness in his heart. With the boys, he was always gentle. Always.

Virginia sighed. If only she could chase thoughts of Simon from her mind. Then she might be able to drift off to sleep. With a weary heart, she had to admit that thoughts of Simon Honeycutt troubled her not only at night but during the day as well. She closed her eyes, praying for sleep, hoping she might escape any more troublesome worries of Simon Honeycutt.

Chapter Twenty-Three
Silence After Two Shotgun Blasts

Simon

After the ladies retired to the wagon, and after the young boys fell asleep in their bedrolls, Simon and Zach talked by the campfire. Simon wanted to ask about the sawmill Mama acquired recently.

Mama hadn't intended to become the proud owner of an East Texas mill, but the owners had defaulted on the loan. They'd given up on the mill, claiming it was a loss and abandoned the entire operation, forests, sawmill and surrounding shops and businesses. In the blink of an eye, Mama became the proud owner of one more venture.

As if she needed more properties to tend to. There was a time when she'd enjoyed new ventures. Not so much anymore. What she really wanted, in her heart of hearts, was a grandbaby. Not a timber mill.

No one else in the family much wanted to take on a new venture either. Simon was intent on starting his own brand, raising the Brahmas his mother disliked so vehemently. Daniel had just married. He and Molly expected a child. Zach didn't want the responsibility of a timber mill, clear on the other side of Texas. He preferred a more leisurely pace. More like the life of a cowboy.

"It's funny how things work out," Zach drawled, gazing into the dying fire.

Somehow, Simon understood they wouldn't be talking sawmills. Or timber. Or forestry. "What are you getting at?"

Simon knew his reply sounded ornery. Guilty of something or other. Which would only make his brother more intent on discussing the topic of how things worked out. Sure enough, Zach grinned in triumph.

"No need to get your nose out of joint," Zach said. "I only wanted to mention a peculiar going-on, the type that I might not have expected."

"Why don't you quit dancing on hot coals?" Simon snapped. His words sounded more irritable than from a moment before. His voice must have carried across the campfire for even Ellwood shifted around in his bedroll. Tuck muttered in his sleep.

Simon recalled that the main purpose of the camping trip was to treat the boys. They needed a reprieve from their worries of their father. Poor kids. He could hardly imagine their burden. He softened his tone, but only slightly. "Quit messing around already," he growled. "Get to the point."

"The point?"

Simon shook his head. Zach chuckled, clearly amused by Simon's discomfort. "What I'm saying is that I never imagined – well, actually, I reckon it's safe to say that *no* one ever imagined you'd get friendly with Virginia Childress."

"Quit talking that way. *Getting friendly* – sounds unseemly." Simon gritted his teeth. "I'm just being neighborly."

Zach regarded him with a thoughtful expression. "That so?"

Simon said nothing.

"Neighborly?" Zach asked.

Simon kept his gaze fixed on the campfire.

"That's funny."

Simon knit his brow. "What's funny? You keep saying this, that and the other thing is funny. Make up your mind. A moment ago, you were carrying on about how it's funny how things work out. Now something *else* has you tickled."

Zach held out his hands. "Whoa. Hang on a cotton-picking moment. What I'm trying to point out is how you claim you're just being neighborly, but you wouldn't ever help out the McCords like this. And we've been friends with them ever since I can recall. And yet, I doubt you'd invite them to stay in Mama's guest room."

"Course I would."

"You'd repair their house if a pecan tree fell on the roof?"

"No question."

Zach's lips curved into a devious grin. "You'd stare at them all afternoon while riding beside their wagon. Like some love-sick schoolboy? So distracted you don't notice *three* low-hanging branches and plum near get knocked out of your saddle?"

Simon clenched his jaw. He glanced toward the wagon, hoping Virginia remained asleep or in the very least couldn't hear Zach carrying on. Zach sure knew how to try a man's patience. While Simon loved his brothers something fierce, there were times when Daniel and Zach tried the bonds of family love. Especially Zach.

"You'd do all that for the McCords?" Zach inquired with a look of exaggerated surprise. "Would you now?"

"No, I reckon I wouldn't," Simon said grudgingly.

"Right. See, that's the part I found sorta funny. How you were doing all this for Virginia Childress, a girl you always loved to tease. Suddenly, you can't do enough to help out. Not to mention you can't hardly tear your eyes away from her. Can you?"

Simon didn't bother to reply.

"And while I'm talking about Virginia." Zach's voice dropped a notch. "As one man to another, I can't help observing how lovely she's turned out. Know what I mean? Have you noticed? Wait. Let me think on this a spell. I reckon you *have* noticed which would account for how you *didn't* notice the tree limbs this afternoon."

Simon gave his brother a dark look to warn Zach that he'd best tread carefully. Simon might not object to Zach poking fun at *him* but wouldn't tolerate his brother talking about Virginia. Not in that way.

His brother took no notice. His eyes sparked with amusement as he gave a low whistle. "I tell you one thing... the governor's little gosling is all grown up."

"You better quit. Right now. I'm not even kidding."

"Don't get all sore. You always tell Mama that you want to start your own brand before you get married. What do you care if I notice how pretty Virginia turned out?"

"I care. Virginia's kind and sweet and innocent. I want to protect her."

Zach's jaw dropped. Simon had to admit he was as surprised as his brother. Despite his astonishment, he knew that it was true. He did want to shield Virginia. He'd do anything to keep her from harm or strife. He'd realized that very thing earlier that day when the topic of guns came up.

For a long moment, neither spoke. Simon kept his attention fixed on the fire and studied how the embers shimmered with heat. The glow mesmerized him for a spell, providing relief from his turmoil. His thoughts drifted to Virginia as he imagined her asleep in the nearby wagon. In his mind's eye, he could picture her lying under the blankets, her eyes closed, her lovely hair loose and framing her pretty face.

Suddenly, he realized his thoughts had drifted. He pushed away his notions of Virginia asleep in the wagon. He turned to find Zach watching him with a thoughtful expression.

"Don't take this the wrong way," Zach said.

Simon scowled. "Whenever someone tells me not to take something the wrong way, I want to bust them in the chops. I don't even need to hear a single word."

Zach chuckled. "Really? What a surprise."

"I figure they're fixing to say something rude, wrong, or out of line."

"Not this time, brother. What I want to say is that I've heard rumors about Virginia."

Simon tightened his fist. "Then keep them to yourself. Act like a gentleman. Just how Mama raised us."

"It's nothing terrible. The rumor I heard from a few fellas in Austin is that Virginia Childress hasn't ever kissed a fella."

Simon turned to stare at his brother.

Zach shook his head. "Don't shoot the messenger."

"She's never been kissed?" Simon asked. "Never?"

He wasn't sure what he thought of the news. Part of him felt a tad pleased. He didn't care to imagine Virginia allowing some rascal to kiss her. She seemed above such frivolous notions. On the other hand, he didn't approve of men talking about Virginia kissing or not kissing a fella. It seemed untoward for men to discuss such a topic.

Zach shrugged. "That's what I've heard. Virginia hasn't ever let one of those city slickers steal a kiss. Seems a shame. Such a pretty gal."

"It's not a shame," Simon grumbled. "It's not a shame, at all. What's more, it's no one's danged business."

Zach shrugged. "I never really believed it. And now that I've seen how pretty she is, all grown up and all, it seems a tad unlikely, wouldn't you say?"

"Virginia is pretty." Simon said quietly. He eyed the covered wagon and tried to imagine the cultured, society girl sleeping on the rough wagon board. "But considering her serious nature, I'd say there's probably some truth to the rumor."

"There's more to the rumor."

Simon didn't reply. What did he care? He might feel a tad relieved, pleased even that she'd never kissed a fella, but other rumors didn't concern him. The less he thought of Virginia, the better.

Zach went on. "I heard that the governor is willing to barter off his daughter's first kiss. Can you believe that? Her very own father?"

Simon's blood heated. "I don't believe a word. Who ever heard of such nonsense? Did Mama put you up to this? I think you're trying to get me riled up, aren't you?"

"Suit yourself."

Simon tried to tamp down the unreasonable anger burning inside him. He couldn't decide who was worse, Mama or Zach.

"A girl's first kiss ought to be cherished by a fella," Simon said. "Not treated like some prize. It ought to be private and tender. Most of all, it should be the girl's choice."

Zach chuckled. "Seems you're giving this a little thought."

"I'm not either."

"Sorry. My mistake."

"What's more, you don't need to go off telling others about this rumor."

Zach grinned and saluted. Simon's blood heated. The two men lapsed into silence, but the quiet didn't last long.

The sharp, piercing cry of a wild animal rang across the campsite. In an instant, both Simon and Zach jumped to their feet. Before either could speak, the shriek sounded once more. The eerie sound rented the peace of the campsite. Ellwood and Tuck sat up and looked around in terror.

"It's all right, boys," Simon said as he circled the campfire. "Just some critter."

"That noise came from an animal?" Ellwood asked, his voice shaking.

"It sounded like the scream of a ghost." Tuck sputtered. "A lady ghost."

"Or maybe a banshee," Ellwood said. "Do we have banshees around here?"

Zach chuckled. "Nah. Banshees go to bed early. So do the lady ghosts. They don't like to miss their beauty rest. You two go back to sleep."

The boys didn't look convinced. They sat, stock still, eyes big as plums. Simon was about to offer to survey the perimeter, to chase off any critters. Before he could offer, the animal screeched again.

"It's getting closer," Ellwood said, his features taut in the flickering light.

Simon considered getting his gun from his saddle bag but wanted to comfort the boys before he set off into the dark with his weapon. He crouched near the boys. "Don't you worry. This is part of the fun of camping."

The boys stared at him, petrified. Poor kids. Their first night camping would be a memorable one. Well, that was part of the fun of camping. When all was said and done, a fella was left with memories and tall tales. Tuck and Ellwood would have a few good stories to tell for years to come.

"I'm sorta scared," Ellwood said. "Just a little."

"Me too," said Tuck. He gulped and hugged his knees. "More than just a little."

"Now there," Simon said. "That rascal will be on his way soon enough."

"Darn right that rascal will be on his way," Mama proclaimed. She climbed out of the wagon, grabbed her shotgun and crossed the campsite as her robe billowed around her. "Danged mountain lions bothering folks, making a racket when people are just trying to catch forty winks."

"Mama?" Zach said.

"Oh, hush. I've got this matter in hand," Mama replied.

She strode to the edge of the campsite. Coming to a stop, she lifted the gun to the treetops and fired twice.

The boys yelped with terror. The final shot echoed. Sleeping birds fluttered from nearby trees. Mama groused about the pesky critters. The boys muttered about Mrs. Honeycutt giving them bad dreams, worse than the mountain lion. Mama hummed as she returned to the wagon, a satisfied smile on her lips. Virginia peeked out of the wagon, wide-eyed with astonishment.

The night breeze wafted across the campsite, fluttering across the delicate trim of Mama's gown beneath the edge of her old flannel robe. Overall, it made for a peculiar sight. While Simon was accustomed to seeing his mother with her trusted shotgun, Barbara, this was the first time he'd seen her firing the gun while clad in her well-worn flannel robe.

As the silence stretched across the surrounding wilderness, Mama offered them a cheerful smile. "I'll wager that old cat is in the next county. Ellwood and Tuck, you two rest well. It'll do you some good to sleep under the stars. Zach and Simon, reckon it's time to turn in. Morning will be here before you know it."

The two boys, along with Zach and Simon, replied in unison. *"Yes, ma'am."*

Mama gave a brisk nod, climbed into the wagon, and disappeared behind the canvas flap. Simon could hear her tell Virginia all about the mountain lion. Mama explained how the gosh-darned cat had best take his fussing, howling, and caterwauling some distance from the campsite if he knew what was good for him.

Virginia, for her part, said little, probably as astounded as Ellwood and Tuck.

Soon the night grew quiet. Even the boys settled under the covers and drifted off to sleep.

"Ever notice how small she is?" Zach said absently. "Tiny, really."

"Mama?"

"Right."

"Small? No, I don't ever notice." Simon shrugged. "If anything, she seems plenty substantial."

"It's her nature. She seems bigger than she is."

"That ol' mountain cat seemed mighty concerned. He probably thought Mama was ten foot tall."

Zach grinned. "I think he's long gone. Pretty sure he won't be back. Likely happy he didn't wind up with a backside full of buckshot."

The men prepared to turn in. Once again, the night drifted to a restful quiet. The only sounds came from peaceable critters. Crickets chirped. A distant owl hooted. The soft crackle of the fire drifted across the stillness.

Simon lay in his bedroll, gazing up at the stars. Much as he tried not to, he dwelled on various aspects of Virginia Childress. Her laugh. Her smile. Her enticing scent.

It was impossible to stop thinking of the girl, probably because she was just a few paces away, resting in the wagon. He couldn't help himself. Then again, it pleased him to have her near. She slept a mere fifteen or twenty paces away. He wished he could find a way to keep her this close for a lot longer, more than a few nights.

Zach's words had set him on edge.

He didn't like to think about anyone kissing her or even talking about kissing her. Not one bit. And yet, he relished the notion she'd never had a sweetheart. Virginia hadn't ever been courted. That pleased him more than it should, and Simon couldn't help smiling as he drifted near sleep.

Virginia hadn't ever been kissed. Not once.

Not yet.

Chapter Twenty-Four
Crossing the Flooded Bethany River

Virginia

After a cold and uncomfortable night in the wagon, Virginia awoke to Amelia's proclamation.

"It's dawn, Miss Childress."

Virginia groaned softly and tried to open her eyes. Surely it wasn't time to get up.

Amelia went on, speaking in an overly cheerful tone. "If we want coffee, we'll need to make it ourselves. This isn't the governor's mansion."

She laughed at her own joke as she dressed in the first rays of sunlight. Virginia winced, her shoulders aching from the hard bed. Slowly, she rose and donned her borrowed cotton frock and the boots Simon had lent her. Camping, she decided, or any manner of sleeping outdoors, was a terrible idea. She climbed down from the wagon to find the menfolk up and about.

Ellwood and Tuck chattered as they poked the campfire coals. They grumbled about the men leaving them behind. They wanted to help collect the lost cows and calves and bring them across the river.

"That's men's work," Simon said gruffly.

The boys insisted they'd be fine help. Both argued that they were grownups. They'd do anything Simon asked.

Zach shook his head. "The river's too high, boys. Maybe next time."

Virginia fretted as she recalled the swirling, muddy water. Fear clenched tight around her heart. She didn't like anything about this venture, especially after she'd seen the full fury of the river. From the roar of the water, she suspected it was higher and faster than yesterday.

She drank a cup of bitter coffee and fretted. Simon and Zach meant to cross the unruly river, find the cattle, then bring them back across the same span of roiling water.

The risk seemed too great. A handful of cattle couldn't possibly be worth the danger. She knew, however, the rescue of the lost cattle had little to do with money.

For Simon, saving stranded cattle came down to principle. The animals were lost. They needed help. The Honeycutt family owned the cattle and were, therefore, responsible. Simon would do whatever it took to bring the animals home. Despite the risk. Despite the danger. And Zach would be by his brother's side.

They ate a quick breakfast of ham and eggs. The boys helped the men saddle the horses. Virginia stood on the riverbank with Amelia and the boys, watching as Zach and Simon rode into the swirling waters. Silently, Virginia said a prayer for the men. They crossed the river, slowly and steadily as she held her breath. She couldn't have ever imagined she'd one day stand on a riverbank and ask God to protect Simon Honeycutt.

After the men reached the other side, they waved and trotted off, disappearing into the brush.

Tuck and Ellwood complained about missing out on a grand adventure.

Amelia tidied the breakfast dishes and fussed at the boys. "You know what mountain lions especially love?"

Neither boy claimed to know. Amelia laughed and told them mountain lions especially loved pesky, troublesome, grumbling boys. From anyone else, the words would have seemed unkind, but Amelia kissed each boy on the head after teasing them.

Ellwood and Tuck grimaced at the show of affection. Then they laughed, insisting she was wrong. Didn't she know that mountain lions liked to eat ham and eggs?

Virginia only half-listened. She ought to be helping wash up. Instead, she found her gaze returning, time and again, to the stretch of river that now lay between her and Simon.

The hours passed slowly. Amelia took the opportunity to show the boys how to mend a harness. Next, she demonstrated how to clean and oil their boots. Virginia took in a little of Amelia's instruction but mostly kept her eyes on the far bank.

Just the prior evening, she'd fretted about her father selling her birthright. A troubling notion to be sure. And yet, not nearly as frightening as Simon and his brother crossing a flooded river.

Amelia turned her attention to the matter of supper.

"A river crossing takes it out of man and beast," Amelia said. "They'll be tired and hungry, not to mention cold and wet. Nothing like a bowl of chili to chase away the chill."

She set the boys to work, chopping onions at a makeshift table, a board set between two stumps. Virginia was in charge of cooking the beef, browning it in the immense Dutch oven, next to a pot of simmering beans.

Amelia added spices, drained the beans, and added them to the browned meat. While the chili simmered, the women brewed tea for sweet tea. Finally, Amelia made a batch of cornbread. She poured the mixture into a cast iron pan and set it over the hot coals.

The aroma of the cornbread and chili pleased the boys and distracted them from the long wait.

The sun began a slow descent to the west. When it was near dusk, Simon and Zach appeared on the horizon. They waved their hats. Virginia gave a prayer of thanksgiving, adding another prayer for a safe river crossing.

The cattle moved beneath a swirling cloud of dust and grit. The calves bawled piteously as they neared the river. The cows shook their heads, their immense horns white and fearsome against the arid, unforgiving land. The men rode hard, shouting encouragement as they urged the cattle to the water's edge.

Virginia watched, spellbound. The animals plunged into the rushing river. To her amazement, the cattle managed to swim the flooded river. They struggled but made good progress. The youngsters fared almost as well as their mothers. One little calf drifted downstream but Zach rode alongside him and nudged him back to the group.

Amelia came to Virginia's side, patted her shoulder, and gave a kindly smile. "You see. They're fine."

Virginia wanted to argue. It seemed wrong to claim success just yet. She kept her eye fixed on Simon. With each beat of her heart, she willed him across the span of water. The animals drew near. The men shouted. The horses pinned their ears with the effort of the swim.

Finally, they reached the shore.

The exhausted animals pulled themselves from the river. The two men were the last to emerge from the roiling waters. Simon nodded and offered her a weary smile. She smiled in return and tried to hold back tears of relief. Silently, she gave a prayer of thanksgiving.

Amelia went to her sons as they dismounted and held her arms out in greeting. They were damp and dirty and tried to wave her off her attention, but she wouldn't hear of it, insisting on wrapping her arms around both men for a long embrace.

Virginia held back. She wanted to compose herself before greeting Simon. It would hardly do to rush to his side with tears streaming down her cheeks.

Ellwood and Tuck celebrated the men's return, only instead of greeting them as they dismounted, the boys cavorted along the bank. They cheered and laughed. Ellwood somersaulted along the river's edge. Tuck danced upon a span of limestone.

Virginia had to smile.

In their own way, the boys had fretted too. Their concern must have been a considerable burden indeed, especially since they had worried about their father for some time now. Her heart went out to them as she tried to imagine their fears.

Tuck stood atop the rocks and mimicked a cowboy lassoing a calf. Ellwood pointed and laughed. Virginia wanted to call them back. They were too near the water. She lifted her hand to her mouth with the intention of ordering them away from the river.

Her good intentions came a moment too late.

Amidst the tomfoolery, Tuck lost his balance. He windmilled his arms. Staggered. Teetered on the edge of the rock for an instant before falling back into the churning water.

Virginia watched in horror. She tried to shout. Tried to call for help. Words failed her. The men were distracted by the cattle and horses. Instead of calling for help, she set off, running as fast as she could to the river's edge.

Chapter Twenty-Five
Goose Jumps in The River

Simon

Simon yearned to get off his horse and call it a day.

River crossings were almost always plenty dangerous, even without contending with high water and young calves. With that in mind, he felt a wave of gratitude when they made it back to solid ground.

His heart beat a little faster when he saw that Virginia waited and watched on the shore.

He'd spent a considerable amount of time thinking about her while searching for the lost cattle. A smile came unbidden as he admired her, standing on the bank. He urged the cattle to an enclosure where they'd find feed and fresh water.

Once he got the animals settled and tended to his horse, he hoped to tell her and the boys about the day's venture. He assumed she'd remain on the bank, but she didn't do anything of the sort.

Instead, she'd hurried off.

He had no idea what prompted her to rush downstream. What followed was worse. To his shock and disbelief, she leapt into the churning water. He watched in horror. She vanished beneath the surface. An instant later, she surfaced and swam a short distance, fighting the swift current. It was then he saw the reason. One of the boys flailed in the muddy water, ten or twelve yards from the bank.

Shaking off his confusion, he spurred his horse along the riverbank. Despite the long day and the river crossing, his horse obeyed his command and set off in a dead run. A moment later, they reached the rocky riverbank.

Simon slid from the saddle just as Mama pulled Tuck from the muddy river. The boy coughed and gasped. Mama thumped his back, trying to help him clear the water he'd inhaled. Virginia tried to reach the bank. Pale and stricken, she flailed against the strong current.

He rushed to the river's edge and tried to grab a hold of her. She was so close. Just a few feet from the bank. To his horror, she was swept away, the fast river tossing her like a ragdoll. She struggled. As she moved past a partly submerged boulder, she grabbed hold.

Simon ran to his gelding, snatched his lasso and returning to the river's edge, swung it overhead and managed to snare her. She lifted her arm to draw the rope taut. While he'd caught hold of her, the loop could easily slip off. She needed to tuck the rope under the other arm.

He cupped a hand to his mouth and shouted, "Put the rope under both arms."

She shook her head.

"If you don't put the rope around your chest, I could lose you."

Still, Virginia remained frozen, too afraid to follow his directions. She clung to the boulder. Simon prayed she had the strength to hang on.

"She's scared witless," Amelia told him.

Zach joined the group. Without a word, Simon handed him the coiled lasso. He rushed to the water's edge and plunged into the river. The water was deep and fast. After two steps, the water reached his knees. Two more steps and it reached his waist. An instant later, it came to his chest.

The cold water, along with the force of the river, made him gasp with shock. Virginia was likely chilled to the bone. With renewed determination, he forged on. He lost his footing once and then a second time but continued. Fighting the current, he made his way to the rock.

Virginia stared at him wide-eyed. She was too frightened to reason with and yet, she seemed to understand he was coming for her. She shook her head. Began jabbering some nonsense about staying put. He ought to go back. She was perfectly fine.

He couldn't make out more than about half of what she said, but he could tell she was going to fight him. As he drew near, he heard her teeth chatter. She tried to edge away from him.

"Quit wriggling," he shouted.

For an instant, her fear faded from her eyes. She gave him a sullen look, as if resenting his tone. Simon understood he was in for a battle but offered a prayer of gratitude that she did as he instructed.

"Quit shouting at me," she answered.

"Pardon my manners," he replied.

Her eyes shone with the threat of tears.

"Do as I say, Virginia. Don't fuss, you hear?" He reached her side and gently pulled her toward him. When he had hold of her, he tugged the lasso loose and slipped it around the two of them. She shivered. Wrapping his arms around her, he drew her close.

"I d-don't want to leave this rock, Simon. I'm quite fond of it."

"Sorry, darlin', but I'm taking you back to shore."

"Simon. Please let me stay put."

"I'm not leaving you here. Put your arms around me."

She squeezed her eyes shut, hiccupped, and wrapped her arms around his neck.

"Attaway," he said.

She whimpered in response.

"Ready!" he shouted over his shoulder.

The lasso tightened around them. The rope stretched taut across the span of rushing water. Zach had wound the other end of the lasso around the pommel of his saddle. He backed the horse slowly, pulling them to the shore.

"There we go," Simon said gently. "We're almost there."

"Please don't let me go."

"I won't."

"You promise?"

"I promise. No matter what, I'm going to hold on tight."

She rested her head against his shoulder. When they neared the shore, Simon thought he heard a small, ladylike burp.

"Pardon me," she said.

"I didn't hear a thing."

"Liar."

Try as he might, he couldn't hold back a chuckle. His boot heel hit the river bottom. He managed to get a foothold and wade the last couple of yards, carrying Virginia in his arms. Mama and Zach met them at the water's edge.

Once he got them out of the river and determined Virginia was unharmed, he helped her to the wagon. She was trembling. He would have liked to comfort her but knew she needed dry clothes. His mother shooed him away, urging him to change his wet clothes.

"Go on, Simon. I'll tend to Virginia and Tuck," she said quietly.

"Yes, ma'am," he replied.

Tuck and Ellwood both cried and sniffled about the near disaster. Simon did his best to ease their distress. Mostly, he was too tired to talk about Tuck's poor choices. Hopefully, the boy understood how close he'd come to outright calamity.

Over the next hour, things settled back to their normal cadence. Zach tended to the horses and rescued cattle. Simon got out of his wet clothes, changing them for a dry set he'd brought along.

Virginia changed in the wagon, donning some of Mama's clothes. Simon could tell his mother had lent the garments to Virginia when she appeared a short while later, clad in shirt and trousers. Virginia looked mortified, but better that than chilled to the bone.

Mama ordered her to sit by the fire and tucked a blanket around her shoulders. After that, Mama bustled around the campsite, cheerfully serving up bowls of steaming chili. She said a prayer, thanking God for keeping Virginia and Tuck safe.

Amen, the group said in unison.

Dusk fell, bringing a gentle peace.

Simon sat beside Virginia. She shivered but at least her teeth weren't chattering. The urge to wrap his arms around her and warm her flickered through his mind. He wouldn't, of course, but the notion tempted him.

He'd held her close in the middle of the swirling river. And she'd wrapped her arms around him. He'd probably think about that for a long time.

Virginia, bedraggled and spent, spoke quietly. "Simon."

"Yes, Virginia."

She looked at him from under the hooded blanket, a bowl of chili cupped between her hands. "I've come to a decision."

"What's that?"

"I don't believe I care for camping."

"You don't? Well, shucks. That's too bad."

"Never take me camping again. Never."

"Never?" He pretended to look astonished, then smiled at her. "All right."

To his surprise, she gave him a tiny smile in response. A sign that she was feeling a little better. He marveled at her spirit and strength. Maybe Virginia wasn't such a fussy city girl after all, even if she did object to camping.

He pondered a few teasing replies. None came to mind. All he knew for certain was how absurdly pleased he felt. And relieved. Thank the good Lord for His mercy. The boys were safe. Virginia too. Simon's heart brimmed with happiness.

Teasing Virginia always came easy for Simon. With Virginia, he was always up for a round of sparring and joking. Something had changed. He couldn't think of a single joke. Not one. Dusk fell. Stars glimmered. Simon had to admit, if only to himself, his joy and gratitude left him tongue-tied.

Chapter Twenty-Six
Time to Go Home

Virginia

The morning after the cattle rescue, Virginia awoke in her room at the Honeycutt ranch house. She awakened from a dream with a start. Sitting up in bed, she set her palm over her heart to slow the frantic beat. Her heart raced, yet her breathing felt laborious. It took a moment to recall where she was.

Slowly, it dawned on her.

She was in Amelia Honeycutt's guest room, in the middle of the immense four-poster bed, beneath a quilt sewn by Amelia's dear friend, Sophie. Sunshine warmed the room, chasing away the night chill. The fragments of her scandalous dream faded. Heavens. Why had she dreamt of Simon?

She wasn't sure but she knew her quiet yearning for Simon was leading her away from her long list of responsibilities. The list was usually the first thing she thought of in the morning and the last thing she considered in the evening. Ever since returning to Bethany Springs, she'd hardly thought of the list.

She took a deep breath. Her thoughts drifted back to Simon. No. That wasn't what she needed to think about. The events of the camping trip had served to make clear. Thinking frivolous thoughts of Simon would only cause trouble. She pushed the notions aside.

After a long moment, she rose and made her bed, eager to start the day.

She needed to change her plans. Up until that morning, she'd planned to remain two more days in Bethany Springs. She couldn't possibly abide by her plans. Not after awaking from such a scandalous dream. No. After dreaming of Simon holding her in his arms and whispering in her ear, she was certain it was time to go home.

Besides, she had a growing list of things she needed to discuss with her father. The Pecan Tree Misfortune, and the unmarked grave at the family plot. Not to mention Amelia's outlandish claim Papa intended to sell the land. That had to be a rumor, nothing more.

And then there was the topic of Junior Whitson. She made a mental note to bring *that* subject up before any of the others. Tuck and Ellwood had caused her a fair bit of trouble. First, the accident at the homestead, and then falling in the stream. Still, they'd endeared themselves to her, the poor little children. She couldn't help herself for caring about their welfare. She liked to think she might help the boys.

She said her prayers, washed and dressed, all the while fuming about the boys' mother. The woman had discarded them like last week's newspaper. Disgraceful. There ought to be laws to protect children. Perhaps Papa would take up that cause.

The subject would make a fine article for the journal which reminded her she still hadn't managed to write a single word. Yet another reason to go home early. She'd done precious little work since coming to the Honeycutt ranch. Simon and his family were too much of a distraction.

As she left her room and made her way down the hall, her thoughts drifted to the dream that woke her that morning. The dream had been distracting. Shocking.

She descended the stairs and pressed her palms to her face in hopes she wasn't blushing. Hopefully not. No matter. It couldn't be helped. There was no time for such foolishness. She needed to ask Simon if he could take her to Austin.

Savory aromas wafted down the hall. Voices came from the kitchen. Amelia chided Simon, calling him a poor example for Tuck and Ellwood. The boys voiced their disagreement, begging Simon to continue. After an instant of silence, they gave out a cheer.

Virginia turned the corner to find Simon putting on a juggling display. It appeared he used fresh biscuits. A pan sat on the counter, with several missing.

The boys watched; their faces wreathed in grins. Amelia watched too. Instead of smiling and cheering, Simon's mother pressed her lips into a grim line. By now, Virginia knew that was how Amelia kept from laughing aloud.

Simon slowed his antics, catching the last biscuit between his teeth.

Amelia turned to Virginia. "You see what I endure?"

"My very best tricks?" Simon looked affronted.

Amelia shook her head. "You can bake tomorrow's biscuits."

Simon buttered a biscuit and shrugged. "I can do even better. I'll make kolaches. Tuck and Ellwood can help out, right boys?"

Virginia stood quietly in the doorway. If she hadn't made plans to leave for Austin, she might have joined in with the tomfoolery. And if she hadn't just dreamed of Simon whispering tender things in her ear, she might have come up with her own joke or two.

Instead, she remained silent. To her astonishment, tears stung her eyes. She was leaving this home, leaving this small group of family and friends. Going back to Austin. Back to endless to-do lists. A multitude of parties and dinners. All of her father's expectations.

Her heart felt heavy, her throat dry.

Amelia's eyes grew wide. "Are you ill? Did you catch a chill in the river? I should have called a doctor when we got home last night."

Virginia waved off her concerns. She summoned the skills she'd always used at political events and schooled her expressions. She knew how to mask fragile, bothersome feelings.

"I'm feeling quite well," she said. "And hungry too. Breakfast smells delicious."

Amelia nodded. Simon eyed her with some degree of suspicion. The boys simply bided their time, probably eager to eat.

She turned to Simon. "I wondered if I could trouble you."

He nodded. "Course you can."

"I ought to return to Austin."

"To Austin?" His look darkened. "Why?"

"Well," she said slowly, "I live there."

"I know you live there, but you'd planned to stay several more days. You talked about visiting your mama's grave on her birthday which isn't till the day after tomorrow."

She gave a breathless laugh. "You remembered."

"Course I did." His frown deepened.

"You want to go home, dear?" Amelia asked. "Your father depends on you a great deal."

"Yes." Virginia nodded. "He does. Depend on me."

Simon leaned against the counter and folded his arms. "We're depending on you too. Especially the boys. If you catch my meaning."

"I know. I promise to do my very best to help matters."

Simon nodded. "I ought to pay Junior a visit. See if they'll let him speak to the boys."

Tuck and Ellwood both looked pleased.

Simon arched a brow. "Maybe you could come along, Miss Childress. That might cause a stir. Might be a big help."

"I can't." Virginia felt blood drain from her face. "I'm the governor's daughter. I can't visit a prison."

Amelia began whisking a bowl of eggs. "Of course not, dear. Simon's not thinking about a young lady's sensibilities."

Simon replied. "I'm thinking of a good man tried for something he didn't do."

Virginia shrank back, hardly able to meet his gaze. Even the boys regarded her with pained expressions. Silence stretched between them.

Tuck crossed the kitchen and took her hand. "You sure are a nice lady, Miss Virginia. I'll always remember you yanking me out of that river. I'm sorry I caused so much trouble with the house and all."

Ellwood wandered over. "We didn't mean any harm."

Virginia gave them a smile, her heart quaking. "Of course."

Ellwood took her other hand and patted it awkwardly. "Do we still get to see the governor's mansion? Like you said?"

"We can get a tour, right?" Tuck asked. "I'd sure like to see what it looks like."

Virginia frowned. "A tour?"

Simon's lips curved into a smile. "Well, that sounds like a right dandy plan. Maybe Governor Childress would like to meet Ellwood and Tuck Whitson."

Amelia chuckled. "I think I'd better tag along. For supervision. Can't have the Whitson boys toppling old trees or halfway drowning in a marble fountain or whatnot."

Virginia felt faint. She'd forgotten her promise to the boys.

"Although," Amelia added, "I'm certain Tuck and Ellwood will be perfect little angels, won't you, boys?"

"Yes, ma'am," Tuck replied.

"We'll be on our bestest behavior," Ellwood chimed in.

Virginia half-hoped Amelia would swoop in and brush off the plan. She'd explain matters to the boys, telling them now wasn't the time. She said no such thing, however. Simon didn't offer any help either.

Virginia wasn't sure how the morning had gone so wrong so quickly. She'd hoped leaving the ranch might solve her many problems. Instead, she'd added several more to the list. She tried to picture Papa's face when she arrived with her guests. He didn't especially care for children, not even under the best of circumstances. What would he say to Ellwood and Tuck when he learned they were the sons of Junior Whitson?

Even worse, Amelia Honeycutt would come along. Amelia. Honeycutt. Amelia intended to visit the mansion and, even worse, she had an axe to grind with the governor. Poor Papa. She almost felt sorry for him. Heavens. What had she gotten herself into?

The boys wandered to the counter to admire the biscuits. Smiling and laughing, they were happy with the turn of events. When they lowered their voices and bent towards each other, Virginia had to wonder what sort of terrible plans they were concocting.

Tuck reached for a biscuit. He watched Amelia as if waiting her reprimand. She said nothing.

Ellwood covered his mouth to conceal his amusement. Tuck moved slowly, stealthily. Amelia went about her business. She scrambled the eggs, not paying much mind to their shenanigans. Tuck went ahead with his scheme of biscuit theft. Amelia seemed unaware. And yet, she hadn't missed a thing. When Tuck neared his target, she swatted his hand away from the pan. He jerked back.

"You can have a biscuit after you say grace," Amelia explained. "Not before."

Ellwood and Tuck looked remorseful as they trudged to the kitchen table. They sat, folded their hands, and waited for the meal to be served.

"I'll behave too," Simon said softly.

Virginia blinked. She could hardly imagine what Simon meant. "Pardon me?"

"I will as well. Just like Ellwood." Simon's eyes sparked with amusement. He tapped his chest and winked. "I'll be on my bestest behavior too."

Chapter Twenty-Seven
Wagon Ride to Austin

Simon

If Virginia hadn't been in such a hurry to leave Bethany Springs, Simon would have borrowed the McCord's carriage. It was a fancy carriage Robert had bought for his wife anytime he squired her to town. There was no time, however.

Simon would have to take Virginia to Austin in the buckboard. She'd already ridden in the old wagon, of course, several times. Just the same, he wished they were traveling in something a little more respectable.

He ordered a ranch hand to hitch the wagon and bring it to the house. A couple of his cowboys loaded Virginia's trunks. Ellwood and Tuck clambered aboard. Simon helped Virginia up. A pang of regret struck his heart as he considered this might be the last time he'd ride alongside Virginia, at least for a while.

Standing beside the wagon, he gazed up, watching her for a long moment.

"Thank you, Simon," she said quietly.

"The boys and I are going to miss you." His voice was gruffer than he intended.

"I shall miss you too." She folded her gloved hands. "I certainly appreciate your kind hospitality."

Her words and tone were cool. Distant. He frowned. He wanted to point out that he'd shown a little more than mere hospitality. He'd sent a work crew to her home. Brought her to his family's home. Plucked her from a raging river. Meanwhile, she sounded like he'd invited her for glass of lemonade.

"It was my pleasure," he replied, his voice a tad gruffer than before.

She lifted her chin and leveled a prim gaze his direction.

"Now, now. No fighting on the wagon, children." Mama said as she descended the steps, a basket in one hand.

To his surprise, his mother wore a dress. And a bonnet. He stared in disbelief.

Mama ignored his stunned expression and carried on as if nothing were the matter. She petted one of the horses. "I remember when my boys were young. The three of them would get to squabbling and I'd stop right there in the middle of the road. I'd tell them straightforward and simple, 'Gentlemen, the horses refuse to pull a wagon of bickering children.' I'd blame the horses, you see."

She laughed. "Worked every time. Almost every time. Once, Simon and Zach got their blood up about who knows what. They were around ten or eleven. I stopped the wagon. Gave them my standard lecture. They ignored me. Jumped off and went from bickering to brawling. Little heathens. When they were all done, they climbed back into the wagon like nothing happened."

Simon didn't recall that particular day but didn't doubt his mother's words. Hopefully, she'd quit talking about him fighting with his brothers. He didn't want Tuck or Ellwood to hear too much of this. Or Virginia, for that matter, though she probably had a pretty good idea about his past.

"They both had black eyes," Mama said. "But at least they weren't bickering."

"We're not bickering," Virginia said. "At least I'm not."

Mama smiled, clearly not buying Virginia's words.

Virginia pursed her lips. "Simon started it."

"I've heard that one before." Mama sighed. "Once or twenty times."

Simon wanted to disagree with Virginia's claim. He hadn't started anything, but he held his tongue. If he argued, he'd simply prove his mother's point, and Virginia's too. Instead, he wisely changed the subject. "You look mighty pretty, Mama."

"Thank you," she said. "This is one of Sophie's castoffs, but it'll have to do."

She set her basket on the wagon beside the boys. "That's for your daddy if we manage to pay him a visit after we pay the governor a visit. I fixed your daddy some of his favorites. I packed sandwiches in wax paper for you two."

The boys thanked her. Simon helped her to the wagon.

"I'd better sit between you two," Mama muttered. "Keep you separated."

"We aren't bickering." Tuck sounded like he was boasting. Trying to show off. "Are we, Ellwood?"

"Nope. We're going to be good all day."

"That's what I like to hear," Mama said over her shoulder. "Let's avoid as much excitement as possible today."

The trip to Austin went quickly, but not fast enough. Mama spent much of the time regaling Virginia and the boys with more tales from Simon's childhood. How he'd pitched a fit when Daniel got a horse for his birthday, while Simon still rode a pony. Or the time he'd tricked Zach into doing his chores which included cleaning the chicken coop and painting the toolshed.

Virginia and the two boys laughed. Simon clenched his jaw.

Amelia went on. "Simon and Junior got into a fair number of scrapes too."

"Our daddy?" Tuck asked, leaning against the larger trunk. "What did he do?"

Mama sighed. "Your daddy never *wanted* to get into any mischief. He just sorta fell into trouble."

Virginia's smile faded. She looked away, her eyes troubled by the mention of Junior's name.

"I can't wait to see him," Ellwood said. "Do you think they let kids see their father?"

"I hope so. Poor Junior," Mama said under her breath. "Can't help feeling sorry for him. His two boys as well."

Virginia knew the comments were directed at her and responded. "Amelia, please. I promise to speak to my father. I give you my word."

Simon heard the tremble in her voice. He might feel a little sorry for her but would not allow himself to offer a word of comfort. She might change her mind which was a risk he couldn't take. So much depended on Virginia's help. Even though he yearned to ease her worries, he said nothing, keeping his gaze fixed on the road ahead.

Chapter Twenty-Eight
Governor Childress Barters Virginia's First Kiss

Virginia

They arrived in Austin mid-afternoon, stopping at the back gate to find the posted guard dozing in his chair. Virginia drew a sharp breath, astonished that the fellow didn't even stir when Simon brought the horses to a halt with a hearty, 'whoa there, boys.'

Amelia gave her a wry grin. "Tax dollars hard at work?"

"Not exactly," Virginia murmured. She prepared to get down, but Simon stopped her.

He set the brake, got down and approached the wrought-iron gate. "Pardon me, young fella."

The sentry opened his eyes, scowled, and grumbled. "Governor Childress don't have time. He's a busy man."

Virginia's heart sank. How often had she uttered those very words? Quite often, she was sorry to admit. And now a lazy guard dismissed her and her friends with the same phrase and twice the indifference. Even more exasperating, the man closed his eyes and went back to his nap.

"You might want to take a gander who's in my wagon," Simon said.

"Don't much care. Governor's not home. He left with some other stuffed shirt."

Virginia huffed and gathered her skirts around herself to get down from the wagon. Simon came to the wagon to help her down.

"That's my girl," Amelia said cheerfully. "Give 'em heck."

Virginia went to the gate, trying to tamp down her irritation. Papa had always insisted she keep perfect poise, especially in public. It wouldn't be ladylike to give this rascal a piece of her mind.

"I don't know who you are." She schooled her features to look agreeable but firm.

The man opened his eyes and blinked with confusion.

"I don't recognize you. Perhaps you're new. You might not realize that I am Virginia Childress. I live here with my father. Open this gate at once or I'll personally see to it you're dismissed."

The guard scrambled to his feet and jerked the gate open while stammering an apology.

"I'll walk ahead," Virginia told Simon.

Virginia strode up the cobbled path. While she'd only left a few days before, it seemed like an eternity since she'd been home. Probably because so much had happened during her stay in Bethany Springs.

Two servants greeted her with surprise. She gave them a brisk nod and instructed them to tend to the horses and wagon. When Simon arrived and the group had gotten down from the wagon, Virginia ushered them inside, down a narrow hall to the kitchens.

"Is this a castle?" Tuck asked. "Does it belong to a king?"

Virginia laughed, a little of the tension leaving her shoulders. She smoothed Tuck's hair, noting his wide-eyed amazement as they stood in the kitchen doorway.

"It's not a castle. And while the governor of Texas gets to live here, the home belongs to you, and Ellwood, Simon, and Miss Amelia."

The boys looked astonished.

Virginia went on. "This lovely home belongs to the citizens of Texas. The governor just gets to borrow it."

Edith, the cook, entered the kitchen with a tray and let out a startled cry. "Why, Miss Virginia! What a nice surprise. We didn't expect you for several days."

"I came home early. I've brought some friends along for a tour of the mansion."

The woman grew flustered. "How lovely. Would your guests care for refreshments?"

"No, thank you, dear," Amelia replied evenly. "We can't stay long. We're on our way to the jail."

Edith set the tray down with a nervous laugh.

"Thank you anyway, Edith," Virginia said as she led the group out of the kitchen. The rest of the house was as quiet as the kitchen with scarcely any servants about. Why that was, Virginia couldn't imagine.

The boys marveled at the grand rooms. They spoke in hushed tones. Simon and Amelia lingered to admire the oil paintings of Sam Houston and Lucadia Pease.

"Do any children live here?" Tuck asked.

"Not at the moment. But Sam Houston and his wife lived here with eight children. The youngest one was born right here in the governor's mansion."

She led them down the hall to the grand staircase. The boys could hardly believe their eyes.

"There's a funny story about one of Governor Houston's sons." Virginia lowered her voice for dramatic effect. "The five-year-old, Andrew Jackson Houston, locked the members of the legislature in their chamber."

The boys looked to each other and back at Virginia, frowning slightly.

"The legislature is a group of men who help run the state," Amelia explained. "Not all of them manage to run things very well, mind you, but that's what they're supposed to do."

Virginia smiled. "That's right. They're important men."

Amelia scoffed.

Virginia went on. "And young Andrew knew he'd be in trouble for locking them in their office. But he wasn't bothered. His father threatened to whip him if he didn't give back the key."

Tuck's eyes widened. "Did he give his daddy the key back?"

Virginia shook her head.

"So, his daddy whipped him." Ellwood gulped. "I woulda given the key back."

Tuck nodded.

"Not me," Simon offered. "I'd let them sit a little longer."

Virginia smiled at Simon, warmth blooming in her heart. Of course, Simon would have a mischievous response. She shook her head, returning to her story. "Governor Houston couldn't bring himself to beat his boy."

"Whew. That's good." Tuck let out a heavy breath.

"Instead, he threatened to *arrest* his son." Virginia laughed softly. "That did the trick. Young Andrew promptly gave the key back and that was the end of that."

Ellwood rubbed the banister and eyed the railing. It stretched up the grand stairwell and curved around to the second story. "I wonder if Andrew ever slid down this banister."

"I'll bet he did," Simon murmured, studying the span of polished wood.

"Now, Simon. Don't suggest something so reckless." Virginia turned to the boys. "Don't listen to your Uncle Simon."

"Reckless sounds fun," said Tuck.

"You certainly know a lot about Texas governors," Amelia said. Her eyes sparkled with amusement. "Do you know much about American presidents?"

"A little," Virginia replied.

"Is it true that President Washington had wooden teeth?"

"I never heard that," Virginia replied, a smile tugging at her lips.

Amelia nodded and directed her attention to the boys. "I heard the poor fellow only had one single tooth when he was inaugurated."

"How dreadful," Virginia said.

Ellwood looked delighted at this bit of news. "One tooth! How did he eat corn?"

"Slowly," Simon said, smiling at Virginia.

She gave him an answering smile.

The boys quickly forgot about President Washington. They were far more interested in the matter of the grand staircase and begged for permission to slide down. Virginia nodded, wondering if she'd somehow taken leave of her senses. Amelia gave her an approving look. Simon chuckled.

Ellwood went first, keeping a tight grip, slowing his descent. Tuck mocked his cautious approach and zipped down so quickly even Amelia gave a little gasp.

"Can we go again?" asked Ellwood, not to be outdone by his brother.

Before Virginia could reply, she heard her father's voice. He was with another man, talking about the upcoming election. Their voices grew louder until a door closed, muffling the sound.

"That's my father," Virginia said. "I ought to tell him I'm home and that I have company."

She excused herself and hurried down the corridor to find her father. When she reached his study, she paused to listen. From the foyer, she heard Amelia telling the boys how she'd slide down such a fine banister. Simon offered his own advice. Virginia couldn't make out his words, but the boys seemed to approve, judging by their delighted laughter.

She sighed, debated going back to forbid any more sliding of any sort. Instead, she crept closer to the door to listen. Her father's companion spoke of a railroad in East Texas. Papa didn't have much to say, other than he had more pressing matters. The two men went back and forth. One or both smoked cigars, judging from the acrid smell wafting under the door.

Wrinkling her nose, she recalled how her father used to disapprove of tobacco. Now he puffed away merrily, indifferent to the effects of the smoke. Virginia made a note of airing his jacket and trousers later that day to get rid of the stench.

The smell overwhelmed her. She waved her hand in front of her face as if that would help. It did nothing, of course. She resolved to return to her guests when the stranger spoke.

"Orville, I didn't come to talk business." He laughed before going on, his voice a lazy drawl. "I'd prefer to talk about your lovely daughter. The pretty girl who's never kissed a fella."

Virginia couldn't believe her ears. She held her breath, waiting for her father to chastise the man. Papa would set the rude man straight, probably drive him from the mansion. A long silence followed.

"You want to talk about my daughter? And the fact she's never been kissed?"

Papa didn't sound as angry as she'd expected. No. He didn't sound at all angry. Virginia leaned close to the door, pressing her ear to the cool, wood panel.

"I do. Me and many of your other benefactors."

Virginia held her breath.

Papa went on. "She has a mind of her own, Phillip. What can I say?"

What could he say? That was hardly the reply she expected from her dear, kindly father. Did she need to give her father a list of what to say? Silently, she considered the possibilities. *Get out of my sight. You'd better shut your mouth. Never speak to me again, you filthy cur.*

She also imagined a few replies from Amelia Honeycutt, none she'd suggest to her father, of course, but pleasing, nonetheless. They included specific threats to a man's private affairs.

Phillip, whomever he was, grunted in response. A moment passed. Then another. "Surely you can rein her in, can't you? Most men know how to manage uppity womenfolk. I can't support a candidate who doesn't know how to rule his own home."

"Now, Phillip," Papa spoke soothingly. "When I win my second turn, I promise you Virginia will gift you with her very first kiss."

Virginia felt her blood run cold.

Her father burst into loud laughter. "Heck, I might kiss you too."

Her world spun. She slumped against the doorframe, not caring if her father discovered she'd been eavesdropping.

Distantly, Amelia's voice echoed across the house. "Are you even listening, Tuck Whitson? You need to go slow at the end. That way you land on your feet. Not your backside. Go on, Ellwood. Show him what I mean. Land sakes, why did I wear a dress today of all days?"

Virginia ought to stop the boys from their pranks. What was more, she shouldn't eavesdrop on her father and the stranger. And yet, she remained rooted to the spot, powerless to do the things she should. The voices of her father voice and the stranger faded from her awareness as her heart quaked.

A movement distracted her. Simon stood in the corridor. In an instant, she knew he'd heard her father's shameful bargain. Simon's eyes sparked with fury.

"Virginia." He clasped her shoulders. "What in tarnation is your father talking about?"

The betrayal stole her breath. She managed to recover after a long moment. She squared her shoulders and looked Simon in the eye. "My father says a number of things to woo supporters. He's determined to win. It doesn't mean anything."

Grim understanding came over Simon's features. "I won't leave you here," he said. "Not if you're in danger."

She recoiled. "I'm not in danger. I'm certain I'm not. My father says things he doesn't mean." She spoke in a hushed tone, mindful of her father in the next room. Anger and shock twisted inside her, but she couldn't bring herself to criticize her father. She clung to the hope that he'd explain away his scandalous offer.

"Come with me," Simon urged. "You don't belong here. You belong in Bethany Springs."

His words tore at her heart.

"I belong here. Helping my father. I'd never dishonor him. Never."

Before he could argue, she retreated a step. "I'll need to speak to my father about several things, especially about Junior Whitson. I think you should go."

He narrowed his eyes.

"Please, Simon. Do this for me."

She watched as he wrestled with how to go forward. Finally, he gave her a resolute look. He nodded. "That's what you want?"

"Yes," she said, unsure if she spoke the truth. "It's what I want."

Chapter Twenty-Nine
Back to the Ranch, Without Virginia

Simon

Simon could hardly bring himself to leave Virginia behind. Everything inside him told him to keep her close, to protect her from the scandalous propositions he heard outside the governor's study. A man spoke of kissing Virginia. The very words made him see red. He wanted to take her with him, or at the very least, stay with her to shield her from such untoward notions.

But Virginia had sent him away. She didn't want his protection. Maybe she didn't trust *him*. The idea that she might not think he was trustworthy hurt his heart.

Despite this quandary, he fixed his attention on the two boys in his care. They needed him. Junior needed him. He couldn't tend to the matter of Virginia. Not now.

With that in mind, he left the governor's mansion.

He took his mother, Tuck and Ellwood across town to the jail, in hopes of seeing Junior. His mother glanced his way a few times but said little. The children skipped up the steps and into the dreary brick building, eager to see their father. Simon ushered them to the desk of a weary-looking clerk. Mama followed a few steps behind, a grim expression etched on her features.

Before Simon uttered a single word, the clerk shook his head. The man knit his brow and glared at the boys. "No children permitted in the jail," he barked. To make his point clear, he followed with a muttered curse.

"These poor little boys only want to see their father," Amelia snapped.

The man's gaze darkened. "And no women allowed either."

"I'm certain Junior Whitson's mother has come to visit," Simon replied.

"Not on my watch. Now git out of my sight."

The boys began to sniffle. They looked up at Simon with tear-filled eyes. Simon wondered if their tearful response might soften the clerk's heart, but no such luck. The man scowled first at the children and then at Amelia.

"Someone woke up on the wrong side of the bed today," Amelia said, her tone icy.

"We don't allow skirts in the jail," he snapped.

Mama sighed. "I just knew I should have worn trousers to town."

The man scoffed. "Trousers, eh? Wish you were a man, or something?"

"Not at all." Amelia smiled coldly. "Do you?"

Her question went over just about as well as expected. Bystanders laughed. The clerk erupted. A moment later a guard escorted them out of the jail. Before they knew it, they stood before the buckboard, wondering what to do next. They'd intended to visit Junior's parents who stayed at a nearby hotel. The children were so distraught, Amelia suggested they simply head home.

"No need to upset Franny and Sheldon," she said. "Heavens knows they have enough to contend with."

Simon wondered if the day could possibly have gone worse. He hadn't told his mother what he'd heard in the governor's home.

"I hope Virginia can convince her daddy to help Junior," Mama said when they were a few miles from home. "I might need to appeal to Wade McCord."

"Boy, things are getting desperate," Simon muttered. "What can Wade do for Junior?"

Mama snorted. "He's friends with Orville. Orville might not take kindly to his daughter calling in favors. Probably respond more favorably to a voter. Old toot."

"Are you talking about Orville or Wade?" Simon offered a tired smile.

Mama gave him an answering smile. "You going to tell me what happened?"

"I will. Soon. Maybe when the boys bed down this evening."

"You're doing a fine job with them, Simon. I'm mighty proud of you."

Simon heaved a heavy sigh. "I don't know how you managed raising the three of us all by yourself. I'm sorry I was such a rascal. I regret it now."

Mama gazed at him with misty eyes as she patted his arm. "Sweetheart, those were trying times, but I'd do it all over again if I had the chance. I loved having little ones."

Simon's throat tightened. He nodded, unable to say much in response.

His mother continued. "Mind you, I love having grown sons too. Makes my heart glad to have my family near. That's why I'd like to see all three married. One day."

Simon thought of the deal she'd offered. Get Junior out of jail and she'd let off about taking a wife. What would happen if he failed? Would she go back to her prior demand? Of course, he might have the boys to care for if Sheldon and Franny couldn't manage. And that would certainly complicate matters.

Everything had turned around.

Marriage suddenly sounded wonderful, especially since he had found the girl he wanted to spend the rest of his days with. Sadly, the girl he yearned for had no use for marriage.

They got home shortly after nightfall to find Daniel and his family waiting inside. Molly and Elsie had brought supper. Daniel and Molly had taken Elsie in when they married. The young girl, an orphan of twelve years or so, was a solemn earnest child. She'd blossomed in the last few months, her serious nature giving way to sunny smiles. The family gathered around the kitchen table to pray. Molly dished up the meal, chicken pot pie, green beans and dinner rolls. Elsie served the plates.

There was a little polite discussion, but no mention of Junior or even Virginia. Simon noticed Elsie looking at Molly with confusion as if to ask where Virginia was. Molly held her finger to her lips and shook her head. Simon was dead tired. So were the boys.

Daniel and Mama chatted about the Childress homestead repair.

"Tell the Collins' brothers to send me a bill when they're done," Mama said. "By then I hope to own the property. Just waiting to hear back from Jim Cassidy."

It took a moment for Mama's words to register. Jim Cassidy worked for Mama whenever she had a land deal. She often hired a man to negotiate a sale, especially if she figured the seller would balk at working with a woman.

"What's this?" Simon asked.

Mama looked at him wide-eyed.

"You're buying the homestead?" Simon asked with disbelief. "The Childress homestead?"

"Yes. I hope the sale goes through. I'll know in a few days' time."

Simon stared in stunned silence. He couldn't imagine how Virginia would greet the news. She'd likely view it as an enormous betrayal. He winced as he pictured the wounded look in her eyes, the same one he'd seen earlier that day as they stood outside her father's study.

"You didn't know?" Daniel asked.

Simon gritted his teeth. Daniel had a fine gift for asking obvious questions. "Does it look like I knew?"

Daniel shook his head and offered a wry grin. "Not really. Now that you ask."

Molly gave him an apologetic look.

"I meant to tell you," Mama said.

"What? It slipped your mind?" Simon demanded.

Mama arched a brow. "Don't sass, Simon Honeycutt."

Simon pushed his plate aside, muttering a few half-hearted words of thanks to Elsie and Molly.

"We made dessert," Elsie said brightly. "I made pie for Miss Childress."

Molly shushed her with a gentle word.

"Sorry," Elsie said softly.

"That's very sweet, dear," Mama said. "I'm sure you'll get to meet her one day. Why, she might even invite you to the governor's mansion. Be sure to ask about the grand staircase and especially the banister, isn't that right, boys?"

Elsie looked bewildered. "Yes, ma'am."

Mama turned her attention back to Simon. "As for the homestead, Simon, I sent an offer the moment I'd heard the news. I did that because it was a good deal. Secondly, I wanted to keep Orville's cronies from snapping it up. And thirdly, I imagine Miss Childress would very much like to live there one day."

She laughed softly. "Surely, you understand my meaning."

Simon rubbed the back of his neck, wincing at the painful crick. "We'll see. Virginia might not want to speak to me ever again."

Chapter Thirty
Lying Through Omission

Virginia

Virginia watched Simon leave from an upstairs window. Her heart thudded heavily as she watched the wagon roll down the road. She would have dearly left with him but couldn't leave her father or her responsibilities at the governor's mansion.

After they left, she waited. And waited some more.

Pacing her room, Virginia paused every few moments to open the door to listen. Her father still talked with his guest downstairs in the study. She waited for the stranger to leave. Meanwhile, she made a list of the issues she intended to discuss with her father. Some items were mere concerns. Like the sale of the homestead. She felt certain it was just a rumor. Probably wishful thinking on the part of Amelia Honeycutt.

Along with her concerns about the homestead lay the question of the small gravestone. Who was buried near her mother? She had a right to know.

Next, there was the problem of Junior Whitson. In her heart, she felt certain he was innocent. She'd never say as much, not to her father. He'd dismiss her feelings and explain that was the very reason women had no business in the world of men. Still, she'd press him to investigate the matter himself.

She wouldn't relent until he promised that Junior's case followed the letter of the law.

Last of all, she wished to speak of the issue that burned in her mind. A grievance, really. She'd have to confront him. Tell him how he'd caused her pain and humiliation every time he discussed her private matters with strangers.

Thirty minutes later, her father's guest left the mansion. Her heart quaking, she descended the steps, trailing her fingers along the banister. Her thoughts drifted back to Ellwood's and Tuck's wide-eyed wonder as they took in the grand staircase. The memory seemed a lifetime ago. In a way it was. It was before she'd listened to her father's shameful words. She might never be able to see him in the same light.

Simon had witnessed her shame. She'd seen the pity in his eyes and sent him away. After everything that had happened, she hadn't imagined parting from Simon Honeycutt in such a rude manner. She regretted her words, wished she could have thanked him and said anything other than giving him a rough dismissal.

Her heart ached. A sudden urge came over her. She could return to Amelia's home and nurse her wounds. Amelia would take her in and give her advice. It might not be good advice, but it would certainly get results.

Pausing outside her father's study, she said a silent prayer, asking for God's guidance. She yearned to explain her concerns and prayed her father would listen patiently. He often dismissed arguments by quoting the commandment about honoring thy father and mother.

She knocked on the door and entered.

"You're home early, Dumplin'!" He rose from his desk and embraced her. "What a nice surprise. Are you all right?"

"I'm fine, thank you."

"You look like you've seen a ghost. I suppose that's because you just visited your mother's grave." He burst into laughter, but immediately saw her shocked response and made an effort to look solemn and attentive.

"That was unkind, Virginia. I'm sorry."

Unkind? His words struck her as barbaric. She would never have imagined her father making light of such a thing. She pushed aside her astonishment. She crossed the room, intent on getting answers to burning questions. "I did visit her grave, in fact. While I was there, I happened to notice another headstone."

"Well, how about that. Did you finish your little article for the journal? I've got some good news. The Austin Legal Society intends to throw a gala next week in my honor. Now don't look so concerned. You won't have to do a thing. Just look pretty. That's all."

"Papa, who is buried on the hill next to Mama?"

He frowned. "Let's see now. Not sure. It might belong to a little one your mama lost at birth."

Virginia heard his words but struggled to make meaning of them. A little one. A child? "Mama had another baby? How come you never told me?"

Her father turned away. Standing before the window, he remained motionless and silent.

"Why would you keep such a thing a secret?"

"Don't question me, Virginia. It's not your place."

"I don't accept that. You haven't been to see her grave in years. I think you ought to stand before her headstone and explain all this. You owe it to me, and to Mama."

He shook his head. "I'm not going back. Neither are you."

"Why not?"

When he didn't answer, Virginia felt herself grow faint. She sank to a nearby chair. Blood rushed in her ears. Her skin grew clammy. "You sold our land."

"Our land?" He turned. "The land was *mine*. It was mine to do with as I pleased. I need the money."

Falling back, she tried to draw a breath. Tears pricked her eyes. A curious sensation stirred inside her body. It grew and bloomed into a burst of laughter, a desperate sound she hardly recognized.

Her father grew red-faced. He snarled. He shook with rage.

"You'd better not be laughing at your father," he bellowed. "I won't tolerate your disrespect."

"Congratulations, Papa." Virginia wiped tears from her eyes. "You sold your land to Amelia Honeycutt. She gloated about the quick sale."

"Silence!"

Virginia rose from the chair. She stood unsteadily. Facing her father, she noted that he too seemed more than a little shaky. Pale, perspiring, he gripped a nearby chair.

"I won't be silent," she said quietly. "Not anymore. I understand a little more about the graves, more than you'd like me to comprehend."

"Stop."

"That baby was born *after* me."

"It's none of your concern. Let it be, Virginia."

Virginia nodded and made her way to the door. Setting her hand on the doorknob, she paused. Without turning around, she spoke. "Mama died in childbirth, but not giving birth to *me*. You lied to me. My entire life, I've carried that burden."

"I didn't lie," he spat. "You assumed she died giving birth to you. That's hardly my fault."

She closed her eyes and tried to slow her racing heart. The temptation to correct him lay on the tip of her tongue. She wanted to throw a final charge at his feet. He was a man of law. He ought to know the concept of lying through omission. The accusation burned inside her, then slowly faded. Sorrow filled the empty spot.

"Was the baby a boy or girl, Papa?"

"Get out of my office." His voice was cold. His words, final.

Virginia did as she was told.

The discussion was over.

Chapter Thirty-One
A Hasty Conversation
with a Dusty Headstone

Amelia

Desperate times called for desperate measures. The grim thought woke her just before dawn and reminded her she hadn't visited her late husband's grave in an age. She said her morning prayers, dressed and saddled her horse in the quiet moments after daybreak. She was halfway up the ridge before she recalled she hadn't made breakfast for Simon and the boys.

"Simon will just have to crack a few eggs in a pan all on his own. He might be doing a lot more of that if we don't get Junior out of that dad-gummed jail," she said to no one in particular.

When she reached the gravesite, she had another realization. She'd forgotten to bring her cleaning supplies. Normally, while talking to George she would wash the grit and dust from the headstone. She chided herself, recalling the rags and scrub brushes she'd left in the foyer. Well, that chore would have to wait for another day.

She dismounted, left her horse tied outside the Honeycutt family plot, strode to her husband's grave and began speaking without preliminaries. "George, I'm sorry but I've got a big dilemma. I know what to do but still felt it proper to explain my plan along with my reasoning."

Crossing her arms, she paced back and forth. "First off, I'd like to make it clear that you are, and always will be, the love of my life. I certainly have no time to dally with gentleman callers." She snorted before continuing. "Unfortunately, I have little choice."

She stopped in front of the headstone. "Did I already tell you have a dilemma? I ought to have said that I have two of them."

A gust of wind kicked up out of nowhere and swept her hat from her head. The breeze tossed the hat high in the air then caused it to tumble across the family plot. Amelia muttered and chased after her hat. When it came to stop at the gate, she picked it up and set it carefully back on her head, tucking stray wisps of hair under the band.

"Very funny," she grumbled as she returned to the gravestone.

"Last week I only had one problem and that was Junior getting himself arrested. This week I've got another. Simon's plainly smitten with Orville Childress's daughter, if you can believe. Never imagined Simon would finally come to his senses. Funny how so many girls have pined after him. Now he's pining after the girl he loved to torment back when he was just a boy. Anyway, I've done all I can to help things along. I'm praying that the sale of the land goes through. Even if I end up with that pretty little homestead, I'm not sure I'll be able to help Junior."

She paused and held her breath. Half-expecting another gust of wind, she reached for her hat brim and held firm. "Which leads me to a desperate plan."

Her heart thudded. "There's one person who can help me get old Orville's attention. One person who loves to attend the same parties and goings-on."

A gentle breeze stirred. She had to laugh at herself. Her guilty conscience made her imagine a tornado barreling across the meadow, making a beeline for her.

"That one person is Wade McCord," she said softly.

The sun cast a warm glow across the pastures. The wind rustled across the sea of grass, rolling, and dipping like so much ocean water. It always struck her as a peaceful sight.

"He's a rascal, to be sure." She let go of her hat and lowered her hand. "He'll likely think I'm looking for a beau. Imagine such a thing, at my age. And he's older than me. The worst part will be putting up with Sophie's pestering and bothering."

She traced her fingers across the top of the headstone. "I think about you every day. Time marches on. I'm still your devoted wife, but please understand I need Wade to take me to one of Orville's shindigs."

A smile tugged at her lips. "Could be fun. I intend to cause a little dust-up if need be. Anything to get old Orville to find it in his heart to help Junior Whitson."

Slowly, she lifted her hand, pressed a kiss to her fingertips and brushed the top of the cold granite. "I'd best be going, my sweet. Would you believe folks are starting to enjoy my cooking? Not only do they like my food, but I likely have a few waiting on breakfast this very moment."

With that, she returned to her horse and rode home.

Chapter Thirty-Two
A Visit to the Travis County Jail

Virginia

While she and her father had quarreled in the past, they'd never remained angry with each other for long. This time was different. After the argument, her father sent word he'd dine alone. She promptly replied that suited her fine.

A day passed. Neither gave an inch.

The morning of the second day, he sent a similar message. At the bottom of the note, he added terse instructions that she finish her article. He wanted it published before the Legal Society Gala.

She tossed the note aside. Before she wrote the article, she had work to do, a very specific task. She fixed her hair in a simple arrangement and dressed in a dark, somber velvet gown. She pulled out a pair of her mother's pearls and affixed them to her lobes. After a brief word with the ladies in the kitchen, she slipped out the back and instructed the guard to summon a carriage.

Once aboard the carriage, she told the driver to take her to a nearby art gallery. As soon as they'd driven a short distance, she explained her true intent. She didn't wish to visit the art gallery. No. She intended to visit a very different sort of place. A place that wasn't particularly fitting for decent womenfolk.

"Take me to the Travis County Jail," she instructed.

The driver paled but offered no argument. Perhaps because she'd spoken in the same manner as Amelia Honeycutt, without a glimmer of doubt or shred of hesitation.

The horses' hooves clip-clopped at a brisk pace. They drove down Congress Avenue, past the shops and offices. Continuing further, they turned off the main road and wound through the modest neighborhoods and soon into the rougher part of the city.

Papa would faint if he knew she'd ventured into such an area. It would come as a severe shock. There were parts of Austin too disreputable for polite conversation. Saloons, of course. That went without saying. Not to mention the seedy areas like Guy Town. But jails and prisons were more than disreputable. They posed a danger to gently bred ladies.

She felt a flicker of growing unease but dismissed her worries. The day's mission concerned grave matters. She needed to forge ahead if she had any hopes of righting a wrong.

When they arrived, Virginia gave her driver further instructions. "You're to wait for me. I won't be more than twenty minutes."

"Yes, miss," he said hurriedly, looking askance at the surroundings. "I won't leave the likes of you in this area. The governor would have my hide if he ever learned who left his daughter at the county prison."

Stairs led up to the front door. All manner of men loitered along the side of the steps. Ruffians. Tramps. Drunks. She noted them in her peripheral vision but kept her gaze straight ahead. Striding inside, she went directly to the front desk. The clerk scowled and prepared to send her on her way.

Before he could fling an insult and dismissal, Virginia spoke. "My name is Virginia Childress. My father is Governor Childress."

The man gaped.

Virginia was ready. She forged ahead. "James Hotchkiss, your superior, is the director of Travis County Prison. And a friend of my family's. I happen to be well acquainted with him as well as his wife and two children. I know how he takes his morning coffee. Cream. No sugar. And I'd like to see Sheldon Whitson. Immediately."

The man's eyes widened and then narrowed. He studied her carefully. Virginia narrowed her eyes. "And you never saw me. Do you understand?"

For a long moment, the two of them held their locked gaze until finally the man relented.

He grunted and motioned for a nearby guard to escort her. She followed the guard. They came to an iron door. Another guard swung it open, let them pass and shut it behind them. The clang echoed down the dark passageway. The noise faded, leaving nothing but the sound of their footsteps.

She felt a strange tremor of fear mixed with surprise. Her plan had worked. She'd gained entry to the jail. Lord help her. To her dismay, she met with another setback in the next instant. At the bottom of a narrow, grimy staircase, she found herself face to face with another armed sentry.

"No ladies allowed down here!" he roared.

She kept her gaze level, trying to look brave even as her courage fell away. "I'm here to see Sheldon Whitson."

"Who?"

"Junior."

The sentry scratched his ear and stared at her. "Junior, eh. You?"

"I only need a few minutes of his time. I'm writing an article for the *Texas Ladies Journal*."

The sentry and her escort both stared in stunned disbelief.

She wondered if she'd come this far only to be turned away just a few steps from Junior's cell. "I suppose you don't get many journalists down here, do you?"

"Journalists?" The sentry said almost to himself.

Her escort leaned in close as he smirked. "She says she's the governor's daughter."

The man's lips twitched. "Governor Childress? Virginia Childress?"

The guard jerked his thumb toward Virginia. "I reckon so. Here she is."

She pressed her lips together. While she hadn't known what to expect, she resented the men's ridicule. "I'm Virginia Childress."

The sentry's jaw dropped and hung open for a long moment before he laughed. Her escort snickered. Their amusement grew boisterous and raucous until both had tears in their eyes.

Their response galled her. "I can assure you that I am indeed Virginia Childress." She had to practically shout to be heard.

They laughed all the more, wiping tears from their cheeks. The sentry finally composed himself, barely. "Sure, you are, darlin'. Of course. And I'm Davy Crockett."

His comment inspired more laughter from the escort. Thankfully, the sentry relented, unlocked the door, swung it open and invited her past with a grand flourish. "Your highness."

Without bothering to reply, she stepped past and waited for him to lead her to Junior's cell. She held a handkerchief to her nose. The stench was overwhelming. Rats scurried into dark corners. She walked past cells, making her way to the end of the hallway. As she passed, the other inmates came near, they gripped the bars and stared in astonishment.

Junior slumped against the corner of his cell. When he saw her, he slowly straightened and crossed the cell to draw near. He stood silently. Watching. Waiting.

Instantly, she saw how much the boys favored their father. He had Ellwood's sweet expression around his eyes and Tuck's shy, tentative smile.

"Governor's daughter to see you, Whitson," the sentry bellowed. "Mind your manners."

"Governor's daughter?" Junior squinted. He gave a slight, disbelieving shake of his head.

The announcement set off a flurry of talk among the other prisoners. Every one of them doubted the sentry's words. They seemed to believe she was some no-account judging from their laughter and shouted insults. None said anything too offensive, thankfully. After a few moments the shouting died down. They quieted, eager to hear what she came to say.

The sentry set a chair near the cell door and returned to his post.

Junior gazed at her for a long moment. "Well, Miss Childress. I thank you for coming. I surely do."

He didn't seem as surprised about her visit as she might have guessed. Probably because he didn't truly believe she was the governor's daughter. They chatted quietly, she asking questions about what happened, and him explaining all that he remembered about the man he met outside the town of Victoria and how he still expected this friend to return and claim the money. She jotted a few notes on a small scrap of paper.

Junior was forthright. Solemn and subdued. It wasn't until she mentioned his boys that his composure faltered.

"Ellwood and Tuck are both delightful," she said quietly as she prepared to leave. "You have two very fine boys."

"You know them?" His voice shook. "Ellwood and Tuck?"

"I do. I met them through the Honeycutt family." She kept various details to herself, such as the tree that crashed through her family homestead, or Ellwood almost getting washed downstream of a raging river. She almost smiled at the outrageous antics of his boys, but her amusement faded quickly as she noticed his distress.

Junior's eyes filled with tears. "I love my boys. Their mama had no use for me. She made that clear early on. She wanted a rich, fancy husband. I'm sorry she caused them so much pain, but I'm grateful for a chance to raise them up."

Virginia, suddenly overcome, could hardly find the words to respond.

Junior went on, his voice choked. "I've never been in jail before, Miss Virginia. *Never.*"

"I believe you. With all my heart."

"And yet... I might lose my two sons. Lose them. Before I get a chance to be their father."

She looked down at her flimsy scrap of paper, a sudden wave of self-doubt coming over her. She tried to summon the memory of Amelia's bravado, but nothing came to mind. Instead, she spoke from her heart with her own words. "I'll do what I can to set you free. I promise."

He nodded, clasping the bars as he held her gaze.

She set her hand over his hand, wrapping her fingers around his. "I'll do my very best to bring you home."

Chapter Thirty-Three
Mama's Scheme

Simon

Simon knew that Virginia's mission was to help her father get reelected. He respected that and had intended to wait until the election to call on her. He'd bide his time. Up to a point.

Along the way, his patience ran out. He couldn't bear the idea of her all alone in that grand house, surrounded by men who didn't appreciate her kind heart, quick smile, and gentle spirit. He hated the humiliated look in her eyes he'd seen when they parted, and he wanted to shelter her somehow.

He also couldn't bear the idea of Junior going to trial and sticking his enormous foot smack-dab into his mouth.

With those two concerns swirling in his mind, Simon woke in the predawn darkness with notions of finally carrying out an outlandish scheme. He'd entertained the idea for some time. He'd grown desperate enough to set the plan in motion. He'd ride into Austin, break Junior out of jail, then steal Virginia from the governor's mansion.

He'd carry Virginia out of the governor's mansion, over his shoulder, if necessary. He preferred the idea of her coming without too much fuss. Maybe she'd even come gladly, her arm linked through his. He liked that scenario quite a bit.

Still, it didn't matter, so long as he returned to Bethany Springs with both Junior and Virginia.

After he made the mistake of sharing his plot with his mother, he realized, (along with Mama's keen powers of observation), that they'd wind up with not one, but two folks in jail.

"Orville might shoot you. There's that," Mama said.

"Maybe," Simon said carelessly.

"I have my own scheme," she confessed later as they stood by the corral railing. "I'll go directly to my old friend Governor Childress. I'll appeal to his sense of honor and explain he'll look a right fool if he allows Junior to go to trial."

Simon watched Ellwood and Tuck spin their lassos. As much as he hoped horsemanship and roping might be in the boys' blood, things weren't looking too promising that morning. Tuck had managed to rope his brother, so that was saying something, just not much. They giggled and tossed the lasso toward the gate post. Once more they missed.

Amelia applauded. "There you go. Keep at it. Relax your wrist a tad."

"That's nice of you," Simon said quietly. "Praising their meager efforts."

"Now, now," Amelia said with a grin. "They're twice as good as you and Junior were at that age."

Simon propped his boot on the lower rail. "You hurt a man's pride with your jokes."

She laughed. "What jokes?"

Tuck tossed the loop lightly. It flew through the air and dropped down over the post, light as a feather. He grinned at his brother, taunting him. Ellwood looked annoyed as he twirled his lasso overhead, intent on showing Tuck a thing or two.

Simon glanced at his mother. "Well, Mama. I've got to ask about this scheme," he drawled. "You plan on waltzing up to the front door of the mansion and asking if the governor's home? This sounds almost as bad as my plan."

"I've asked Wade McCord to take me to a party at the mansion."

Simon wondered if he heard correctly. Wade? Mama's nemesis? Take her to a party? He considered asking if she intended to wear a dress but wisely set the question aside. The boys squabbled about roping techniques. He ought to step in, but he still tried to understand what his mother had just told him.

"I didn't think you liked Wade," Simon said.

His mother smacked his shoulder. It had been a while since she'd smacked him so he couldn't help feeling a little affronted.

Ellwood and Tuck eyed him with curiosity.

"Keep practicing," Simon said, rubbing his shoulder. "If you stand there with your mouth open, you'll end up catching flies, not calves."

The boys went back to twirling and throwing.

"I *don't* like him," his mother said resentfully. "He's a lady's man. I'm a widow. We get along about as well as oil and water. But I'm willing to attend a party at the governor's mansion with him if it helps Junior and these two boys."

"That's nice," Simon said, keeping his gaze fixed on her.

"Nice?" She scoffed.

"I mean it. I know that must have cost you something to ask Wade McCord for a favor."

"You have no idea." She grimaced.

"Well, he's a likeable fellow. Smart. Kind. He doesn't have a family, but he's devoted to Robert, Sophie and their three boys."

"He's a rascal. He's older than me and never been married, and in my book that's a strike against him."

She gave him a pointed look. Probably a small dig about him getting married. He wasn't quite sure why she'd mention Ward's age but sensed he ought not to ask. He'd never imagined his mother heading off to a party or anywhere, for that matter, with a gentleman-friend. None had dared show interest. Except for Wade.

Simon spoke. "I hope you can sweet-talk the governor into helping Junior. And I hope you enjoy a nice evening with Wade."

"Hush," she chided. "I'll enjoy nothing at all. And don't you dare tell your brothers that Wade's squiring me off to a party at the governor's mansion."

"If I did, they'd call me a liar."

She narrowed her eyes.

"Won't say a word, Mama. Not a peep."

His thoughts drifted to the same subject that had tormented him since returning home.

Virginia.

He didn't understand it, but just the thought of his sweet Virginia made his breath catch.

Virginia...

His mother might catch a glimpse of her at the party. She probably would. He felt a strong sense of envy. What he wouldn't give to see her again. They'd parted on troubled terms. He didn't have the chance to say a real goodbye or ask if he could call on her. Or anything. She'd asked him to leave, and he'd complied, mostly because he didn't want to cause her more trouble or heartache.

Now his mother, who disliked parties almost as much as she disliked Orville Childress, made plans to attend a party at his home. Simon tried to imagine how the evening might play out.

Virginia worked behind the scenes to help her father. If she weren't in charge of the party, she'd likely spend the evening chatting up the guests. He was certain his mother would make a point of talking to her if only to offer a quick compliment.

His heart ached.

Virginia.

How he missed her. As much as he yearned to see her again, he needed to stay put. He had a duty to the boys. Once the boys were situated, he intended to go to Austin and speak to Virginia. She might not want to see him, but he'd tell her what was in his heart. If she heard him out and turned him away, well, he'd tried his best.

Not that he'd give up easily. If she sent him away, he'd come up with a new plan. He wouldn't give up until he'd talked Virginia into accepting his hand. But first he needed to tend to the boys.

Ellwood and Tuck squabbled. Somehow their lassos had gotten tangled. One moment they fussed about whose fault it had been, the next they collapsed with fits of laughter.

Simon wasn't sure how much they fretted about Junior. There'd been a few nights where he'd awoken to one of them weeping. He'd comforted them best he could, all the while praying for the good Lord's guidance. What did he know about caring for a couple of youngsters? Nothing. That's what.

So, despite feeling like he had no good options in front of him, or perhaps because of it, his heart warmed to watch as the boys practiced cowboy skills. Nothing like a little fun, mixed with a little hard work, to distract a boy from his troubles.

Tuck stopped arguing with his brother for a minute when something distracted him. He pointed off into the distance. "Is that our daddy?"

Simon followed the boy's gaze. Off in the distance, a man and rider traveled along the road. The pair were no more than a spot on the horizon. Despite the distance and the sun's glare, Simon thought he recognized the man on horseback. Maybe it was just his imagination but something about the rider reminded him of Junior. He didn't want to say as much for he hardly dared hope.

For a long moment, no one spoke.

The rider disappeared from view as he rode down a dip in the road. Time seemed to come to a stop. They waited. Finally, the rider came over the hill, closer now but still too far to be certain.

"I think it's him," Mama said softly. "I believe Junior's finally home."

Ellwood let out a whoop. "That's our daddy. It's him. I know it."

Tuck agreed, offering a cheer to match that of his brother.

Simon began to think they might just be right. The rider had Junior's same posture and style of riding. His shoulders slouched a little. His Stetson tipped at the very same angle. It had to be Junior, Simon decided. It had to be.

"I'll be darned." He shook his head with amazement. "Finally."

Junior spotted them, shouted a greeting, and spurred his horse into a lope.

Chapter Thirty-Four
Orville and Virginia Make Amends

Virginia

After Virginia visited the jail, she returned home directly. She hoped her father hadn't noticed her absence. Fortunately, he was away that morning, attending a meeting and, as it turned out, it hardly mattered. Little had changed. In the following days, he kept a frosty distance. They continued to take their meals alone. If they happened to meet in the corridor, or in the garden, they'd offer a few cordial words of greeting but nothing more.

Despite the circumstances, Virginia knew, without a doubt, her father expected her to play hostess at the gala in a few days' time. That much was clear. For a change, she did not need to play a part in the planning of the event, choosing the menu, ordering flowers, or triple-checking the guest list. No, the Austin Legal Society had organized the event and would be seeing to all that. All she needed to do was to attend the event, and to play her role of the doting daughter.

What would her father expect? She had to wonder. Especially after she submitted her article for the *Texas Ladies Journal*. They'd promised to publish it before the gala, and true to form, they came through on that promise. Papa was among the first to read the article. She knew the moment he'd read the last line.

"*Virginia!*" Her father's voice echoed down the marble halls.

Virginia sat at the desk in her room, writing notes. She paused to listen, waiting for the thud of his footsteps.

An instant later, he flew through the door, waving the journal, red-faced and shaking with anger. "You. You wrote an article about a man charged with a serious crime. It's not possible."

"No. I did not. I wrote an article about a man who was *once* charged with a serious crime."

He knit his brow and lowered his gaze to the journal, open at the article she'd written.

"The charges have been dropped," Virginia said.

Her father looked aghast.

"I can't claim much credit. It had little to do with my article. Perhaps it was my visit to the jail that got the judge's attention."

Her father grew deathly pale. He stared at her, unblinking. His throat moved as he swallowed. After a moment, he staggered to a nearby chair and plopped down. "You… you, my only child, went to the jail?"

She nodded. While she'd expected his disapproval, she hadn't expected he might be distraught to the point of passing out, but that's how he looked. She was grateful he'd sat down.

Lowering his gaze, he tugged a handkerchief from his pocket. Slowly, he lifted it to his brow and wiped away a soft sheen of perspiration. For a moment, he stared at the linen square as if unsure what to do next. He tucked it back into his pocket, then laid the magazine across his lap and absent-mindedly smoothed the edges.

"I'm the governor of Texas," he said quietly. "And even I have never set foot in that jail."

"I know."

"That place..." He coughed and cleared his throat. "That's no place for a lady. All I've ever wanted was to shield you from rough elements, the world of men and whatnot."

"I understand your concern. I'm fine." She held her palms out. "You see? I'm completely unharmed."

Her effort at levity went unnoticed. He looked stricken as he rubbed his forehead. "Lord help me, I haven't slept in days. I probably won't fare any better after hearing this."

"I was trying to help a wrongly accused man," Virginia said.

"I know," her father spoke quietly. "You were trying to do the right thing. More than I can claim."

Her breath caught. Had she just heard her father admit to some shortcoming? Before she could ask, he went on.

"After your mother died," he said, his tone sober, "I made a vow to protect you, no matter what. I figured I'd make sure you never married so that I could shelter you from harm."

She wanted to explain how much he'd made her suffer. The guilt. The lies. All the accusations, they died in her throat. Despite the painful past, she loved her father. She knew he loved her too. And yet... everything had changed, and neither he nor she could fathom the path forward.

He sighed as he cast a furtive glance her way. "It was easy when you were small. You were happy spending time with your dull, old father. But the years passed, and you grew into a young lady who began to attract a fair bit of attention. The fear of what happened to your mother unnerved me."

He paused, closed his eyes and shook his head. With a weary sigh, he continued. "I ought to have told you the truth right then. That your mother died a year and a half after you were born. Instead, I let you believe the worst. It was cowardly."

Before she could speak, he stopped her with an upheld hand. "I only wanted to keep you safe. I reckoned I owed that much to your mother."

"Protect me from marriage and a family?"

"Protect you from men who think they need a son to carry on their name."

Virginia drew a sharp breath.

Her father lowered his gaze. "Your mama passed, trying to give me a son."

"Oh, Papa," she whispered.

He rose from the chair and crossed the room, moving slowly as if he'd aged twenty-five years in the last five minutes. Pausing at the door, he glanced back. "Your mama wanted to name him Orville."

It all made sense now. The unfinished inscriptions on the headstones. Her father's grief mixed with profound guilt. His desire to sell the homestead. As much pain as he'd caused her, she couldn't find it in her heart to be angry for she knew he too suffered.

Instead of anger she felt hollow, bereft.

Later that afternoon, he sent a bouquet of flowers, yellow roses along with a note. He asked her forgiveness and promised to do whatever he could to halt the sale of the homestead. Virginia was sure that Amelia wouldn't give up the property. Despite her heartache, she was relieved to be back on speaking terms with her father.

When it came time for dinner, he met her at the dining room door with a box of candies. He arranged for the kitchen to prepare her favorite dishes. Over dinner, he offered outlandish schemes to get Amelia Honeycutt to sell the land back. "I'll speak to her in person. Tell her I'm desperate to make amends with my daughter, even if it costs me the election."

Virginia shook her head. As much as she appreciated her father's offer, she knew it would come to nothing. The land was good as gone. "Amelia will never sell. She jokes about becoming a cattle baroness. And for that, she needs as much land as possible."

He gave a dismissive wave of his hand. "As governor, I possess various means not available to regular citizens. For instance, I could offer to name a flower after her."

"A *flower*?"

"Yes, a flower. It ought to be one with sharp thorns. Or maybe not a flower. A thistle!" He snorted. "That would be fitting."

Virginia smiled. "Perhaps you shouldn't attempt to negotiate a deal with Amelia. I have the feeling it might end badly."

"Leave it to me, sweetheart. You shouldn't negotiate *anything* with the Honeycutt family. I know you don't care for them. Particularly Amelia's boys. Never you mind. I won't rest until I've fixed this."

It dawned on Virginia that she hadn't told him a word about the pecan tree incident or that she'd been a guest in the Honeycutt home. Best leave sleeping dogs lie, she decided. And if Amelia couldn't be persuaded to part with the land, Virginia would try to convince Simon.

She'd start by explaining a thing or two about Junior's release from jail. Simon might not care. Especially if he'd made plans to use the Childress lands for his own herd. If that were the case, the homestead was as good as gone.

Chapter Thirty-Five
Mama Offers Simon a Gift

Simon

In the days leading up to the gala in Austin, his mother grumbled, complained, and fussed about everything under the sun. Every so often, she circled around to talk about how deeply she regretted asking Wade for anything, especially something as significant as an invitation to a grand party.

"I've never so much as stepped foot into the governor's mansion and yet, look at me. Going twice in the span of a few short weeks. I'm not happy. Let me tell you."

You told me, Mama. A couple dozen times, Simon wanted to say. He didn't. Instead, he listened patiently. Her complaints helped him forget his own concerns.

"And now there's no reason for me to go a party at the mansion. Not anymore. Junior is home. The land sale has gone through which means that I own the Childress Ranch. And that fool, Wade, will want to talk to me and get to know me. Lord help me."

"Tell him you don't want to go," Simon suggested while they rode the perimeter of the Childress homestead.

"I can't do that."

"Why not?"

"Because I intend to sweet-talk you into going with me."

His stomach dropped.

Mama went on. "I hope to convince you to go with me as a chaperone."

Simon felt a strong pang wrap around his heart. It seemed like years since he'd seen Virginia. He missed her terribly but had resolved to wait until the election was over. Then he'd call on her. He'd pursue her with all the fire that burned in his heart. Until then he'd wait because he knew she felt a deep obligation to her father.

So, his mother's words about taking him to the party sent his thoughts stampeding the very opposite direction. He liked that direction. Very much. He envisioned a grand party, imagined finding Virginia amidst the crowd, taking her hand in his and drawing her close for a sweet kiss. Finally.

"I'll have to get a new dress," Mama said, yanking him from his thoughts.

"Yes. Sounds about right."

"Sophie's offered to help. You'll need a new suit."

His thoughts wandered back to kissing Virginia. Meanwhile, his mother went on about the party. She talked like she was about to undertake some monumental task instead of attending a simple evening event. Most of all, she grumbled about spending the evening with Wade.

"I'll go with you," Simon said. His mind raced with possibilities. He imagined Virginia's joy upon finding him at the party even though she might be too angry to speak to him. She'd view the sale of her family's land as a grave betrayal, and he could hardly blame her.

"I assumed as much," his mother huffed. "Wade McCord is a rogue, and a lady has to safeguard her reputation."

Simon smiled inwardly. If Wade were fool enough to try anything with Mama, he'd likely wind up injured and severely humiliated.

"I'm not keen on parties," Mama said. "But if I *don't* go to this party, Sophie will have my hide. She is acting like Christmas has come early. And she's not even going to the shindig. Despite all that, she's probably already picked out a dress, shoes, and jewelry."

"Sounds nice," Simon said absently as he imagined Virginia's sweet smile. His thoughts returned to the fellow talking about her first kiss. If Simon heard a single word about Virginia's kisses, he'd likely cause a scene right there in the mansion's drawing room.

Mama went on. "Sophie expects us to stay in their family suite at the new Driskill Hotel. You'll need to pack a bag. Robert and Sophie will get their feelings hurt if we don't stay a few days."

"Sure." Simon said.

They rode to the top of a ridge and stopped their horses to take in the view. The wind skimmed the lush pastures below. In the distance stood the Childress home, with its new roof and rebuilt back wall. The view was mighty pretty, but Simon found little joy in the sight.

The past few days, life had gone back to the way it was before Virginia's visit. Junior had taken the boys to his home. Simon found himself missing Tuck and Ellwood, much to his surprise. The Childress home had been repaired. Simon had returned to his cabin on the far side of the ranch.

Things were back to normal and yet entirely different.

Everything, it seemed, depended on him sweet-talking Virginia into returning to his life. He'd have to convince her how much she meant to him and get her to forgive his family for buying the Childress homestead.

"Orville Childress wants his ranch back." Amelia snorted.

It was as if she'd understood his thoughts. Sometimes he suspected his mother did actually know what he was thinking. He frowned. "Really? Wonder why?"

"Virginia's probably giving him heck. I'm not selling, of course," she said. "I've decided to give it to you."

He stared, wondering if he'd heard correctly.

She shrugged a shoulder. "I'm not keen on those ugly critters you call cattle, but I don't want you to claim some spread clear across the other side of Texas. I like having my boys nearby."

"Mama, I don't know. Seems wrong to take the Childress ranch."

"No need to say anything at all." Her eyes watered. She sniffled.

He couldn't recall ever seeing his mother on the verge of tears. "I appreciate it," he said. "Don't get me wrong, but part of me wants to hand it right back to Virginia."

"Fine."

Fine? He waited but she remained silent. He could hardly imagine his mother giving him an entire ranch, especially when she didn't approve of his plans to start a new brand. Even more surprising, he'd just talked about giving the land away and she'd hardly batted an eye. What in tarnation was going on?

He tipped his Stetson back and scratched his head. "You're not dying or something, are you?"

She glared. "Hush now."

His heart stuttered. His mother had always been a constant, permanent presence in his life. He could hardly imagine her getting ill, or worse. Swallowing hard, he awaited some explanation.

Brushing her finger below her eye, she swiped a tear before it slid down her cheek. Then, she hiccupped, which only made him worry more.

"Something's wrong," he said quietly. "That's why you wanted to go for a ride. Am I right?"

He waited.

Instead of dissolving in a puddle of tears, she squared her shoulders which he took as a good sign. And then all heck broke loose. Shaking her head, she lit into him something fierce. "There are a few things wrong! You, son, are the most ornery, impossible rascal I've ever known. I'm offering you a fine ranch and you're still acting ornery and impossible. What does it take to get you to be agreeable?"

His worries vanished. His mother was fired up. Thank goodness.

They continued, riding down the path as she proceeded to get good and mad. With each step she got more and more perturbed. Simon let out a sigh. What a relief. For the first time in days, his heart felt a tad lighter. Unable to resist, he allowed himself a small chuckle. His amusement only served to provoke her more.

"Dang, you know how to try a mother's patience," she snapped.

"You're looking a little pale," Simon teased. "You off your feed?"

His mother lifted her gaze to the heavens. "I don't know where I went wrong with this one, Lord. Help me to understand."

They made their way down the ridge. Riding beside his mother, Simon endured a stern lecture. She made her opinion clear. On account of his sass, she'd changed her mind about the land. Instead of giving it to him, she'd offer the property to

Zach who likely had the sense to appreciate the gesture. As far as Simon was concerned, she explained, he could just go ahead and raise his ugly cattle in Timbuktu.

His mother always enjoyed grousing any time one of her boys set out on his own path. That was just her way. She simply figured they'd fall in line. Daniel had. Zach likely would. And, eventually, Simon would too.

He knew good and well that she wouldn't go back on her offer of land. Oh, she'd act put out, but deep down, she mostly just wanted him, along with his brothers, to remain nearby. She yearned to be able to see their homes from her porch. To his surprise, he wanted the very same thing. To his great surprise.

Family, it turned out, was pretty comforting, even when brothers acted a tad troublesome.

He scanned the broad pastures. In the distance he could just make out the Childress Ranch. The land was prettier than any of the spreads he'd considered buying. And the property included a home. Not just any home but one that meant so much to Virginia.

Virginia...

Quietly, he dared yearn for the dream he held deep in his heart. The hopes he held dear brought a smile to his lips. And as much as he disliked wearing fancy clothes and attending fancy parties with fancy people, he could hardly wait for the gala at the governor's mansion.

He was ready. Mama wouldn't need to sweet-talk him much at all to get him to agree.

Chapter Thirty-Six
Through God All Things Are Possible

Sophie McCord, Amelia's Best Friend and Wade McCord's Sister-In-Law

Sophie McCord was no country girl. Born in New Orleans, she was accustomed to fine things. She appreciated the new Driskill Hotel in downtown Austin for that very reason. Austin was a long way from the refinement of New Orleans, but the bustling, up-and-coming town offered a lovely reprieve from life on the ranch in Bethany Springs.

And a stay at the Driskill always made Sophie feel like she'd stepped back into the world of her childhood.

The Driskill boasted a number of amenities that Sophie appreciated. One in particular. Each suite had an attached bath. While that sort of feature was commonplace in New Orleans, the Texans considered attached baths a luxury.

"I know you won't approve of my dress." Amelia's voice came from the adjoining bedroom. "I'm sure it will do just fine."

Sophie smiled. They still had several hours till the party, but she knew Amelia fretted. Her dear friend worried about her dress, her jewels and most especially about attending an evening event with Wade.

A moment later, Amelia appeared in the doorway. She wore the same tattered robe she favored, the one that belonged to George. She'd wrapped her wet hair in a towel and, looking irritable, held out a dress for Sophie's inspection. "What do you think?"

Ever since they'd arrived that afternoon, Amelia had grumbled about getting dressed up. It wasn't something she did very often. This was a special night, however. Amelia and Wade would be in the same room with many of the most powerful people in Texas. More importantly, they would be there *together*. There was a chance, a slim chance, that Amelia would think more fondly of Wade after the party. Sophie knew that might happen.

Sophie also knew that Amelia was prepared to endure almost anything to help Simon woo the governor's daughter.

That dress, though. It was too much. *Quelle horreur!*

Sophie set her hand on her heart and drew a sharp breath. The dress Amelia held was one Sophie had given her at least fifteen years ago. Sophie could hardly recall where she'd gotten the dress but the sight of it sent a shudder down her spine.

"It's very beautiful," Sophie said, wincing.

Amelia rolled her eyes. "You're a terrible liar. It doesn't matter, though, because that's all I brought, so that's what I'm wearing."

Sophie shook her head and tried her best to suppress a smile. All along, she knew that Amelia would arrive, intending to wear some travesty. Sophie knew Amelia's taste, or rather her indifference. Which was why Sophie had come to Austin prepared.

Sophie cast the dress aside, tossing it over a nearby chair and presented Amelia with a new frock. "I had a dress made just for you."

Holding up the gown, she held her breath, praying that Amelia wouldn't let loose her legendary temper. Amelia gazed at the dress, a smile tugging at her lips. She didn't get angry. Far from it. Instead, she trailed her fingers down the delicate fabric and let out a soft sigh.

Sophie smiled. Every so often Amelia Honeycutt showed her feminine side. Sophie would never say as much, of course. Amelia would never forgive her. Instead, she waited patiently for Amelia to allow herself the small luxury of attending a party with a man who wasn't George Honeycutt.

"It's a nice color," Amelia allowed.

Sophie heard the note of hesitation in her voice. She narrowed her eyes, hoping to look both stern and sensible. "It's a fine dress. Nothing too pretty, of course."

"Of course." Amelia recoiled. "I'm a widow. Not a young, innocent girl, looking for a beau."

Sophie waved a dismissive hand. "Poo. I know you're not looking for a beau. The dress is eh... how do you say, very serious. Very conservative."

"All right," Amelia said. "If you say so."

"Trust me."

The two small words seemed to have the opposite effect. Amelia narrowed her eyes. She pressed her lips together.

Sophie gave a huff and strode across the room to hang the dress on a hook. She fluffed the material and muttered a few choice phrases in French. After a long moment, she turned to find Amelia watching, her eyes wide and tear-filled.

"Amelia," she murmured. "George would want this. It's been a long, long time. You deserve a little fun. *Non?*"

Amelia shook her head. She sniffed. "I'm going to the party. I might have a little fun."

"Perhaps so."

"But I'm not planning on any fun."

Amelia looked offended by the notion of fun. Sophie hastened to sooth her ruffled feelings. "Of course not."

Amelia smiled. "Then again, I'll probably enjoy seeing Orville fidget and what not."

Sophie smiled even while her heart ached. She had to smile at Amelia's steely nature. Of course, she wanted to give Orville Childress a bad time. She disliked the man a great deal. On the other hand, Sophie couldn't help feeling badly for Wade. She knew how much he admired Amelia, how much he'd yearned to court her and make his feelings known. Wade hardly dared, however. He didn't want to offend Amelia or risk her wrath by suggesting something untoward.

"I'll wear your dress," Amelia said on a sigh. "I might as well get dolled up to go to the governor's mansion."

Sophie let out a breathless laugh. She hoped and prayed the evening would be everything Amelia and Simon and Wade hoped for. Could it be? Could it be that their hopes and dreams would align?

Par Dieu tout est possible.

Through God all things are possible.

Chapter Thirty-Seven
Love's First Kiss

Virginia

The day of the party arrived. For most events, Virginia had a long list of things to do. Not today though. The only thing she had to do today was to pick out a dress. Not a dress from her wardrobe, but a new dress. Her father insisted on it.

Her seamstress and an assistant came to the governor's mansion mid-morning with five frocks for Virginia to choose from. Marcy was an excellent seamstress and knew Virginia well, knew her size and tastes. The frocks were laid out across the bed for Virginia to consider.

Virginia ran her fingers across the fabric of each dress and noted the fine material, but her heart wasn't in it. If it weren't for a deep sense of obligation to her father, she would shoo Marcy out and climb back into bed with the morning newspaper. But she could not do that. She selected a dress and the assistant gathered it off the bed and held it in front of her.

Virginia turned to the mirror and gazed at her reflection. She didn't particularly like it, in spite of the encouragement and compliments from Marcy and her assistant.

"Oh, I don't know," Virginia said wearily. "The dresses are all lovely, but I don't know that I can choose. Can you choose one for me?"

Marcy blinked and drew back. "Well, I can. But if none of these dresses appeal to you, I can send for others."

"No, Marcy. Heavens. It's nothing to do with the dresses. I just don't know that I can choose this morning."

Marcy shooed her assistants away and spoke quietly as she peered over her spectacles. "Usually, you have such clear notions on the sort of dress you want. If I had to choose for you, I would choose this dress. The pale blue complements your eyes. The lace neckline is especially delicate and beautiful. You must make a decision. I won't decide for you."

"I must choose?" Virginia asked absently, gazing in the mirror. For some reason, she wondered what color Simon might find pleasing. It was absurd. Simon Honeycutt wouldn't care one way or the other. She needed to chase thoughts of Simon out of her mind.

Virginia tried to coax a cheerful smile to her lips. "Marcie, darling. Let's go with the blue one. I don't know why but I cannot get excited about tonight's party."

Marcie's brows lifted. A smile tugged at her lips. "I understand perfectly."

"What do you understand?"

Her seamstress began gathering her materials, humming as her assistant gathered up the remaining dresses. "You've met a gentleman. It's time you enjoy life a little instead of working as your father's lackey."

"I beg your pardon?" Virginia tried to summon an ounce of outrage, but her words sounded flat and uninspired.

Marcy's smile widened. She spoke deliberately, and louder than a moment before as if announcing matters for the benefit of her assistant. "You've made a lovely choice, Miss Childress. As always it is my great pleasure to serve you. Danielle, please gather up the other dresses and load them in the carriage."

For a good thirty minutes after Marcy left, Virginia mulled Marcy's comment about being her father's *lackey*. When Marcy first said it, Virginia was stunned, but also in agreement. The more she thought about it the more she realized, Marcy understood the situation perfectly. For prior events, Virginia worked non-stop to make sure everything was ready. Today's party, however, organized by the Austin Legal Society, turned Virginia into just another guest, with no responsibilities prior to the start of the party.

Even her father had fended for himself. When she met with him an hour before the party, she found he'd already selected his own clothes and cufflinks, and he was fully dressed. There was nothing for her to do.

She couldn't help feeling a little lost. She'd always enjoyed the notion she was indispensable.

So much for that last shred of pride. Indulging in self-pity, she wondered if Simon missed her at all. Maybe he was managing just fine on his own and had hardly noticed that she left. This new idea made her self-pity fade. She pushed her shoulders back and studied her father's attire.

Her father stood before his mirror admiring himself, dressed perfectly from his shoes to his cravat.

Even Virginia had to admit he looked quite respectable.

"I suppose you don't need my help," she said.

Her father smiled. "I managed this all by myself, thanks to your help over the years."

"You look very nice."

"As do you," he replied. "Your blue frock is very becoming."

Virginia had hardly paid attention to her frock as she dressed that afternoon. She was so used to Marcy's fine work. Papa liked her blue dress? She noted it was, in fact, blue. What did she care? She swept the thought aside. The evening would be long, drawn-out ordeal with dull people, none of whom she cared about. She felt tempted to excuse herself from the entire affair.

He picked up a comb, hesitated and leaned toward his reflection. "I'm a little balder with each party."

"Not at all."

"You're a terrible fibber," he grumbled. "Though I do appreciate the sentiment."

Virginia drew back the drapes to look out the window. In the gathering dusk, the lamplighter worked to light the gas lamps across the front of the mansion and along the drive to the road. The first guests would soon arrive. Usually, she enjoyed preparing for a grand evening but felt none of her usual happiness. The notion of spending the evening chatting with strangers filled her heart with a dull ache.

"You look a little under the weather," her father said as he finished combing his hair.

She let the curtain fall. "I'm feeling fine. Just a little preoccupied. I'd hoped to hear some good news about the land."

"I received an interesting note today, from a young man asking permission to call on you."

A wave of irritation came over her. In the last few days, she and her father had come to a tentative truce, or so it had seemed. Now he'd return to his old ways. He likely planned on making a show of her in front of his political friends. Once again. Perhaps there'd be mention of her first kiss. She hoped not.

"I hope you told him no," she replied sharply.

"You can tell him so yourself. He's attending the party this evening."

Virginia hardly believed what she was hearing. She stared at him in utter disbelief. Her father had clearly forgotten or dismissed her feelings about this matter, he seemed almost amused by her expression. He chuckled.

A knock came at the door. A servant announced the first guests were arriving. With that, the evening was underway. There was no time for argument. No time for anything other than to play her role. Her father tucked her hand in the crook of his arm and escorted her downstairs to the grand foyer.

Burning with resentment, she couldn't bring herself to play the gracious hostess. She refused to pretend. What did it matter? She wasn't in charge of the party. After greeting two elderly couples with a few mumbled words of welcome, she excused herself and left the foyer. Her father barely noticed. He carried on with his usual charm, greeting each guest like an old friend.

She retreated from the noise and hubbub and sought refuge in the kitchen. She expected to find some measure of chaos there too, but at least she wouldn't have to keep a happy façade. To her surprise and slight disappointment, the kitchen staff had matters well in hand. They didn't seem to need her direction either.

Feeling desolate, she retreated to the garden. After a short while, the cool evening breeze revived her spirits. Instead of returning to the festivities, she lingered in the shadows of the house. She listened to the laughter and merriment coming from inside. Every so often, she thought she heard her father's booming voice.

She rubbed her arms to chase away the chill and wandered to a nearby rosebush. Most of the late-summer blooms had faded but a few remained. She bent her head to inhale their perfume. A noise broke the quiet of the garden. To her dismay, it was the sound of the door behind her. Someone came to disturb her peace. Without thinking, she darted behind a mid-sized hedge. Holding her breath, she waited, praying the intruder would return to the party.

Chapter Thirty-Eight
Amelia Attends a Party

Amelia

Amelia traveled to the governor's party in Wade McCord's elegant carriage. It was just her and Wade in the carriage. Simon chose to go alone, riding his favorite gelding. She didn't press him to join her since she knew he preferred to keep his own company before talking to Virginia.

Wade had arrived at the Driskill, slightly rumpled from a busy day at court. Thanks to Sophie's quick attention, he'd managed to change into an elegant coat and vest but still wore a four-in-hand tie. His wavy hair, tinged with gray, looked as though it was in need of a visit to the barber. Still, he cut a handsome figure, tall, erect, and always on the verge of a smile.

Wade and Amelia kept a light-hearted conversation as they drove to the mansion. Wade knew all about Simon and Virginia. He knew that Simon hoped to propose to Virginia. And on that note, she appreciated the way he spoke of the weather and the fine accommodations at the Driskill and avoided the subject entirely.

The last time she'd come to the mansion, she'd driven up the back road. This time, they approached from the front, and the view of the mansion in the last rays of sunset struck Amelia as a grand sight.

"What a pretty home," she murmured.

"Very pretty," Wade agreed. "The columns lend a lovely symmetry. And the wide porches give a southern charm."

"Why, Mr. McCord," Amelia teased. "I declare. I actually agree with you on something."

Wade grinned. She almost thought that he'd blushed at her words. To think she could make a rogue like Wade McCord blush.

For weeks Amelia had dreaded this day. The only reason she had wanted to come to this party was to convince Orville Childress that Junior was an innocent man, and that it would be a travesty of justice if he was convicted of a crime he didn't commit.

She had all her arguments ready and had rehearsed them in her mind many times. And then Junior came home, and no arguments were needed. And she no longer needed to attend a party at the Governor's Mansion either, but here she was, keeping her obligation to Wade McCord, because that was the right thing to do.

Even more important, she'd come to the party to help Simon.

Carriages filled the curving driveway as guests alighted. Attendants hurried to take care of the horses. Laughter drifted across the lovely Texas evening. Wade's carriage drew near the front steps. The driver halted the horses. A servant opened the door and set a small step down for Amelia. Wade helped her from the carriage and tucked her hand in the crook of his arm.

"Isn't this nice?" he murmured.

"If you say so," Amelia replied. She tried to sound bored and did her very best not to give in to a silly burst of girlish laughter. It *was* nice. More than nice. The evening would be perfect if only Simon could convince Virginia that they were meant to be. She could hardly bear to think of Virginia refusing him. She'd break his heart. And then what? Amelia hated to think of Simon getting hurt. A mother was only as happy as her least-happy child.

Wade was the perfect gentleman. Amelia had to admit as much, if only to herself. He escorted her inside the governor's mansion and introduced her to his friends. She said hello and visited with each person for a spell before she and Wade made their way around the crowded salon and spoke to other acquaintances.

Her heart felt light. She didn't want to admit it, but she felt happy. She felt better than she had in a good long while. Perhaps it was Wade's kind attention, or perhaps the fine gown Sophie had made just for her. The silk and lace were of the highest quality.

Possibly, her contentment came from visiting the city of Austin and the Governor's Mansion. It pleased her to be out and about amongst all the fine and fancy folk and away from the dust and the grit and bellowing Longhorns.

Then again, it was just as likely, her excitement came from her dreams for Simon. She didn't see Virginia amongst the crowd and prayed that Simon had drawn her to a quiet spot.

Amelia wouldn't allow herself to dwell on dreams of a new daughter-in-law. Not yet.

Instead, she needed to keep her wits about her. By and by, she and Wade came face to face with the governor. Orville looked pleased to see them, or perhaps that was just how he acted with all his guests. Friendly, cordial, wearing a mask of politeness. Wade began to explain how highly he esteemed the Honeycutt family and how much he cherished their long friendship.

Orville looked bemused.

Amelia grew impatient and cut Wade off. "Would you listen to Wade McCord talk about me and my family? A person might think one of the Honeycutts was running for governor."

Orville chuckled and briefly took her hand in his. "Mrs. Honeycutt, it's an honor to have you come to the governor's mansion."

Amelia resisted the urge to explain a few things. For one, when she agreed to come it was because Junior needed her. Two, this wasn't her first visit to the mansion. And three, she had intimate knowledge about the foyer staircase and how well varnished and slick the handrails were. She kept her poise and held her tongue. "Seems you expected me."

"I confess that I had an inkling."

Amelia arched a brow and gave Wade an inquisitive look.

Wade held up his hands. "I didn't say a word."

Orville shook his head. "No, no. It wasn't Wade. It was your son, Simon. He wrote me a letter. Perhaps I'll let Simon tell you the details himself."

Amelia planned on discussing her offer of the land she'd bought out from under Orville Childress, an exchange that might help Junior's predicament. In the end it was Virginia who'd secured Junior's freedom. Just the same, Amelia wanted to discuss the matter with Orville. She understood, however, that now was not the time. If the evening proved to be a success, there'd be plenty of time to talk about the property.

Instead, she kept her conversation cordial. She commented on the lovely party, the beautiful home and impressive array of notable guests.

"I look forward to visiting with you a little more, Amelia," Orville said. "I feel certain we'll have a great deal to discuss."

"I'd like to think so," Amelia said.

"Time will tell," Wade added in a sing-song voice.

Amelia frowned at him. He immediately sobered and did his best to look solemn.

"For now, I'm afraid I need to play the part of host." Orville looked regretful with a quick flicker of remorse that came and went in the blink of an eye.

"Nice to see you, Orville," Wade said.

Orville's brows lifted. "Nice to see you too, McCord. You're looking mighty well. It must be the fine company you're keeping these days."

Orville excused himself. Amelia gave Wade an inquiring look. He responded with an expression of exaggerated innocence. Amelia would have dearly liked to interrogate Wade on Orville's meaning but refrained. It would be best to let sleeping dogs slumber.

In the meantime, she'd make the rounds and see how many of her fellow ranchers attended the governor's shindig. It amused her that few recognized her since she was dressed in Sophie's fine gown, as good a disguise as any.

She hoped to find Virginia amongst the crowd. Then again, if Simon's plan worked, he might have managed to entice Virginia to a quiet spot away from the festivities. Amelia said a quick prayer that Simon had inherited a small fraction of his father's gallantry.

It was at such a party, so many years ago, that George Honeycutt had stolen her heart.

"Would you care to dance?"

Wade interrupted her reverie. She was about to say no. An excuse was on the tip of her tongue. Wade seemed to anticipate her reply and was ready with a quick rebuttal.

"Sophie says you're a terrible dancer," he said. His mouth turned down with a hint of regret, but his eyes sparked with humor.

"She doesn't know what she's talking about," Amelia replied with irritation. "I'm a better dancer than Sophie."

"Sure you are." He gave her an indulgent smile. "Of course."

"There's not even any music, Wade."

His lips quirked as the first few notes of music floated above the sound of talk and laughter. With a sheepish look he explained. "I'd heard the Austin Legal Society hired a quartet for this evening's party."

He held out his arm and waited.

She sighed, trying her best to look put out as she accepted his invitation.

Chapter Thirty-Nine
The Intruder

Virginia

Music drifted across the garden. Virginia had forgotten about the quartet the Legal Society hired for the evening. She had to admit the music added a great deal. She'd often wanted to hire musicians, but her father had vetoed the idea.

She lingered in the shadows, waiting for the intruder to return to the mansion. She felt absurd. As much as she disliked hiding in the garden, tonight for some reason she most assuredly disliked the notion of speaking to the guests. What she needed was a few moments to compose herself. Hopefully, the intruder would soon leave. But no. That was not to be. Just her luck, the stranger drew close, footsteps crunching the gravel path. Ducking down, she held her breath. The footsteps drew closer.

Go away!

The footfalls sent a shimmer across her senses for some reason she couldn't imagine. Probably because the stranger seemed intent on disturbing the peace of her secret escape. He stopped a few paces away on the other side of the hedge.

"I'm looking for the governor's daughter."

Virginia gasped, quickly clasping a hand over her mouth. Slowly, she straightened and peered between the bushes. Her heart thundered behind her ribs. Unable to glimpse the stranger, she parted the branches. In the near darkness she could make out a form, a silhouette against the night sky. The voice and the teasing intonation made her imagine Simon. Even the height and wide span of shoulders made her think of Simon.

And yet, it couldn't be. Her imagination played tricks on her. Surely.

"Have you seen her?" he asked.

She heard the lilt of his voice, could practically see the smile tugging at his lips.

Simon. Her childhood nemesis, her recent knight in shining armor. Simon had returned. He'd come to the party despite his dislike of such events. He was there, standing just a few steps away, in the shadows of the garden. Her doubts faded. A wild surge of hope swept over her. "Simon," she breathed. "You're here."

He circled the hedge, stopping half a pace away and taking her hand in his. "I'm here, looking for Virginia Childress. A friend of mine. A girl I've come to realize I can't live without."

"Oh." She gulped. "Oh, my."

Inwardly, she cringed at her clumsy reply.

Simon laughed softly, the sound a warm rumble emanating from his chest. "I've heard she's never been kissed."

Holding her breath, she awaited some teasing comment. Simon, of course, couldn't resist giving her a bad time.

He spoke, his tone thoughtful. "Maybe she's like President Washington."

Of all the things he might say, a comment about Washington had to be the furthest she'd ever imagine. "W-what?"

"President Washington. Surely you've heard of him."

"Yes."

"Well, maybe she has wooden teeth. That's the reason she's never been kissed."

Simon... Heavens, he was impossible, really. And yet, he stole her breath clean away. How she'd missed him. So very much.

She gave a breathless laugh. "Simon. You're incorrigible."

He wrapped his arm around her waist and pulled her close. She drew a sharp breath of surprise. His arm resting just beneath her shoulders felt warm, strong yet gentle. His scent, clean, reminiscent of spice and sandalwood, sent her thoughts adrift.

She wanted to draw even closer to inhale his masculine scent. Part of her wondered if it was all a dream. After all, how else could she explain Simon appearing at a party there in the governor's mansion?

"Think she has wooden teeth?" Simon asked, his tone earnest. His teasing pulled her back to reality.

"I doubt she does." Virginia replied, trying to sound disapproving but failing miserably as soft laughter fell from her lips.

Simon went on. "Maybe the governor's daughter needs a good reason to kiss a fella."

"A good reason?"

"Or maybe some sort of barter." He lifted her chin. "Trade you?"

She could feel her face heat with a blush. "What will you trade?"

"A homestead for a first kiss."

His words made her heart race. She could hardly breathe, much less reply. He had to be teasing. Surely. And yet, she knew he'd never tease her in such a cruel manner. He'd never taunt her about her family's land or certainly not about her very first kiss.

"It's a pretty place," he whispered. "But I don't want it. Not unless I have you by my side. It's yours for a kiss."

She nodded. He lowered and brushed a soft kiss across her lips. Her breath caught in her throat as she awaited what he might say next. His kiss was her first. His kiss thrilled her. And yet, just as quickly, she had some doubts. While he'd touched his lips to hers, she wasn't entirely sure if that brief caress counted as a kiss. Would he expect more? Or would he walk back his outlandish proposal. She couldn't imagine he'd offer her family's land.

"You can't be serious," she murmured.

"I'm not playing around. My mother gave me the property. Now I'm giving it to you."

She tried to keep hold of her frantic thoughts.

"But why?" she asked.

"Because I love you. And I'm hoping to call on you, maybe kiss you a little more, then get married and start a little family. What do you think?"

Her heart raced, beating with every hope she'd ever dared imagine. "I'm certain I'd like that very much."

He lowered and kissed her again, only this time, Virginia knew without a doubt this was indeed a true kiss. Simon gathered her close, claiming her with a gentle but strong embrace. His kiss, warm and tender, sent a rush of emotion across her heart. He scattered more kisses across her cheek and temple.

With her hand resting on his chest, she felt his heart drum under her palm. For a long moment, it was just the two of them, embracing outside the mansion. The sounds of the party floated on the breeze, a distant reminder of the evening's purpose. Virginia knew her father would be looking for her soon. For once, she didn't care. She only wanted to remain in Simon's arms.

Sighing with contentment, he spoke softly, his mouth next to her ear. "I've missed you. So much. I came to this party with one, single aim. All I want is to take you back to Bethany Springs."

He waited for her reply, but she didn't need to consider the offer. She knew her answer. She knew at once. "Yes, Simon. That's what I want as well. Take me home."

Chapter Forty
Wade Brings Biscuits and
A Letter from the Governor

Amelia

Everything had turned out beautifully. After the party at the governor's mansion, Amelia had two entire days to revel in the satisfaction. Simon had proposed. Virginia had accepted. The plan had worked.

For the price of a homestead, she'd gotten her most troublesome child engaged to be married. She thanked the Good Lord each night at bedtime and each morning when she woke. There'd been a time when the price of a homestead would have been too steep. Not anymore. Now she viewed the price she'd paid as a bargain.

Her delight didn't last, however. The end came swiftly, with the sound of a knock at her front door. A visitor? The thud weighed upon her heart. Surely, she fretted for no reason. Surely. Deep down, she wondered.

With a quick glance at the clock on the mantle, she confirmed it was far too early for company. The sun had scarcely skimmed the eastern horizon. Who on earth called at such an hour?

She set down her pen and pushed her ledger aside. Another knock broke the silence, but she ignored the rude sound. Silently she reviewed the list of her most near and dear.

Daniel and Molly would be still sleeping. Molly didn't rise too early on account of her advanced condition. Simon had returned to his cabin for the time being, eagerly awaiting the wedding just a few weeks off. Zach had traveled to the new logging venture in east Texas.

Junior and his boys were happily settled in a brand-new cabin.

So, who on earth could have come calling so early?

Slowly, with trepidation, she left her study and went to the front door.

"Morning, Amelia." A man's voice called. "I brought you some fresh biscuits!"

"Wade McCord?" she muttered.

She peered through the window, hoping she might be wrong, but no. To her dismay, Wade peered back. A wide, dazzling smile lit his face. He held up a basket as if to prove his claim of fresh biscuits.

Amelia groaned as she rubbed her forehead. "It's too early for breakfast."

His smile vanished. His brow knit. "Should I come back? Say in a half hour?"

"How about this time next year?"

He cupped his hand to his ear. "Didn't catch that."

This was her penance for asking Wade to help out with Junior's dilemma. Wade had happily agreed to squire her to the governor's party. He'd behaved admirably. She couldn't complain. But now Wade felt entitled to some promise of friendship. The fool. He might even imagine she owed him. She considered taking the offered basket and chasing him off her porch as she pelted his head with a flurry of fresh biscuits.

"Did you say something?" Wade bellowed.

"I'm sure you're laughing, George," she muttered. "This probably seems a fine joke."

"A fine joke?" Wade shouted. "Not sure what you mean. I'm not the best baker. Is that what you're referring to?"

"Oh, for heaven's sake." Amelia unbolted the door and let it swing open. "Would you like to come in, Wade?"

"Thank you kindly, Amelia."

She admitted him to her home even though it was entirely untoward. Especially at this hour. She bid him welcome from between gritted teeth, not because she wanted to have breakfast with Wade McCord, but because she wanted to avoid hurting Sophie's feelings. Sophie was her dearest friend. A kind and generous woman, but one inclined to hold grudges.

"I just put some coffee on." Amelia gestured to the kitchen. "How about we sit and visit a spell?"

Wade swept his hat from his head and stepped inside with a grateful smile. "I just won a nickel from my brother."

Amelia strode before him, stalking down the hallway. "Let me guess. You bet Sophie I'd refuse."

"I bet Robert a nickel. Sophie doesn't know. Besides, she'd never place a bet on you, her dearest friend. She'd view such a thing as a betrayal of sorts."

"Hmph. Not so sure. She might, especially since she's convinced that she knows me better than I know myself."

Inside the kitchen, she set out mugs, plates, and silverware. Wade set the basket down on the table and took a chair near the stove.

Wade spoke. "My brother's wife keeps a ledger in her head of every relation she has. She knows more about me than my mother ever knew, and she pulls up facts and stories from my past to *persuade* me into agreement with her, on all sorts of subjects."

"Really?"

"Yes, really. In fact, when she realized she had you in a corner and you needed the governor's help with that cowboy of yours, Sheldon Whitson, she told me to plan to attend that party a week before she even spoke to you about it."

"Darn. *Now* you tell me. That's the only reason I agreed to your company. I try to pick my fights with Sophie McCord."

"You and me both," Wade said as he chuckled.

Amelia poured coffee into the mugs, setting one in front of Wade. "Listen Wade, I don't mean to appear ungrateful. I certainly appreciate your taking me to the party. I had a lovely evening and things all went the way I'd hoped, but I don't want you to start calling on me. I'm a widow. George is the only man I've ever loved and the only man I'll ever love. Ours was a once-in-a-lifetime romance."

Wade sat back in his chair and offered another one of his dazzling smiles.

She folded her arms and glared. How could a person be so darned cheerful so early in the morning? Or ever, for that matter. She eyed the basket of biscuits and considered lobbing one at his sunny expression.

He folded his hands. "I didn't come to call on you, Amelia."

Blood warmed her cheeks. Her breath stalled. Goodness, had Wade McCord made her blush? Again? He'd already made her blush when he escorted her into the post office. Now he was doing the very same thing right in her own kitchen. Thankfully, he had the decency to avert his gaze as he took a sip of coffee.

"Although, I must say, I very much enjoyed escorting you to the governor's party. It was an honor. And if you don't mind my saying, you looked perfectly lovely. I felt very lucky to have such a pretty lady on my arm."

Amelia sighed heavily. Wade could charm the whiskers off a tom cat.

He coughed and took another swallow of coffee.

"Go on," she said, her tone cool but unwavering. "Why have you come? What's so urgent that you've arrived at the break of dawn?"

"Orville asked me to speak to you."

Her heart dropped. Orville? This couldn't bode well for the wedding plans. She edged to a nearby chair and sat down. Scarcely able to breathe, she nodded. She pictured Simon's face and the sweet, happy smile he'd worn all the way home from Austin. If Orville Childress dared hurt her son, she'd...

Well, she didn't know what she'd do but it would be grim. Severe. Merciless. She could summon all the ferocity of a mama bear even though her boys were grown men. Maybe that sort of thing never went away.

Wade guessed her fierce thoughts. He held up his hands in a conciliatory gesture. "It's nothing terrible. No calamity, thank goodness."

She waited.

"He simply wanted to ask your family if the wedding could be postponed till right after the election."

Closing her eyes, she willed herself to take a deep breath. Her heart slowed. Her worry faded. She opened her eyes and studied Wade. "Why postpone till after the election. He's a shoo-in."

"I think so too. But he's nervous. He's fretting that without Virginia, he'll lose."

Amelia stared in stunned disbelief. She wasn't sure what surprised her more, the notion that Orville Childress finally appreciated his daughter's value, or that he'd sent Wade to negotiate the wedding date.

"Why didn't Orville come ask me himself?"

Wade gave another aggravating smile as if the answer was perfectly obvious. "Our governor is a little afraid of you, Amelia. Plenty of menfolk are."

She didn't bother to comment. He took her silence as encouragement and elaborated on his argument. Typical lawyer. Liked to hear himself talk about everything under the sun.

"You're like a bird," Wade explained. "A small bird, of course. Small but fierce. A sort of bird that likes to puff her feathers out to look bigger. You fool plenty of the other birds, but not me."

Various comebacks drifted through her mind. Birds? Feathers? If Wade wanted to compare her to a bird, she'd like to return the favor and compare him to an old turkey buzzard.

She sipped her coffee as she considered the wedding delay. Simon would be disappointed. He'd storm around, threatening to steal Virginia from the governor's mansion and marrying her in a hasty ceremony in some two-horse town.

Simon might not care about the niceties of a fancy wedding, but Virginia certainly did. Amelia knew that for a fact because the girl had written letters to Simon, telling him about her dreams. All her life, she'd been led to believe she ought not marry.

Now that she understood the truth, she envisioned every detail of her wedding day, from the church and the music to her vows and gown.

Virginia's wedding plans struck a tender part of Amelia's heart. Amelia wanted the girl to have her special day. A beautiful dress. A lovely, delicate veil. Flowers. Music. Friends and family gathered to break bread. The very things Amelia enjoyed at her own wedding so long ago.

She pushed the memories aside. "How long, exactly, does Orville Childress want to wait? Till after he wins? Till he starts his new term? How long?"

Wade removed a piece of paper from his breast pocket and unfolded it. He patted his other pockets. "Dang. I forgot my spectacles."

She hid her amusement. Wade McCord needed spectacles. What would all his female admirers say?

He grumbled as he searched every pocket two and three times. As he grew increasingly agitated, Amelia fought the urge to laugh. It was as if the entire notion of spectacles perturbed the man's sensibilities.

Made sense. Men were every bit as vain as women, often more so. Everyone considered Wade McCord a handsome fellow. Especially Wade McCord.

His failing eyesight hurt his pride. She watched him grow more and more agitated. His face reddened. He pressed his lips to a tight line of aggravation while peering inside his coat pocket. Quietly, but with marked irritation, he muttered, "Darn, darn, darn. I must have left them on my bedside table."

Amelia murmured a few words of sympathy as she held back her laughter.

After letting him flail and fluster, Amelia noted more and more pity and resolved to do what she could to ease his masculine suffering. "I think we can agree you failed to bring your eyeglasses. Give me the note. I can read the message aloud, Grandpa."

Wade grumbled as he pushed the note across the table. "I'd like to say one thing."

"Fine by me. Go ahead."

"I'm no one's grandfather, I can assure you of that."

"All right." She straightened the creases of the note. "Let's just take a gander and find out how long Orville wants to hold off. He probably wants to keep Virginia working her fingers to the bone for years to come, right up till he runs for president of the United States."

"Doubtful. He's feeling guilty. I don't know the details. He wished he'd encouraged her to follow her own interests instead of helping him day after day. He mentioned misleading her about her mother's passing."

"I believe the word is lying, counsellor. Not misleading."

"I'm sure he's guilty as charged, Your Honor. But he's showing remorse and wants to make amends."

"We'll see about that."

He nodded but didn't reply.

She read Orville's short note and studied the suggested dates. Orville's note was a tad blurry but as far as she could tell the dates weren't more than a few weeks after the election. That seemed reasonable enough. Hopefully, Simon would agree without too much fuss. She squinted, trying to make certain she'd read everything correctly. Last thing she wanted to do was to tell Wade she approved of a date three years off.

Wade's chuckle distracted her.

"What's so funny?"

"You are, Mrs. Honeycutt." He held his arm straight out and narrowed his eyes to read a make-belief note.

The cad. He was mocking her, pointing out the way she held out Orville's note. She hadn't even noticed her outstretched arm and had to admit she must look a tad silly. Just the same, she didn't care for his amusement. Not one bit.

Wade probably figured turn-around was fair play.

She didn't use spectacles. Not because she was vain but because she didn't need them. Fact was, she could read perfectly well, or she could when there was enough sunlight. Sunrise hardly counted as such. The poor light was the problem. Not her eyes.

She gave him a stern look, but he ignored her.

"I might not be the only one who needs spectacles." He looked solemn. "Maybe someone else needs spectacles, Grandma."

His lips curved into a smile and widened to a grin. His laughter filled the kitchen. His shoulders shook as he muttered the word a time or two more. *Grandma...*

Amelia's blood warmed considerably. She narrowed her eyes.

Slowly, his laughter faded. He shook his head and wiped his eyes. When he saw her expression, he sobered. Or tried to, anyway.

She folded her hands. "How is it possible you and Robert McCord belong to the same family?"

Wade offered no hint of repentance.

She went on. "I can see perfectly fine when there's good light."

"Why sure, you can. I'll bet your eyes are just fine. It's your arms that are too short. That's all. Give me that danged note. I'll hold it out for you, maybe from the other side of the kitchen.

"Oh hush." She slapped Orville's note to the table. "I'll agree to a delay in the wedding if Simon agrees. He won't be happy, though, especially after he asked the governor for Virginia's hand."

"I understand."

"And we need to stick to the plan that they get married right there in the mansion. That's not on my account but because Virginia would like to say her vows there, right at the bottom of the stairs."

"No question. Orville wants what Virginia wants."

She scoffed. "Since when?"

Wade looked thoughtful. "I know you don't like Orville Childress. But I can assure you he loves Virginia."

Amelia wasn't convinced. "I think Old Orville just can't stand the notion of losing the governorship."

Wade shook his head. For a long moment, he said nothing. "Orville is starting to realize how little he cares about being governor. He's not sure how he'll manage without Virginia's help."

"That so?"

"It most certainly is so."

"Well... I'll be," she said in astonishment.

"Sophie told Robert she intends to find him a nice lady to settle down with. That's what he needs."

"Maybe that's true."

"He better not get ideas about calling on you," Wade grumbled.

"It would be a cold day in Hades," Amelia scoffed.

"Darned straight."

Wade smiled again, only this time he didn't give her his too-bright smile, the one he used to deliberately charm folks. Or sweet-talk the unsuspecting. She had to admit she liked this smile a lot more than the usual variety.

She took a biscuit from the wicker basket and nudged it back across the table. He selected a biscuit and set in on his plate. She then offered butter and a jar of peach jam. She found a knife in the drawer beside the stove and set it near his plate. The early glow of dawn cast a soft light across the table.

Outside, the birds twittered. In the distance a herd of yearling cattle mooed. Her ranch hands called out morning greetings. Sheldon gave orders somewhere by the main barn. Junior whooped over some delightful goings on. She hoped that Tuck and Ellwood worked alongside their father. A sense of peace settled over her heart.

She took a bite of the warm biscuit.

"Your biscuits are very good," Amelia said. "They might be better than mine."

"You don't say."

"Pains me to admit it."

"I'm sure your biscuits are mighty fine."

"They're as tough as a pair of old boots."

He looked thoughtful. "You're kneading them too much. Biscuits need a light touch."

"Hard to believe Wade McCord is teaching me about biscuit baking."

"They need a light touch." He arched his brow. "Along with a secret finish."

"A secret finish. And what's that?"

She waited for him to reply. What sort of secret finish could Wade McCord have up his sleeve? She didn't even know he knew how to scramble eggs, much less bake perfect biscuits. How had this arrogant, impossible lawyer learned how to *bake.*

He didn't say a word. Instead, he pretended not to notice that she awaited his answer. He ignored her, took another biscuit, buttered the flaky insides, and heaped a generous dollop of peach jelly.

"I'm visiting Bethany Springs for a few days." He spoke in a casual tone. "Perhaps I could call again and bring you some more biscuits. What do you say? Shall I stop by tomorrow morning?"

Her jaw slackened.

"No need to look so surprised. I enjoyed taking you to the governor's party. Very much. Sadly, we didn't have much chance to visit." He gestured between them. "Like this. It's a treat to have you all to myself."

She blinked.

He looked at her with an expression of exaggerated innocence. "I can bring you another basket of biscuits. Should I come around at the same time?"

"The break of dawn?"

He shrugged a shoulder and offered another shining smile. "Early bird gets the biscuit."

"I don't think so, Wade." She folded her hands and gave him a cool look. "Your biscuits aren't *that* good."

He chuckled, then set his hand over his heart to show how much her words wounded him. She tried to school her features, to keep from smiling at his antics. Wade McCord could be charming every so often, but she was determined not to let on.

If Wade McCord thought she approved of him, there'd be no living with him or Sophie. For years now, she'd snubbed his attention and she wasn't about to change her mind now. Even if he was trying to help Simon and Virginia. Amelia was too old for such foolish notions. Too long widowed to change her ways.

Sophie was her dearest friend. Amelia knew she hoped something might come of her and Wade. She didn't want to disappoint Sophie, but it couldn't be helped. Sophie would have to accept her decision. Amelia would never agree to risking her heart. Not again.

"I could even bring a little bacon and fried eggs," Wade offered.

The rascal. He likely tried this ploy with all sorts of women folk. She wasn't going to fall for his schemes. Or his baking. She wasn't going to fall for anything Wade offered.

When she didn't bother to reply, he shrugged. She waited for more charming offers, but he said nothing. To her surprise his mouth tugged downward, and he looked a tad dejected. With a heavy sigh, he drained his coffee, let the matter rest, and he said nothing more about it while he ate his steaming, perfect biscuit.

Chapter Forty-One
A Heartfelt Gift

Simon

It had been weeks since the party at the governor's mansion. Weeks since he'd seen Virginia and held her in his arms. It seemed an eternity. Each day stretched endlessly making him miss her more and more. He wanted her nearby, not living in Austin.

At times he understood the need to remain patient. Other times he felt a deep need to wrap her in his arms, to hear her voice, to make her laugh.

Ranch business carried on as usual and kept him occupied. Thank goodness. Otherwise, he might have lost his patience and made a plan to bust Virginia out of the mansion late one night, like he considered doing for Junior at the jail. Likely he'd have more luck at the mansion.

Today, though, there were things to tend to on the ranch, which made the wait tolerable.

Three Brahma bulls arrived from Galveston. He brought them to the ranch and put them in a nearby pasture. Friends and neighbors came to see the new breed of cattle. Not one missed the chance to point out he wouldn't get far with a trio of bulls. If he wanted to grow a brand, he ought to think of buying a few more Brahmas, folks suggested.

"I don't believe you need any more bulls," Junior explained.

Simon groaned inwardly. While he was mighty pleased that Junior was out of jail and back home with his family, Junior's gift for pointing out the obvious wore on Simon's nerves more so than ever.

Simon replied from between gritted teeth. "Mighty helpful. Thank you kindly."

"I have a good idea," Junior said, brightening.

"I'll bet."

"How about you get some *cows?*"

"There's a swell idea. I'll look into it soon as I get a chance."

Junior grinned, bid him goodbye, and set off to eat supper with his parents, Elliot and Tuck flanking him on his left and right. Simon watched them walk away. A tug pained his heart as Junior joked with the boys. They laughed. Junior offered another teasing remark.

The sweet moment left Simon feeling more lonesome than ever.

By now he'd assumed he and Virginia would be married and starting a new life at the Childress homestead. But no. He and Virginia lead separate lives. Still. Everything hung on the election. Once that was over, their lives could proceed.

She wrote every day, talking about the wedding plans and the work she did for her father's reelection. He wrote back, telling her about the ranch and the growing herd of Brahma cattle. He didn't mention the fact that he only had a few bulls.

When his spirits sank, even lower than he could have imagined, he came up with a plan. An idea that would, Lord willing, please Virginia. He decided to include Tuck and Ellwood in his project. Both were plum terrible at keeping secrets, but that didn't matter. Virginia wouldn't return to Bethany Springs until they were man and wife.

It was a cold October afternoon. He and the two boys set out after lunch with winds whipping across the pasture. The trees bent and swayed under the onslaught of a blue northern.

The boys rode behind him, grumbling about their father taking a new wife. The kindly lady who'd tended to Junior in jail had remained as a tender spot in his heart.

Velma and Junior were now man and wife. The boys weren't so sure what to make of it.

She'd come to visit, gotten to know Junior's parents and children and in the space of one short week she and Junior got married. Normally, these sorts of things didn't turn out well for Junior. Mama had said as much and made a point of questioning Velma before the nuptials.

Despite Mama's vigorous interrogation, Velma remained agreeable to the marriage. A little shaken, but agreeable. She vowed to honor Junior and care for the boys as if they were her own.

"At least she cooks all right," Tuck muttered.

"She makes good fried chicken," Ellwood agreed.

"She makes us say prayers every night," Tuck sighed.

"She likes to kiss the top of our head. And calls us little angels."

Tuck spoke in a high-pitched voice. "What would my pair of little angels like for breakfast?"

Both boys groaned.

"I always thought you were a pair of angels," Simon explained. "Even after that time you swapped the salt and sugar on Mama's kitchen table."

Both boys quieted. Simon grinned and looked back to find them both pale and stricken.

"Does Mrs. Honeycutt know that was us?" Tuck asked.

"Who do you suggest I blame it on?" Simon asked.

"How about Elsie?" Ellwood suggested.

Simon laughed. His heart warmed to have the two boys along. It helped keep him from missing Virginia so much.

"I wouldn't blame Elsie if I were you," he cautioned. "You two might just as well admit you're the guilty parties."

"Right," Ellwood muttered. "No one will blame Little Miss Perfect."

"Elsie's a good girl, but I doubt she thinks of herself as perfect. She lost her parents and her grandma, and then she was abandoned by the last of her family." He glanced back. The boys looked solemn.

"For a long time, she was convinced we didn't want her around, just like her other kin," Simon said gently. The boys looked almost teary-eyed. "You see? Sometimes family is who God puts in your life, not just folks you're related to."

The path took them along a high ridge where the wind blew hard enough to chill him to the bone. He tugged his collar up to protect against the cold. He stopped his horse and waited for them to catch up. "You best give Elsie a chance. While you're at it, give Velma a chance too."

"Yessir," the two boys said as they bent against the wind.

He smiled inwardly as he noted their ease in the saddle. In a short time, the boys had taken to spending long stretches on horseback. He and Junior worked with them every day. The prior week, Simon presented them with chaps and their own boots. They'd been overjoyed. It was as if he'd given them some sort of priceless treasure. He considered their response and how they'd likely viewed the gifts as a sign they belonged there on the ranch.

They did. He'd told them as much, as had Junior, of course, but the cowboy gear had somehow made things official.

They rode further, none of them speaking as the Childress homestead came into view. His breath caught. The cabin was a handsome structure, well-built and sturdy now that the Collins twins had made repairs.

In less than two weeks, he and Virginia would live in the old homestead. In the meantime, he did what he could to prepare for her arrival. He'd had the house properly cleaned. The pantry stocked. Molly had sewn new curtains and even embroidered a pretty tablecloth and matching napkins. Mama had polished a set of silver she'd been saving for him and had sent off for new pans.

There was only one last detail he needed to tend to.

When they arrived at the homestead, Ellwood tended to the horses while he and Tuck dug holes on either side of the porch stairs. The ground was muddy and heavy from the recent rains. He finished quickly but Tuck's progress was slow. Simon set his shovel aside and waited. He knew better than to offer help. The young man needed to finish the job on his own.

Ellwood trudged to the cabin, struggling under the weight of a couple of shrubs. They were bare root, clad in only a few leaves but armored with an array of sharp thorns. The boy tried his best to avoid the thorns while still handling the shrubs gently. He set them down by the bottom step.

Tuck finished his task and eyed the plants. "Uncle Simon?"

"Yes?"

"Are you sure these straggly things are roses?"

"I'm sure. Miss Sophie brought them back from her family's home in Louisiana. She babied them all the way back and made me promise I'd plant them right away."

Ellwood scrubbed his hand over his face. "They look like goners."

"That's because it's almost winter. Let's just see what happens come springtime."

Both boys looked doubtful. Simon couldn't blame them one bit. The straggly shrubs looked pitiful and lifeless. The only part of them that looked half-way hardy were the fierce thorns adorning the spindly branches. Sophie had wrapped the roots in burlap and hopefully they remained strong enough to revive the rose bushes. When Sophie gave him the plants, she confessed she knew nothing about gardening.

"Zee plants might not leeve," she'd murmured sadly. "Zay might already be dead."

Simon hoped Sophie was wrong. It seemed a small thing, but in his mind the roses might mean a great deal to Virginia. That was enough for him.

"Let's take off the burlap, Ellwood. Tuck, you bring a pail of water from the handpump."

The boys did as he asked. Simon noticed the skeptical looks they shared whenever they thought he wasn't looking. He winced, wondering if the effort would pay off. The idea of surprising Virginia warmed his heart more than he could say. And yet, he hardly dared hope the wilted plants might recover.

The three of them worked diligently. Simon settled the shrubs gently in the ground and held them as the boys eased dirt around the exposed roots. Together, they patted the dirt down. When both shrubs were planted, Tuck tipped the pail to give the roses a little water. When he'd watered both plants, they stood back to admire their work.

"Think she'll like them?" Simon asked.

Both boys nodded.

"Why sure she will," Tuck said.

"What's not to like?" Ellwood asked. "Roses are pretty. Ladies like pretty things."

"I picked them because her mama liked yellow roses." Simon touched the nearest shrub. "It seemed fitting. I just hope they grow."

The boys both grew quiet. The wind stirred and made them all shiver. It seemed far-fetched to imagine the poor little shrubs would survive, much less grow and blossom, but a man had to have a little faith. That's what he told himself.

The boys seemed overcome by the plight of the rose transplants. They teared up and said little as they prepared to leave the quiet homestead. After they saddled up, Simon glanced back at the lonesome house and the new rose bushes.

He tried to think of a few words of prayer. Although he yearned to say something that pertained to the cabin and his marriage to Virginia, he could only summon a simple sentiment.

Thank you, Lord.

The simple words seemed paltry. Especially considering how full his heart felt. Ever since he'd kissed Virginia, he'd yearned to exchange vows. He'd agreed to wait to marry her because he knew she wanted to see her father reelected. Only then would she be free to start a new life.

Even if Orville Childress lost, Simon would claim his promised bride. He'd told her as much in a letter. She'd replied that she counted the days until they said their vows. He'd read the letter a dozen times after, running his fingertips over her words.

The wind buffeted them as they left the homestead. The boys quickly recovered from their fretfulness. They rode home, flanking Simon on each side, giving him all manner of grief as if trying to draw him from his pensive mood.

"What if that shrub ends up a potato plant, Uncle Simon?" Tuck asked. He knit his brow. His cheeks looked red and chapped against the cold, but he was clearly pleased to have a chance to tease Simon. His eyes sparkled with amusement.

"Guess we'll have us some potatoes," Simon replied, hiding his smile.

"Might turn out to be corn stalks," Ellwood offered mournfully. "That would be something, wouldn't it?"

Simon heaved a heavy sigh as he tugged his coat sleeves down.

"How about bean plants, like Jack in the Beanstalk?" Tuck suggested. "I bet Miss Virginia would think that was mighty fine. Probably even better than a bunch of thorny roses."

Simon merely shook his head and gave the boys a stern look. Unfortunately, he'd given himself away somehow. Perhaps a look in his eye or the tilt of his lips. Something had told the boys he was trying not to smile at their tomfoolery.

They laughed with delight. Of course, they did.

He ought to have known they'd only be encouraged. Over the course of the last month or better, he'd learned a lot about the boys, and they'd learned a lot about him. He'd grown to appreciate their tender hearts and boyish yearnings. They just wanted a place to belong. What was more, they wanted to belong forever.

They in turn had learned they could rely on him to teach them a thing or two. He could guide them, expected respect but at the same time they understood Simon could take a little ribbing. In fact, the teasing banter served to bond them in a way that was a world away from the types of talk that women seemed to relish.

The three of them rode down the hillside as the boys carried on with more and more outlandish ideas of what they'd planted that afternoon. Ellwood and Tuck insisted the two ugly and mostly dead shrubs weren't roses. No sirree. The plants were anything *but* roses.

They came up with a multitude of theories.

By the time they'd returned to the ranch, the boys had run the entire gamut of possibilities, from every sort of fruit or vegetables along with a few dozen imaginary and whimsical plants just for good measure. Not one included roses, of course. Not one at all.

And Simon didn't mind. Not one bit.

Chapter Forty-Two
Something Old and Beautiful

Virginia

In the days before the wedding, Virginia had encountered three very different surprises.

The first surprise involved news that two of her dearest friends intended to come the day of her wedding to help her with her hair and wedding dress. Virginia was overwhelmed with gratitude.

Even though the wedding had been delayed, she hadn't imagined any of her old friends could make the trip to help. Over the past few years, she'd neglected her friends terribly. Ever since Papa first announced he intended to run for governor, Virginia had been too busy to write or visit. So, it came as a lovely surprise when Millie and Victoria traveled to Austin to attend to her on her wedding day.

The second surprise came when her father insisted that she remove herself from any cooking, baking or food preparation for her wedding. She knew he fretted about expenses. In a burst of nervous energy, she offered to cut costs by helping with a small part of the cooking.

Her father had agreed tentatively. His demeanor changed drastically the evening she'd prepared a few sample dishes. Upon tasting the dishes, concocted from recipes she'd invented, he insisted she stay out of the kitchen entirely.

"Your cooking is simply too delicious," he'd gasped as he set the slightly charred roast aside. "We don't want to distract attention from the lovely bride, now do we?"

The third surprise arrived in the late afternoon, less than an hour before the wedding. A soft knock at the bedroom door was followed by the appearance of Amelia Honeycutt. Virginia almost didn't recognize Simon's mother. Amelia was dressed in a soft, gauzy gown of lavender, her blonde hair swept up in an elegant arrangement. The afternoon sunlight seemed to subtly illuminate her lovely features.

"Amelia?" Virginia stammered. "Look at you."

Simon's mother gave a coy smile and followed with a demure curtsy. "What? Me?"

Virginia knew Amelia would attend her nuptials but hadn't imagined the actual sight of Simon's mother there at the wedding. She gaped and tried to make sense of the vision before her.

Amelia Honeycutt. Simon's mother. The woman stood at the door of her room. She wore a dress. A dress! Not pants, boots and a tattered Stetson. Why, Amelia even wore jewelry. A glittering pair of earrings adorned her ears. A delicate bracelet circled her wrist.

Sounds of the wedding party drifted past Virginia's door. Normally, she'd be downstairs directing the festivities. She'd be certain to manage things so her father could fully assume his role as governor. Not today. Papa had demanded she enjoy her day and let others tend to matters, for this afternoon, she was the center of attention, as much as she disliked that role. Her father insisted that she needed to stay put and wait and even *worse*, depend on others.

Waiting was very uncomfortable.

Making matters worse was the fact that she hadn't seen her fiancé in what felt like ages.

All day, Virginia had fixed her attention on Simon. Even though her friends fussed over her, Virginia's mind kept drifting to Simon, her betrothed. The girls reminisced about past boyfriends and girlhood prank of years ago, but Virginia only thought of Simon.

Where was he? What would he wear to their wedding? Would he like her simple ivory silk gown? Would he think she looked pretty? Was he as nervous as she?

Probably not.

Simon was never nervous.

Still, the entire day had seemed surreal. She'd already sent her friends down to find their seats in the ballroom and had been trying to collect her frantic thoughts before her father came to escort her down the grand staircase.

In the midst of the quiet and confusion, Amelia had arrived.

All afternoon, she'd shooed people away. She didn't want visitors. In truth, she didn't want her dear friends Millie and Victoria to stay longer than necessary. She wanted to be alone to think about Simon and their life together. All she wanted was to be alone, or so she thought.

A deep, satisfying warmth spread across her heart. Amelia was here. Thank goodness.

"I brought you something," Amelia said in a hushed tone.

Naturally, Amelia would suggest something outrageous.

Virginia shook her head. "I don't care for anything to drink. I won't indulge in spirits. Everyone, even my father, claims a small nip will help with my nerves, but I'm certain it will only make my nerves much, much worse."

Amelia laughed as she drew near. "I'm not bringing you whiskey. Or anything to addle your mind. I'm bringing you something better. I'm bringing something old. Something from George's family."

Amelia's expression grew solemn as she held out a jewelry box and slowly opened the lid. "George's parents had a fine love affair despite starting off badly."

Virginia held her breath. She still couldn't see the contents of the box.

"Quit fretting, child. It's nothing as terrible as the bride cooking for her own wedding. I declare!" Amelia gave an inelegant snort. "The stories of you cooking are making the rounds and we're all a little frightened for Simon."

"What?"

"Never mind about that." Amelia waved a dismissive hand. "I'm trying to show you the necklace George's mother wore when she got married. The same necklace I wore when I said my vows."

Amelia drew nearer to show Virginia what lay inside the box. A string of pearls rested on the delicate, velvet lining of the box. The white pearls gleamed. An intricate, gold clasp glinted in the afternoon sunlight.

Virginia lifted her hand to her bare neck.

"Yes," Amelia said as she set the box on the vanity. "You're not wearing a necklace. Works out well. Mighty glad I don't have to talk you out of some hideous piece old Orville bought you. Lord knows he likely hasn't got a modicum of taste. Sorry, dear. I promise not to fuss about your father this evening."

Her lips curved into a cheeky smile. "Now that Orville and me are kin, I'm saving up for all the holidays to come. Won't *that* be fun?"

"I'm sorry but I don't quite understand."

"Oh, never you mind." Amelia leaned close and draped the necklace around Virginia's neck. Amelia winced as she struggled with the clasp. "Darn. It's hard to see the tiny clasp in this light. Sometimes I' think I might even need... Oh! There we go."

Virginia ran her fingertips across the pearls. They were lovely. Perfect. Just the right shade of ivory to match her dress.

"My word," she breathed.

Amelia stood silently behind her. She rested her hands on Virginia's shoulders and gazed at the reflection in the mirror. Her eyes shone with a soft tearful gaze.

"Pearls don't just appear out of nowhere," Amelia murmured. "They begin with a hard, sharp grain of sand inside the oyster. Over time the oyster turns the discomfort into something beautiful. Something lasting. And that my sweet girl is the story of you and Simon. I always think that's so-"

The door snapped shut behind Amelia making both of them startle. Sophie McCord crossed the room, her pretty face etched with dismay. "She is telling you her oyster story, no?"

Virginia blinked, unsure what to say.

Sophie gathered her fingers together as she held her hand outstretched. "Wis a small piece of sand and then the pain. Yes? What an 'orrible story! Do not listen, Virginia."

"All right," Virginia murmured. "I won't"

Sophie forged on. "The pearls are perfect together. And so are you and Simon."

Amelia nodded and began to respond but Sophie shushed her with a sharp look.

Sophie returned her attention to Virginia as her expression softened with a gracious smile. "Your father, zee governor, is on his way to your room." Her smile faltered. "He is not crying. Not too much."

Neither Virginia nor Amelia replied. Sophie gave an elegant sigh and gestured to the door. "Come, Cherie. It is time to get married. Poor Simon. He looks as white as ze ghosts."

Chapter Forty-Three
The Wedding

Simon

All anyone wanted to know was if he was nervous. Some folks had a sure-fire remedy for wedding jitters. Wade McCord offered a cigar. Sophie suggested a small glass of cognac. Mama might have been the most jittery of all of them. She either prayed or paced or at times did both.

The Honeycutt Family was ensconced in an elegant, quiet room situated away from the staff and other guests. Sunlight flooded through tall windows. A blaze crackled cheerfully in the hearth. Burnished wood paneling lent added warmth to the tasteful quarters.

At first, Simon thought the room was spacious and plenty comfortable. Once his mother began pacing to and fro, the accommodations felt cramped and crowded. She and Sophie stepped out briefly to speak to Virginia but returned a few moments later and Mama resumed her nervous pacing.

Finally, the time arrived. The group left the room and filed into the foyer. Daniel ushered Simon to the front of the room, near the violinist. A profusion of flowers adorned the mansion. Wicker stands overflowing with blooms lined the walls. Garlands hung the length of the banister. The perfume of a thousand flowers filled the air.

In the letters she wrote Simon, Virginia had promised the wedding would be a modest affair. Clearly her father had overruled her requests. The mansion held a profusion of flowery festoons and flourishes.

Inwardly he smiled, imagining his mother's approval.

He crossed the foyer and came to a stop at the bottom of the grand staircase. His brothers flanked him. He could almost feel their nervous energy. The guests sat in the foyer, some spilling over to the hall. They spoke in quiet, hushed tones.

Simon had to admit, if only to himself, he too, felt a tad fretful, part of him wishing to be done with the wedding and back home in Bethany Springs along with his bride. As the violinist began to play, the guests quieted, and Simon's thoughts scattered like leaves on a morning breeze.

Orville Childress, dressed in a dark three-piece suit and pale-yellow tie, escorted Virginia down the stairs. Simon watched them descend, entranced as he could take in more and more of Virginia. Each step revealed a little more of his sweet bride.

As she turned the corner, Simon's breath left him. Virginia, his lovely, captivating sweetheart, looked more beautiful than he could have imagined. Radiant. Her white gown clung to her slim frame. From beneath her veil, she smiled sweetly at him. He managed to give her an answering smile, but only after Daniel nudged him in the ribs and knocked him out of his daze.

Virginia came down the steps gracefully. When she reached the foyer, she turned to her father. He lifted her veil and kissed her forehead. Taking her hands, he held them for a long moment before setting them in Simon's hands.

Virginia looked up at Simon, a shy smile tugging at her lips. He wanted nothing more than to lean down and kiss her right there in front of everybody. Zach seemed to understand his thoughts. He cleared his throat, sending the clear message that Simon needed to pay attention.

The minister, a friend of the governor's, began to say the vows. Mercy, the man droned on. And on. Simon was beginning to wonder if he'd ever finish. The minister asked both he and Virginia for their I do's. To Simon's thinking this ought to be the end of the matter, but no. The minister still had miles to go, probably on account of a few stories he felt called on to share.

Virginia's lips curved with a mischievous smile. Simon squeezed her hands and gave a small sign of his impatience. Her smile threatened to widen.

Finally, the elderly gentleman warbled the last words. "I pronounce you man and wife."

"At last," Simon said softly so just Virginia could hear. He lowered to press his lips to hers. His arms wrapped around her and drew her into a firm embrace. If he'd had his way, he would have lifted her in the air but one of his brothers murmured a few words of caution.

Steady, there, Simon.

The minister announced the new couple. "I present Mr. and Mrs. Simon Honeycutt."

The guests clapped politely. Mama grumbled about the windy pastor. Wade remarked on the lovely service. Daniel and Zach marveled that Simon had actually gotten hitched. Sophie dabbed her eyes with a lace hanky and murmured a soft flurry of tearful, happy words in French. Governor Childress blew his nose and assured everyone he wasn't weeping. Of course, he wasn't, he blustered. Just a slight cold, that was all.

"Is this a dream?" Virginia asked.

"If it is a dream," Simon replied. "It's the finest dream I've ever known."

In the next instant, Zach and Daniel tugged Simon from his bride and shook his hand, each congratulating him. Mama, Sophie, and several other ladies flocked to Virginia to offer best wishes. It seemed that no sooner had he and Virginia become man and wife when they were pushed apart by well-wishers. Simon had to smile at the irony. Virginia must have been struck by the same idea, judging by the wry smile she gave him.

Simon didn't mind a few moments apart from his bride. Even if she'd been whisked away by friends and family, she belonged to him now. Nothing could change that, and he'd never known such a deep and abiding contentment.

Chapter Forty-Four
Hiraeth

Virginia

Orville Childress had won his re-election, which was no surprise to Amelia. What *did* come as a bit of a surprise was that he was as cantankerous and argumentative as ever. And that was on a lovely Easter Sunday afternoon, no less. The man delighted in argument. They stood in Simon & Virginia's parlor studying a lovely piece of embroidery.

Orville seemed to think her pronunciation of the word, *Hiraeth*, was the most hilarious thing he'd heard in a good long while. He laughed and laughed, wiping tears from his eyes as he mocked her pronunciation.

"Why, Mrs. Honeycutt, you need to roll your r's. You can't say the word with a Texas accent."

"I say everything with a Texas accent," she snapped.

"Try again." He sobered, cleared his throat, and repeated the word, exaggerating the enunciation.

Virginia peeked around the corner of the kitchen, her face flushed from cooking.

"Papa, don't tease Amelia."

He frowned petulantly.

"It's Easter Sunday," Virginia said, trying to look stern.

Orville relented. "Well, fine then. I'll try to behave myself, considering."

Virginia smiled, her hand drifting to her midsection. Amelia noted the gesture and with a small rush of happiness, noted the small curve beneath Virginia's palm. Simon and Virginia expected a baby sometime in the Fall. Amelia had hoped for a granddaughter but was so pleased about the news, she found she didn't much care if the baby was a boy or girl.

So long as it was healthy.

A boy would be a blessing. Even if they ended up naming the poor child Orville.

Tuck and Ellwood called a greeting from outside. Amelia went to the porch to find a surprising sight. Tuck stood beside one of Simon's Brahma bulls, while Ellwood sat astride the animal, bareback, holding the reins of a makeshift bridle. Both boys grinned at her, eagerly expecting her shock and dismay.

Junior had done a fine job with the two boys, working with them every day to show them what he knew about cowboying. The boys had taken to their lessons, partly because they enjoyed learning as much as they could, and partly because they loved their father very much. That didn't mean they weren't still a pair of incorrigible rascals.

She had to admit, the boys had behaved admirably through the extra-long sermon that morning. They were capable of being good as gold. Both of them a head taller in the last few months, the boys were growing up before her very eyes.

"What do you think of our new pony, Miss Amelia?" Tuck asked in a cheeky tone.

"Would you like to take him for a ride?" Ellwood added.

"No. Thank you kindly," Amelia replied, trying to keep from smiling. Tuck and Ellwood hardly needed any encouragement.

Simon sauntered out of the house and chuckled at the outrageous sight. Orville and Virginia followed. The boys could hardly contain their amusement. The bull, for his part, seemed entirely unperturbed by the turn of events. He hardly noticed his audience. His only response was a slight flick of his ear. It appeared the animal was on the verge of falling asleep, judging by his drooping eyelids.

"You two better never try that with a Longhorn," Amelia advised.

The boys frowned.

"Why not?" Tuck asked.

Amelia sighed. "You know perfectly well why not. A Longhorn would never put up with such foolishness. A Longhorn would have the sense to buck you off and stomp on you a time or two."

The boys looked affronted as if they found such behavior rude and outrageous.

Amelia went on. "These silly Brahmins don't have an ounce of good sense. They don't seem to realize that they are cattle."

Simon folded his arms and leaned against the railing. "They're gentle animals. So long as they're treated well, they're quite docile."

For the last few months, Amelia and Simon had kept a running debate about the virtues of Brahmas and Longhorns.

Amelia continued. "For some reason they're under the impression that they are dogs. Ranch dogs."

Simon chuckled. The boys joined in.

"Yes, ma'am," Tuck said. "This one is our favorite dog in the whole herd."

Ellwood laughed at his brother's fine joke. Tuck hopped onto the bull's back and settled behind his brother. The two boys took their leave, wishing Simon and his family a happy Easter.

Amelia stood on the porch and watched them leave while the rest of the group filed back inside. She made a point of talking to Simon about getting each of the boys a horse of their own. They were too big for the ranch ponies and ought to have sturdy mounts that weren't as old as Rooster and Dusty.

As the years passed, she found satisfaction in giving away things. She'd given Virginia the parcel of land that she'd bought from under Orville's nose. A passel of ugly Brahma's grazed the land now, but that was a small price to pay.

"Mother, we're ready to eat," Virginia called from the door.

Amelia smiled, touched by Virginia's address. Molly, her other daughter-in-law, called her by her given name, but not Virginia. Virginia hadn't ever known her own mother, so it struck Amelia as especially poignant.

She came to the table, taking her seat beside Simon and across from Orville. The group wasn't as large as it usually was at Easter. Zach was working at the Honeycutt Sawmill in East Texas. Daniel and Molly had stayed home. Molly expected a baby in the next few weeks and the doctor had ordered her to remain in bed. Amelia intended to bring them a basket that evening and to check on Molly.

The group clasped hands and bowed their head. Simon's voice filled the quiet.

"Heavenly Father, may the grace of our Lord be with us this day. We ask that you watch over the rest of our family, especially Molly. May this meal be blessed as we gather to celebrate. May Your love be shared amongst us as we enjoy the gift of fellowship. May we remember to offer the grace and forgiveness that You have freely given us, and may we always give thanks for Your sacrifice. Amen."

A peaceful quiet fell over the group as each offered their silent prayer and gave thanks.

After a long moment, Virginia softly invited the family to begin the meal. It wasn't long before Orville returned to his teasing and arguing. He seemed to enjoy tormenting Amelia about Wade McCord, urging her to explain their friendship.

"Wade's a friend," Amelia explained. "Nothing more. Please pass the scalloped potatoes."

Orville chuckled as if her words proved something he'd long suspected.

"What about you, Orville?" Amelia asked, serving herself some green beans. "Don't you get lonesome in that drafty old mansion now that Virginia's gone."

"I do, in fact," he groused. "I miss Virginia a great deal."

"What a shame." Virginia buttered a roll.

"Being governor's not as gratifying without my lovely daughter helping me along," Orville grumbled.

"That's very sweet, Papa. Thank you." Virginia took a small slice of ham, studied the platter, and then took another.

Inwardly, Amelia smiled, pleased that Virginia seemed to be recovering her appetite. The poor girl had suffered a fierce bout of morning sickness. She was a little too thin for Amelia's liking. Amelia resisted the urge to add a few more helpings of potatoes to the girl's plate.

"What will you do when your term is over?" Simon asked. "Come help raise Brahma cattle?"

Orville chuckled. "Heavens no. I know, firsthand, how hard ranching is. You might recall, I grew up in this very home. After I'm done serving the people of Texas, I intend to spend as much time as I can either traveling or fishing. I might even take up birdwatching. Mostly, I look forward to being a grandfather."

"That's mighty nice," Amelia said. "And I mean that sincerely."

Orville smiled. He looked like he might embark on another round of teasing about Wade. Amelia, acting quickly, cut him off before he could start.

"So, Governor Childress. Tell me something."

"Certainly, Amelia."

"What does the word mean." Amelia gestured toward the frame that held the embroidered, hard-to-pronounce word.

"What word to you mean?" Orville asked innocently.

Virginia laughed and glanced at Simon who gave her an answering smile. Amelia sighed. She was aware that she might be the only one who didn't know the meaning of the peculiar word.

Simon set his fork down. "Mama, *Hiraeth* is the Welsh word for 'home'."

Amelia's eyes grew wet, something that didn't often happen. She used her napkin to dry them before a tear ran down her cheek.

"That's right," Orville said. "My mother was born in Wales. She always said the word also had meanings such as nostalgia and homesickness."

Virginia smiled. "It's a lovely word. To my thinking."

Virginia and Amelia shared a knowing look. Amelia nodded. "It is," she said softly.

The End

Book Three of Brides of Bethany Springs
Vow of the Texas Cowboy

When Zach Honeycutt arrives in Pineville to run the family's new sawmill, he knows he'll have to deal with hard working men, some with big, sometimes bad, attitudes. He's ready for the menfolk. What he's not ready for is finding Daisy and her two sisters living in the foreman's cabin, the cabin where he intended to live. Sorting things out turns into more than anyone imagined.

Books by Charlotte Dearing

Mail Order Providence
Mail Order Sarah
Mail Order Ruth

<u>Brides of Bethany Springs Series</u>
To Charm a Scarred Cowboy
Kiss of the Texas Maverick
Vow of the Texas Cowboy
The Accidental Mail Order Bride
Starry-Eyed Mail Order Bride
An Inconvenient Mail Order Bride
Amelia's Storm

<u>The Bluebonnet Brides Collection</u>
Mail Order Grace
Mail Order Rescue
Mail Order Faith
Mail Order Hope
Mail Order Destiny
Love's Destiny

Sign up at <u>www.charlottedearing.com</u> to be notified of special offers and announcements.

Made in United States
Troutdale, OR
04/18/2024